The Genius of Desire

The Genius of Desire

A NOVEL BY

Brian Bouldrey

BALLANTINE BOOKS
NEW YORK

Library of Congress Cataloging-in-Publication Data

Bouldrey, Brian.
   The genius of desire / Brian Bouldrey. — 1st ed.
      p.   cm.
   ISBN 0-345-38334-6
   1. Gay youth—Fiction.   I. Title.
PS3552.08314G46   1993
813′.54—dc20   92-97321
                                                                              CIP

Manufactured in the United States of America

First Edition: June 1993

10   9   8   7   6   5   4   3   2   1

For Jeff

I have to see that this baptism carries enough awe
and mystery to jar the reader into some kind of
emotional recognition of its significance. . . . I have
to make the reader feel, in his bones if nowhere
else, that something is going on here that counts.
Distortion in this case is an instrument; exaggeration has a purpose. . . . This is not the kind of distortion that destroys; it is the kind that reveals, or
should reveal.

—FLANNERY O'CONNOR,
MYSTERY AND MANNERS

Thus for a moment, does a lie become the truth.
—FYODOR DOSTOYEVSKI
THE BROTHERS KARAMAZOV

The Genius of Desire

GOING TO THE HOUSE

This is not a story about my parents. My parents always knew when I did something wrong, and used discipline. This is a story about my relatives, my aunts and uncles and cousins, who never punished me, so that when I was in trouble with my parents, I would always say, "I wish I could stay with my grandmother."

The only thing like punishment I ever received from those other relatives was through my cousin Anne, and maybe her older brother, Tommy. Anne would go through my dresser drawers and pull out six pairs of underwear and say, "Is this *your* underwear?" and start laughing before I could answer.

Then her brother would say, "Hey, little man, you've got little ducks on your underwear," and he'd laugh, too. I'd grab the underwear out of Anne's hand and stuff it back in the drawer, and then Anne would pull it out again, and they would both go into more peals of laughter. They repeated this until they were sick of it, and left my room.

CHAPTER 1

Confession

My great-grandmother Kaiser had six children: three girls and three boys. The boys were my grandfather John, and my uncles James and Thomas. There was Aunt Teresa, and her fraternal-twin sisters, Charlene and Charlotta. All of them, but for Uncle Jimmy's fatness and Aunt Teresa's primness, looked alike. As they grew older their bodies stopped growing except for their bellies, and the cartilage and hairs in their ears and noses. They were prone to a beautiful ugliness, which I loved them for. The wrinkles and fat and hair growing from their beet-colored pores made their eyes, wet blue and brown and green, seem reason enough to call them beautiful. They also loved to tell jokes and retell stories until they became outrageous lies.

On my great-grandmother's piano, there was only one photograph of my aunts and uncles together, Teresa, Charlene, and Charlotta, Tom, James, and my grandfather John. They were huddled together on the top of the Empire State Building. They were all young and looked exactly the same—the girls might as well have been triplets—the way all women from the 1930s looked the same to me. They wore a lot of lipstick, which shows up curiously well in those old black-and-white photos. Charlene and Charlotta were wearing fancy pillbox hats, and they were smiling uneasily, as though they were standing on top of a shaky ladder together. My uncles looked no less nervous, their hair parted in the same exact way it was until their old age, and one of them held on to a hat from the front and back, covering his part.

More enjoyable to me was a souvenir phonograph record the six of them made during that trip to New York City. For a dollar, a vendor would cut into wax a recording of your experience at the top of the world's tallest building. My great-grandmother kept it near her doily-covered chair and despite the dozen instances when I begged to hear it, only once did my great-grandmother play it for me—for all of us—because she didn't want to wear it out.

The sound was very scratchy. There was the noise of wind blowing against the microphone, and then that wind rose up like a gale and I could hear one of the brothers saying, "Hey, my hat, I almost lost my hat!" and he giggled, amazed, nervously. Then a sister, I imagine it was Aunt Teresa, spent the rest of the record saying what else they had seen, where they had eaten, and how nice the hotel was. She didn't stop until the wind blew hard again and two of them made a little squeal. Then there was the sound of the man saying, "Time's almost up, kids, better say one last thing." Almost immediately, and without any planning, they yelled out over the blasts of wind at the same time, "Hi Momma and Daddy!" Then the wind turned into static.

My aunts and uncles were nothing like that in real life. The six of them and their children were enough to make up a platoon, and the house was always a detonation of people when I visited. My uncles were in the military or police, and each could take up a whole couch just by sprawling down on it. My aunts were loud and fearless, some chain-smoked and yelled at their children in far-off parts of the house. My aunts could have gone to war, too. Even though they all married men and gave up their last names, they were still referred to by their maiden names when they were together, or drank a little, or bickered, or went bowling, or saved some bauble that cluttered up their homes and lives, or told an off-color joke: "You're such a goddamned Kaiser."

For instance, I remember Aunt Charlene and Aunt Charlotta arguing about the man who made the recording at the top of the Empire State Building. Aunt Charlene insisted he was sweet on her. Aunt Charlotta said not so, he had a thing for Teresa. Aunt Charlene said she was willing to bet money. Aunt Charlotta said she'd be happy to take her money, and why didn't they bring Teresa in to tell her side of the story. Aunt Charlene said *of course* Teresa would agree with her, it would be acting in her own self-interest. Aunt Charlotta said, "Oh, Charlene, you're such a goddamned Kaiser."

■ ■ ■

The summer when I was eight, my father was away most of the time working on oil pumps while the union was on strike. He wasn't a scab, my mother kept explaining to me, even though I didn't know what a scab was. He wasn't a scab, but he wasn't in the union, either; he was a low man on the totem pole and had to leave his office job to fill in where he was needed. He came home rarely, like a legend—out of proportion and wearing gray oil-stained coveralls and a rust-red rag in his back pocket.

My mother was going to have another baby, and now that school was out, I was on vacation, getting in her hair. My great-aunt Teresa agreed to take me off her hands for the summer. She lived with my great-grandmother (Aunt Teresa's mother) in Monsalvat, Michigan, four hours from home. Most of my mother's extended family—the goddamned Kaisers—lived there, even on the same street.

I remember my mother making the arrangements over the

phone, talking to my aunt and trying to glue a broken plate together. She had to concentrate on the conversation, finally, and put the two pieces of plate down on the table.

She explained it to me in my room that night. "We've got a plan, Michael. You will spend the summer with Grandma and your aunt. They've got plenty of room, and your cousins live two doors down. You can play with Anne all you want. That will be fun, won't it?"

Anne was my second cousin. Sharp nose and chin, cruel sneer, she was the first person my age I knew who used swear words. Once, when her father, my uncle Tom, had a metal detector and was running it around my grandmother's yard, we found an old lead toy soldier. Uncle Tom told us it was from World War I, because it was a doughboy, with a wide sloping saucer on his head for a helmet, and a pointed bayonet in both hands. He gave it to me and told me to wash the dirt off it. While scrubbing it in the old porcelain sink where there were two spigots, I found that the soldier was painted orange and green. I was holding him up to the light to say something military to him when Anne burst into the bathroom, grabbed it from me, and broke the brittle lead man in half, at the torso. I saved him anyway.

Things—objects, like the lead soldier—gave me much more than people, then. Alone in my grandmother's house that summer, I took to talking to plates and banisters. I added my own scratches to the nicked molding, my own smells to those already floating in the yellowed halls.

The first day in that house, Aunt Teresa took my duffel bag and suitcase to the extra room behind the kitchen. My grandmother was sitting at the kitchen table. I sat down with her, then, because it seemed more polite than standing and watching her. She smiled but didn't speak. She kept eating a cinnamon roll while she stirred her coffee. On the table were a pair of salt-and-pepper shakers shaped like praying hands, one hand for salt, one for pepper. They sprinkled from the thumb.

I knew that my grandmother didn't like me. I was just another body invading her house. We didn't have anything to talk about. I was glad when the dachshund, Chester, came up and rubbed against my legs. Chester was Aunt Teresa's aging dog, and every time she saw me, she reminded me of the time I had shut Chester's tail in the porch door when I was three, and broke it. I don't remember that. But now Chester had a kinky Z-shaped tail. Aunt Teresa said she was not angry about it. She continually told me that she was not angry about it.

Aunt Teresa walked back into the kitchen and took Grandma's plate away to the sink. I could tell that Grandma was not finished with it, but she didn't say anything. Aunt Teresa said to her, "Why don't you sit here while I show Michael his room." She had the room, just off the kitchen, fixed up just for me, she said. She'd had Uncle Tom repaint it.

The walls were chalk blue, and the room smelled like talcum powder, fresh paint, and dust. There were puffy things everywhere, overstuffed chairs, small round useless items like plastic ashtrays. The trim in the room was pastel pink. I was to live in this soft spot, a supple shell, too easy on my eyes and to my touch. I floated all summer.

"How do you like it?" Aunt Teresa asked.

Just then, I heard footsteps in the kitchen. My cousin Anne tore in. She stopped and looked around. "Geez, Michael. This is a *girl's* room. This is a girl's room. You sure are living in a pretty little room!"

Aunt Teresa nodded. "Yes, isn't it pretty?" she said. Then she left us alone.

"Michael's living in a girl's room!"

"Shut up," I said.

Anne's voice lowered to a punishing hiss. "I'd like to see

you make me, you little wuss. I could beat you until you were bleeding right now, one hand tied behind my back." Then she made her head sit straight on her neck and spoke up: "But you'd tell. You'd go crying to Aunt Teresa."

"You're the one who always tattles."

"Shut up. You live in a girl's room." She scampered out, probably to torture Chester. More than once I saw her take a bed sheet and force Chester to sit in the middle; then she'd scoop up all four corners of the sheet and twirl the bundle of dog over her head.

I stayed to stare in a near stupor at my pastel room, as if I were lost in the pleated folds of a cotton blanket. Aunt Teresa came back in and said, "What's wrong?"

I supposed then that I had to have a reason for looking like that, pouting, the bulb of my lower lip stuck out while I thought. Three years before, in kindergarten, the teacher wanted us to learn our telephone numbers. She went around the room asking each of us what it was. I didn't know my telephone number, but I felt I owed her an answer of some sort. I rattled off several numbers. She shook her head and praised me for trying, then she told me my real phone number.

Now I felt that I owed Aunt Teresa an explanation for my pout, so I made something up, just for her. I told her I had taken two dimes that were on the dining-room table.

Aunt Teresa rushed into the dining room and came back. "Michael. The dimes are still there. Why did you think you took them?" She shook her head and said, "Now come with me, there are a few things I need to show you."

I followed her into the living room, past my grandmother. She was still sitting in the kitchen, not even reading, her hands in her lap under the table.

By special tour of the house, Aunt Teresa explained, room by room, that she was afraid that the rest of the house was off limits to me. I couldn't be in the living room, because that's where my grandmother often napped, and kept all her nice things, and watched her soap operas on the television, very loud. Each day was spent planning around the soap operas, or "her story." My aunt said I would have to go outside for a while, during the weekdays, so Grandma could watch "her story."

Aunt Teresa did not take me bodily to her own bedroom, but pointed up the stairs. "And you can't go upstairs, where I live. The stairs are very steep. What if you fall?" The attic was up there, too, and I could sometimes stand at the foot of the stairs and look into the door. It was usually ajar, and sometimes it was opened wider than other times.

"There's nothing there but rusty nails to fall on and open windows to fall out of. Never let me catch you in that attic." Aunt Teresa's own room was out of sight, her secret place where she only went for sleeping and naps.

I let my eye travel up the long line of the mahogany banister. I rested my hand on the mushroom-shaped pedestal at the foot of the stairs, sunk my fingernail into the old wood polish that had turned gummy over many years. "Who else has touched you?" I asked it.

■　　■　　■

Even before the summer of my mother's pregnancy, I knew Monsalvat well. Monsalvat, Michigan, was always the place we went for holidays: Christmas, Easter, New Year's. A long time ago, a group of German immigrants founded and named the town. There wasn't much of a German community left, but the humiliated girls in the plaza shops on the main street wore lederhosen and pigtails. A lot of tourists visited Monsalvat, because there was a beaded string of lakes where people kept summer cottages. There were seven local hofbraus that proudly served large portions of glutinous potatoes, stuffing, and stroganoff, all attended to by old men in tuxedos. The most famous shop in Monsalvat was Franken-broner's, which sold Christmas decorations all year round. All along the highways up to Monsalvat, there were huge bill-boards in the shape of Christmas ornaments that said, VISIT FRANKENBRONER'S! WHERE IT'S CHRISTMAS EVERY DAY! My parents always stopped there and bought saltwater taffy, but never Christmas things. That summer, we never went to Frankenbroner's, and I hardly ever saw the salesgirls in le-derhosen. Before, Monsalvat had always seemed to be a place where time had stopped on an endless Christmas. That sum-mer, time had just stopped.

Furthermore, it was apparent for the first time that this place was not one in which holidays were perpetual. I had imagined that my aunts and uncles were always at play, goof-ing off, telling their dirty jokes, drinking up a storm. But now it was as if everybody did nothing *but* work—if not as police-men, then in the mall as salesclerks or at the huge gray-windowed auto plant just south of Monsalvat. Everybody seemed weary, older. Most of my aunts and uncles were in their late forties or early fifties, but this didn't account for the haggardness I saw day to day, changed only by week-ends, or maybe a rainstorm that cooled the sticky weather down.

■　■　■

The first evening, Aunt Teresa came into my room to tuck me in. In her hand she had Volume One of the *Childcraft En-cyclopedia*, full of stories and fables. Up close, in lamplight, I could see that the roots of her hair, as red-brown as a crayon, made a quick zigzag before they sprayed out into a big airy mass. Her forehead was tall and white. Her eyebrows had been drawn on like a drawing of a Japanese man, and they were so black they were purple. There was a layer of powder over her oval face, and it showed four firm creases around her mouth, evenly balanced on the line of her lips.

My parents did not, as a habit, read to me. But Aunt Teresa was determined. The story she chose was the myth of Oedipus, the part where he gets challenged by the Sphinx to a riddle match. Aunt Teresa would stop the story in the middle and say, "Can you guess? Can you guess what it is that stands on four legs at dawn, on two during the day, and on three at dusk?" Then she read the part where Oedipus solves the riddle and then turned the book toward me. On the page was a picture of the Sphinx, part beast and part beautiful woman, surrounded by human skulls and rib cages, enraged to death by Oedipus' right answer, flipping over a cliff. Aunt Teresa closed the book and said, "Do you know what happened to Oedipus after that?"

"No," I said.

"He became king of the city." Then she got up, and turned off the lights, and I was alone in the chalky, blankety comfort of my room. In the corner, a night-light burned, and it was shaped like the praying hands.

■　　■　　■

The next day was Sunday, and I came into the kitchen in my slippers and bathrobe. Almost immediately, I noticed that the kitchen rugs had the likeness of praying hands stitched into them. I had been tipped off by the night-light; it was like discovering a stain on my shirt that I hadn't noticed all day, and could not keep my eyes off of, now. The praying hands were everywhere.

Aunt Teresa said, "Goodness, you're still in your bathrobe! We're going to church in less than an hour—get washed, get dressed, good God." She was already dressed, and had put so much hairspray in her hair that it hung in the air around her.

I could tell that her hairspray was taking up all the air, and that sticky gobs were getting into my lungs. I had heard in school that there were little hairs in my nose that filtered, so I closed my mouth and tried to breathe through my nose. It smelled like suffocation and perfume.

I went into my room and put on a shirt and a clip-on tie. Then I saw a mote of dust swirl through an angle of dry, mid-morning light. I sat down on the bed with my hands beneath me, following one speck of dust. Aunt Teresa came in. She saw me sitting there and rushed to her knees before me. "What's wrong?" she said.

I looked at her. I told her, "I've tracked some dirt in through the front door. I didn't mean to, but I did." I'd lied, as smoothly as this room's walls, and she checked for the dirt and didn't find it. It was not long before she stopped believing my imaginary misdeeds. Later, when I cracked the shade on a small lamp, so that it fell apart one day while nobody was around to see it actually break, I told my aunt that I had done it, and she waved it off. My grandmother looked at me in silence.

After church, the entire family came over to Aunt Teresa's and Grandma's for dinner. This was to happen every week, a traditional event. Most of them sat in Grandma's living room and watched golf or baseball.

This was my first real look at the living room. It was a place glutted with mismatched porcelain, collections of stamps from foreign countries, rosaries, newspaper clippings, and pictures of Catholic icons. The Sacred Heart of Jesus was everywhere: that horribly gleaming heart, a fist-shaped heart surrounded by a crown of thorns constricting and cutting into the fleshiness of it here and there and making it bleed. It was glowing, like the sun. Everything in Grandma's living room was breakable, or peeled off in layers. There were patterns on top of patterns, lace over plaid, flower print confusing houndstooth.

These Sunday visits by the family were as much a ritual as mass itself, everybody eating chicken or pot roast and gathering around the television to watch sports, Uncle Tom and Uncle Jimmy and my cousin Tommy trying to know more batting averages and draft picks than the other guy, mumbling numbers, mock experts.

The only relief came from Anne. Aunt Teresa came in with an unclothed Barbie and asked, "Anne, why did you pull the head off of that doll?"

She shrugged, but surely. "I was done with it. It had bad hair that you can't comb. Its hair stuck up like Michael's."

"Anne, what do I have for little girls to play with if they come over?"

"There's no little girls that come over. There's just me. *God*." She was cruel and she was exasperating, but she roused me from that cloudy, timeless stupor, and I settled for it, for her.

I sat in the living room and watched and waited, and smelled the hairspray and baby powder. I sat with my great-aunt Mary, Uncle Tom's wife, with the chronic health problems, who described, while we ate, how she coughed up blood-and-phlegm balls every night. I sat with my godfather, who pointed out that he was also my cousin. (They always reminded me who they were in the bloodline—great-aunt, third cousin, uncle by marriage. It was like they were trying to remember themselves.) I sat with the wayward cousin Tommy, Anne's brother, who was seventeen but smoked cigars, and who used to get into my underwear and made a deep impression on me the previous Easter by accidentally gashing his arm with a pocketknife and taking that opportunity to write in blood on a piece of paper towel for Aunt Mary, his mother: "Love," and then his name. I sat with my immense uncle Jimmy whose wife was dead but to whom he still spoke, at times, to the air: "Well, Barbara," he would say at the end of dinner, "I suppose if you were here, you'd want to go home now." Then he would leave.

. . .

We could only watch educational television in the evening. Aunt Teresa loved to watch the TV nature shows, the National Geographic specials, the "Undersea World of Jacques Cousteau," "Wild Kingdom," and "Walt Disney True Life Adventures." Those were the places where it was okay to see uncovered breasts, strange scarifications, and animals giving birth or killing each other.

Anne liked freak animals, the deep-sea blind fish with feelers that glowed, the platypus, the sideshow animals at the Monsalvat County Carp Carnival.

Anne also delighted in the stupidity of animals, and laughed when a migrating herd of wildebeests panicked and ran headlong into a flooded river, some drowning, some drowning others, but always plowing forward, so that at the other side of the river, only half of the herd survived. "God, they're such morons," she screamed with delight.

Chipmunks flirted with each other, and the male would mount the female just as the camera cut away, me not old enough to understand why, why the true true-life adventure could not be shown.

Men in television studios dressed in safari pants and shorts sat in front of film footage of men shooting tranquilizer darts at elephants in order to tag them. Tall, shirtless men stood on the prow of the *Calypso* and lunged spears into the water, cursing in French at strange exposed lengths of fish flesh as they broke the surface of the water. Australian lizards flipped their scaly manes up like Elizabethan collars and ran at the screen, mouths wide. Elks locked their horns together while butting each other, and died that way. Desert animals perished without water.

We saw a baby zebra caught in a tar pit, scrambling with its gangly legs only to find itself deeper in the muck, over and over, for hours, until it died from exposure or a predator or exhaustion. Anne laughed at that, too. She thought the zebra was doing some stoogey physical-comedy act for her.

I sat agape. "Why is it trapped like that?"

"Well, that's nature," Aunt Teresa said. "It's the survival of the fittest."

"But there's a guy there running a camera, why doesn't he go over and pull it out?"

"Well," said Aunt Teresa, "that would be cheating. That would be upsetting the order of nature."

This was meant to comfort me. And the narrator on the science show had cold comfort for me, too, when he explained that the sun would burn out in a few million years, but by then, man would be smart enough to go to someplace warmer.

Every night Aunt Teresa came in and read me a new story. Most of them I already knew: Red Riding Hood in battle with the Wolf, rescued by a huntsman; Cinderella, who was the only girl who could fit into the glass slipper, rescued by a prince.

And every day I said no more than "good morning" to my grandmother. She smiled, and sat with her hands at rest in her lap, in a calico housedress. Her shriveled, direct, kindly face made me strangely frightened, ashamed because we never talked. I ached to go in the living room again. I ached to see the attic. I was so afraid of those places.

■　　■　　■

I counted weeks by Sundays. Time passed, and Aunt Teresa kept busy in the kitchen, cooking and holding court. She rarely went into the living room. It was not her realm. I became comfortable in the fuzzy stupor of pillows and bedtime stories, the soft glow of the praying-hands night-light. And my fear of my grandmother subsided, and she became only a place at the corner of my view, harmless, voiceless.

One Sunday, there was a particularly wild baseball play on the television, and I chose that chaotic moment to put my plate of chicken down on the arm of an old flower-embroidered stuffed chair and sneak upstairs. The stairs creaked loudly, but the whole house creaked, and I tried to go so slowly that the creaking footsteps seemed to come out of the regular shifts of the house. It was a gradual process as I put more weight, then more weight on the toe, ball, and heel, and again, ascending like arpeggios on the upright piano in the living room.

I was nearly at the top, but just before I made it up, Anne saw me and shouted, "Hey, Michael! Hey, Aunt Teresa!"

I hustled down again, pouting. Aunt Teresa came in, wiping her hands on an apron. "What's wrong?" she asked.

I confessed that I'd spilled macaroni-shell salad on the good carpeting.

"Oh, you did not," and she walked briskly back to the kitchen. I slumped in a chair next to my grandmother, and muttered to myself. I caught Anne, aghast, retract her head down her long neck and leave as if she were participating in a walking race.

My grandmother turned to me. "It's dangerous to go up there," she said.

I was startled by her intense concentration on me. With all of those cousins, aunts, and uncles, I was unnoticed most of the time. "Why?" I asked. I suddenly thought, She is bored with all of these people, too, always eating her food and using her television and not saying anything to her. She was going to take it out on me, I figured. "What's wrong?" I asked softly. "Is there a body in the attic? In Aunt Teresa's room? Is that what makes all those creaking noises?" She never heard me, because I talked too softly. I was speaking to the overstuffed furniture.

After my grandmother warned me about the stairs, I went over to that clunker piano, and tried to figure out some tunes that I might sing attic-wards, to the arched ceiling of water-stained rafters and mouse-chewed corners. Aunt Teresa came back into the living room and pulled a key out, one that locked the piano cover. She gave the lock one quick twist. I watched the tiny set of praying hands attached to the keychain dangle between her own bony hands. They glowed in the dark, in case she dropped her keys at night.

Then my grandmother suddenly got up, with weird energy, arms outstretched out of her thin flowery dress. She knocked over a tintype of her own father, long gone. "There, there," she said to me, putting things in order. "There, there." She handed me a picture of her husband. And then she pulled out another picture of that glowing Sacred Heart, beating and beaten, and said, "Here, look at this."

I figured that this was her way of warning me, showing me a way to get out of her house. I figured she saw me as some kind of rottenness. And even though fat Uncle Jimmy was taking up the entire chair next to me, and the smoke from Aunt Charlotta's cigarette made the room seem even more crowded, this interchange between the two of us seemed very private. I was confused by this close attention, confused and embarrassed, for it seemed to me that the only point of this was to *scare* me—scare me away from that very intimacy.

There was more she had to show me. She showed me her collection of foreign stamps, and we peered at postmarks, dates, words torn in half sometimes on the cancellation stamp. But we knew the meaning of those half words, like "Timbuk—" and "Pakis—" and more from closer places, Italy and Jerusalem, foreign, boring, and a finger pointing outward, to faraway points.

And there was more. In that most endless of the endless Sunday afternoons, she gave me clippings from her son Tom's promotion to police chief and my grandfather's award of a medal for duty in the marines. She said, "I remember I thought he was dead for months, and then he turned up a hero."

I was more interested in the backs of these clips. They were hints of a real world, beyond that house, the more important world in which my uncles were promoted or died. There were articles on the backs of this brittle yellow paper, articles about a child smothered in an attic, portions of a sports section, parts of stats.

My grandmother smiled. "So what's upstairs that you want?" she asked.

"How would I know?" I said, staring at the picture of my great-grandfather on her doily-covered coffee table. Even people cluttered her room. The picture was black-and-white, but it looked more yellow brown. He was dressed in a thin suit, and he didn't smile.

■　■　■

One afternoon, Aunt Teresa was in the kitchen, making toast for my grandmother and talking smartly about limbo. My grandmother sat with her hands on her knees, smiling vaguely. When you get old, I figured, and can't see as well, the room must look less cluttered. My grandmother couldn't see all the porcelain and glass and knickknacks through the thick round lenses of her prescription glasses. Aunt Teresa helped to make it that way. The most cluttered places were far away: her attic, her past, and maybe heaven. In heaven, you can fall and cut yourself, and it won't hurt.

Aunt Teresa said, "I think they got rid of that purgatory stuff in Vatican Two." Vatican II was an invitation to my aunt to come back to the Catholic fold. She had married a Protestant man, and the priest was hard, and said, "How do you expect to go to heaven, when you marry a man who's not Catholic?" That did it. She wanted that dangerous sharp-clawed Protestant even more.

But then he died, and Vatican II told her she had suffered enough, and she went back to mass, and that was that.

My grandmother said, "Oh, bull. Where did all those babies go, that died before they got baptized? They didn't just float off to the devil, you know."

"Well, that's what I heard."

"I just don't believe it. I doubt that the pope would do that to a baby." But she said that last part only to me. Aunt Teresa had walked across the room, and was placing dishes into the sink. She broke a coffee cup, and almost swore. And then Chester waddled up to her, pawed her ankle, and licked the coffee off of her hands when she put them down and together for him. His Z-tail fit perfectly under his rump. I compared her hands with the salt-and-pepper shakers.

I looked at my grandmother and smiled, but I took what she said to me personally.

■   ■   ■

Near the end of the summer, my cousin Anne was confirmed. For her Confirmation name, she chose Saint Teresa, and my aunt was her sponsor. I remember how long that mass was, how the priest put oil on Anne's forehead, how she wore white gloves and put her two hands together in prayer and clasped between her index and middle fingers a white card with the name Teresa on it. My grandmother sat on one side of me and Aunt Teresa on the other. They watched me watch. "Do you want to go up there and do that, too?" asked my great-grandmother.

Did she want me to move to another pew, away from her?

Anne's sharp little nose was pointed to the altar, and her

beady eyes were shut, so the priest couldn't see how mean she could be. She had a rosary in her hand, and I watched her lips move as she said Hail Marys. I think she skipped parts. She held the rosary out in front of her like she was going to put it around her neck. I thought, Why do all these church things—scapulars, rosaries, vestments—go around your neck, like charms?

Aunt Teresa saw me staring at the crucifix. It was a tortured one, painted in flesh tones and blood. She tried to divert my attention. "See that candle up there?" She pointed to a gilt cradle with a candle encased in translucent red glass. "That means that God is here with us right now."

That spooked me, and I looked back at the garish crucifix. Aunt Teresa said, "What do you think of Him? Isn't that something? Would you do that? Would you suffer like that, if you knew it would take away everybody's sins?"

Like my telephone number, I had an answer for Aunt Teresa. I said, and I think I really meant it then, though I wouldn't say it now, "Sure I would, if it would save everybody."

That was probably a sinful thing to say to her, because she showed it on her face. I wasn't old enough to be as selfish as I am now about my own life. She once said, when she caught me climbing in a tree in the backyard, "You kids think you're immortal."

Anne had listened to me, too, her Hail Marys out of the way. She said, "I bet he would." I looked at her to see if she was teasing me, but she looked like she really meant it. She looked at me and smiled, and it looked like a real smile. It scared me.

After the mass, we went back to the house for an even bigger Sunday dinner to celebrate the new Teresa in the family. And she got gifts. She got a pair of new gloves and a picture of the Sacred Heart on a small scapular, and a book of prayers, and Aunt Teresa gave her her own small set of ceramic praying hands, a paperweight. A lot of people just gave her money. This put Anne in an even better mood. She left me alone.

Aunt Teresa had made a buffet, slicing slivers of ham and turkey and piling them neatly, filling celery sticks with cream cheese or peanut butter. I was absorbed in the self-dare of squirting out in mustard bad words on slices of bread, then squashing them quickly into a sandwich so they couldn't be read. I said the words quietly to the figure in the porcelain.

Anne looked at me from across the room. She smiled and made a look like she wondered what I was doing. She had been so nice all that day that I decided to show her. I held out the open slice of bread, and she stood up, daintily smoothed her skirt with white-gloved hands, and walked over. When I showed her the bread, she bugged her eyes as if she were not the first girl I had ever heard saying swear words. "I don't believe what you wrote," she said.

"It's just a word. So what?"

"I'm telling."

"Go ahead."

"I will."

I walked away from her and picked up speed, toward my aunt in the kitchen. Anne followed me, gained on me. "No, that's okay," I yelled back to her as she gained on me, "I'll tell her myself."

"You're totally a dink, Michael," she called, and followed. "You're totally stupid."

I went up to Aunt Teresa and stood deliberately before her with my lip puckered up to my nose. She said, "Michael, what's wrong?"

Anne came in with her white dress, strapped white purse, and white gloves. "I wrote a bad word on the bread with mustard," I said.

Anne glared at me. "He did. I saw him."

"Oh, you did not, Michael. You think you wrote a bad

word, but you didn't. And why are you lying like that, Anne? Didn't you learn anything at church today? Why are you lying?"

So later, when Chester came up and begged by my foot and I gave him some of the turkey out of the middle of that sandwich, Anne didn't run and tattle, she sat staring, stumped and foiled.

Then she must have thought of something. That was when the soft boredom of another Sunday got the best of me. Anne eyed the stairway, and smiled at me. She looked like she wanted me to get in on a secret she had. She hissed, "Michael," and made an upward motion with her head. Suddenly there was an upset all around us because of a baseball play on television. It was as if she willed the distraction herself. She bolted in her white dress up the stairs, making whisking noises as the stiff pleated material rubbed against itself. She hunched on the fifth stair behind the banister, and I followed her.

This is what I found out: You had to go through the attic room to get to Aunt Teresa's room. Anne already knew. She knew the whole place. The cheers downstairs seemed far away, muffled as if under a blanket. The sound of Anne's footsteps on the slatted floors sounded clear, the clearest thing I'd heard all summer. Chester had followed, and I was sure his clicking claws would give us away. "Chester, go away," I said.

The attic was cold, even that summer. It was lit by a bare bulb suspended on a thick black wire from the ceiling. It was not a soft room, it had splintered wooden beams, rusty nails, upside-down chairs with legs like lances, and low windows that opened downward. I liked that place, even with Anne in it.

There was a trunk wide open, with more letters and clippings and porcelain figures. Medals and souvenirs from wars, sashes and silver medallions for unnamed, unimaginable, commemorated bravery. Anne went through the closed door at the other side of the room. "I'm bored," she said. "This is boring. Come this way. Aunt Teresa's got the good stuff."

I caught up with her, followed her into the bedroom, and saw them. Two paintings of praying hands, and a bronze cast, a ceramic statue, bookends, ashtrays, a Bible, shaped notepads, gum erasers, needlepoint pillows, all shaped like praying hands. Even her bedspread had the pale white hands embroidered into the fabric.

Anne casually picked things up and tossed them to me, enamel, porcelain, glass, and I dove to catch them. "Don't drop them asshole," she said. Chester jumped on her knee and caught one of his claws in her skirt. She slapped his snout and played with a snag of thread.

"Look at all this," I said. I stared at a painting of the Sacred Heart framed over the bed. It was so red and dark, like an overripe plum, and the crown of thorns punctured it so many times, it bled all around.

"She plans on being Grandma when Grandma dies." Anne picked up a pair of crystal praying hands sitting on a lace doily. "This one is her absolute favorite."

"How do you know?"

"I read it in her diary. She said she got it as a gift from her best friend in Florida. It was super expensive."

"Let me see."

"Catch—" And Anne threw the crystal hands into the air, across the room, out of my reach. I tried to scramble for it, but Chester was right in front of me. I kicked him and he yelped, and I tripped. The crystal praying hands whumped onto the floor, and I prayed they did not shatter. When I looked up and they were all right, I stood up and looked at Anne and waited for her to laugh so I could laugh with her.

"You stupid ass," Anne said. "Now you're going to get it." Anne tore from the room before I could stop her. Chester ran down with her, his broken tail dragging down the stairs. I did not run, I just sat in the attic room on an empty suitcase. I felt trapped and stupid, but I saw things clearly. There was no place to hide here. The attic was wide open, exposed, strong simple sharp lines, up and down. I waited. I muttered to the trunk, to the fly-spangled windowsill.

"Michael, are you up there?" Aunt Teresa called to me, and moved swiftly up the stairs. I could hear Anne's snappy shoes clicking up behind her, and Chester's paws making a sound like beads falling down the steps, beads fallen from a string one after another. "Michael, come down here right now." She sounded scared.

I heard Anne say, "Wait till you see what he did. You've got to see what Michael did. I told him to come down. Now he'll be sorry. You ought to send him home so he'll never come back here."

I retreated back into her bedroom and picked up the crystal praying hands from the floor. Aunt Teresa walked in and looked at me. She didn't see the praying hands, and I wished she would. She kept looking at me, and I tried to show with my face that something was in my hands.

"What have you got there?" she asked. She took the crystal out of my hands. She stared at it through the light.

"I don't know," I said. "I was downstairs, and I heard a big crash, and I came up here, and Anne—"

"You little liar!" Anne squealed. "You lying bastard!"

"Anne *Teresa Kaiser*, watch your mouth. Do you know what that word means?"

"Yes, it means him. He's lying his head off. He dropped your praying hands on the floor."

Aunt Teresa didn't say anything but sat on the bed and beckoned me closer. She pointed into the glass. Somewhere in its perfect depths, a small crack had started. "See what's happened," she said, and she looked like she was going to cry.

Then we all noticed that my grandmother was standing in the room. She was breathless, in her flowery dress, resting against the treacherous doorknob. I thought the knob might turn on her at any minute and make her fall. We didn't know how long she'd stood there.

"Mother," Aunt Teresa almost shrieked, "what are you doing up here? You know the last time you made that climb you broke your hip. Do I have to watch you like these kids?" And that is how she rescued herself from crying.

My grandmother said, "I sent Michael up here to see what was going on, I heard such a noise, and I was worried somebody had hurt themselves. Did you come up here on your own, Anne?"

We all floated in midair.

Aunt Teresa let herself breathe, and stared into the crystal. "This is my favorite thing in the world," she said, shaking her head, stroking the glass. Chester came up and licked her spotted hands. She said, "Chester."

■　　■　　■

That night, Aunt Teresa did not come in to tell me a bedtime story. My grandmother did. She brought in an old book, its pages foxed and its calfskin binding cracking. "I want to read you a story or two," she said, "from a book they read to me when I was a girl." She peered hard at the page and tried to read but couldn't. Without shame, she said, "Why don't you read it to me."

I read the story of Cinderella to her. I stopped. "I've read this before, I know this story."

She pushed the book toward me. "Read it anyway."

I did. It was like the same story, only a different story. In this version, Cinderella's stepsisters hacked off their toes and heels in order to fit into the glass shoes. Then I read how Red Riding Hood was swallowed whole by the Wolf, only saved when a huntsman slit that big dog open to find that happy ending crouched deep in his stomach.

I said to my grandmother, "These aren't the same as Aunt Teresa told me."

"They aren't?" she said, and she took the book from my hand and started running her old hands over the old pages. "Sometimes, I think your Aunt Teresa has a dirty mind," she said. But she smiled and touched me lightly. "Look," she said, pointing to the alarm clock on my nightstand. "You should have been sleeping ages ago."

CHAPTER 2

The Secret Name of the Carp

Not long after Anne's Confirmation party, her parents, Uncle Tom and Aunt Mary, took us to the county fairgrounds for the Monsalvat County Carp Carnival and Petunia Festival. I remember Aunt Mary wore a dress that looked like first-aid gauze. I studied the dress very carefully, because at first it seemed like it was transparent. Catching a glimpse of her substantial underwear, I looked away. She looked like she had just been crying, or was going to.

The county fairgrounds were on the edge of a lake. It was very shallow, and far out in the middle there were weeds growing out of the water. Anne boasted that she once waded all the way across. From the parking lot, I could see the swoop of the double Ferris wheel and the downhurling loop of a loop-o-plane and the plunge of the "Mad Mouse." On a big sign was a mean-looking rat with eyebrows that looked like the slashes painted onto Aunt Teresa's forehead. My muscles ached to be on all of the rides at once.

Inside the fairgrounds, the motors that ran the rides sounded as if dozens of tractors were tearing up the earth. Somebody kept screaming from inside the haunted-house ride and a man on a megaphone yelled, "Come and see Rose-mary's Baby, with tiny cloven hooves!"

Anne said, "Let's go see that! They have a midget horse and a two-headed cow, too."

"Don't be silly," said Aunt Mary. She kept leaning back and protecting her delicate face from the sun. She pulled the dress away from her skin and fanned herself with it. "It will give you nightmares, and I don't want the heartache. Let's get lemonade."

Uncle Tom, however, wanted to see the carp. All around us was the smell of the carp. I breathed it in over and over, a sad smell, like lakes and sun and leaves rotting. It smelled of going back to school.

In a big clearing by the lake stood two poles with a rope stretched between them. The contenders for the big-gest carp were hung and tagged. I read the tags carefully. Each one had the length and weight of the carp, and then a name. I thought these were the names of the fish, like they were pets. After all, they named racehorses. "Savage," "Seagrave," "Tenderly." I read every tag out loud, to each fish.

Uncle Tom was looking at a fat one, whose eye and fleshy mustachios had dried up into its green gnarled head. I touched its dead eye while Uncle Tom said, "They give prizes for the best carp—tackle boxes and boat motors and even boats. One of these days I'll get the best carp."

I looked at the sunken eye and the slack snouted mouth. "Is this the best carp?"

"Michael, get away from those or you'll catch something." Aunt Mary looked like she thought the whole thing was bunk, the kind of bunk that might make her faint dead away. "I'm surprised they don't have a Carp Queen contest. That would top it off, wouldn't it?"

"You can be Carp Queen, Michael," said Anne, who had

sulked since the Rosemary's Baby. Uncle Tom didn't say anything to her, but looked at me to see what I would do.

"Shut up," I said straight into the face of a freshly caught carp, still dripping. I looked for ears on it, but only found the gills.

"Carp are so ugly, look at their faces," Aunt Mary said to us. "Just ugly. Do you know what they eat? Garbage. Do you know who eats carp? Nobody I know. It's pointless to catch them. It's pointless to have a contest. It only encourages them."

"Encourages who?" I asked. But I was talking to the dead fish again. The best carp's name was Braggart. Behind me, people were screaming as the Mad Mouse whooshed downward.

■ ■ ■

I knew all the people at Monsalvat were related to me, but it took a while to figure out how they were connected to each other (although they were always tracing the connections). So it was a revelation when I realized that Uncle Tom was Aunt Teresa's brother. He came over often, because of all their brothers and sisters, they liked each other the best. Sometimes he made pancakes for dinner, and root-beer floats while he listened to Smothers Brothers records. Whenever there were epic movies on television, he watched them at my grandmother's house because the screen was bigger: *Barabbas*, *The Ten Commandments*, *Ben-Hur*. One night I woke up because the television was blasting, "Thou shalt not commit adultery!" It sounded like God in the next room, with Uncle Tom and Aunt Teresa.

I came into the living room to see what was going on and I caught a glimpse of a red tornado on the screen. Uncle Tom headed me off and led me back to my pale blue room. He lifted the cover like he was showing me something on the surface of the mattress and I climbed in. He turned off the light again. Then he put his head down close to mine and whispered:

> "Listen! Listen!
> The cat's a-pissing!
> Where? Where?
> Under the chair!
> Run! Run!
> Get the gun!
> Aw, shoot, he's all done."

I begged him to repeat it, to get it right in my head. But he slipped out of the room to hear the rest of the Ten Commandments. In the morning, he was back at the house to fix something in the basement, because he was also my grandmother and Aunt Teresa's handyman. He'd built and fixed everything at least once, Aunt Teresa said. I asked him, "Say that Listen Listen thing again."

Aunt Teresa wheeled on him. "Thomas, don't tell him that," she said. He winked at me and was silent. Uncle Tom was full of mysteries and secret words.

■　　■　　■

Somewhere in the summer, near the time of the Monsalvat County Carp Carnival and Petunia Festival, Aunt Teresa realized that I had not been to Confession, and needed to go. She took me during the special children's Confession hours that her church had. Back at home, my mother usually helped me beforehand to remember my sins. When I asked Aunt Teresa for suggestions, she said, "You know what you've done."

I waited until a girl walked out of the confessional booth, and went in. It was different from the one at home, bigger, with dark wood like the interior of Aunt Teresa's Bonneville coupe. It even had a dim light overhead and there was a smell of wood polish. I ran my hand along the ledge and kneeled on the red pad in front of velvet curtains. The confessional window had little holes that radiated out like the pattern of a Chinese-checker board. I forgot the words I was supposed to say. Then they came back: "Forgive me, Father, for I have sinned, my last Confession was two months ago."

I waited for the priest to say something. There was a low, plugged-up mumble. Suddenly I understood that there was one priest shuttling between two booths. If I listened carefully, I could hear the sins of the other person, another boy.

"I made my brother eat dirt," I heard him say. "I was mean to my mom. I don't like hamburgers."

Father O'Hara told him to say ten Hail Marys and ten Our Fathers and he muttered some words that sounded like Uncle Tom's secret rhyme. Then his chair wheels swiveled over, he pulled a board away, and light streamed through the holes. It was bright and I squinted. He said, "Yes?"

"Forgive me, Father, for I have sinned, this is my first Confession. These are my sins. I was mean to my mom. I did not write to my dad while he was away. I made my brother eat dirt." I stopped for a minute, trying to think of more sins.

"Anything else?"

"I can't think."

"Think about the Ten Commandments. Have you broken any of the Ten Commandments?"

I ran through them in my head. My eyes swam in the sunburst pattern of holes. "I think I may have committed adultery."

There was a pause. Then he said again, "Anything else?"

"I missed church last week," which was the one true thing. I had missed because I went with Anne and her older brother, Tommy, in Tommy's car, but we stopped at the lake on the way and never made it to mass. Tommy made me swear not to tell.

"Of all those sins, missing church is the most terrible. You must always go to church. I want you to say twenty Hail Marys and twenty Our Fathers and pray the Apostles' Creed once. Think about the importance of going to church every Sunday." I could hear him thump his fingers on the sill of the window on each word in the last sentence. He muttered those words: "Absolve ... sins." The little piece of board slid over and the booth was dark again.

I walked out of the confessional and knelt in a pew in front of a statue of Joseph, with a lamb in his hand. Which Joseph was that? There were a dozen different Bible stories with guys named Joseph in them.

The mortal sins are strange and arbitrary. It was not my fault I had missed church, and it was the only thing I had confessed that really happened, except maybe for the adultery, which I meant to look up. I would never confess to missing church again.

■　　■　　■

"What do you confess when you confess, Uncle Tom?"

"I don't know. Laziness. Swearing. Drinking. Missing church. Fishing." He was up on a ladder, building a little shed outside my grandmother's house to put the lawn mower and tools. I handed him spike-sized nails from a thick brown bag that you can only get at the hardware store.

"Is fishing a sin?"

"It is when it makes you miss church," he said, with a nail hanging from his mouth. Uncle Tom fished year round, it was what he was most famous for in the family. In the summer he fly-fished in the rivers and cast lines from the ends of docks.

In the winter he augered holes in the ice and set out tip-ups, like miniature oil pumps, white with red flags that tipped to let him know there was a fish on his line. "Listen," he said, handing me the butt of a two-by-four he'd sawed off. "Why don't we go out one of these nights and spearfish?"

I ran my fingers over the sawed edges of the two-by-four. "Spearing? You're going to take me out spearing?"

"Sure. We'll practice spearing the best carp for the next Carp Carnival. If your aunt Teresa will let you."

"She will, I'm sure she will. Do you think she will?"

"I'll ask her. Don't say anything until I ask her." He climbed down the ladder and went over to the bag of nails. He stuck the head of his hammer into the bag. When he pulled it out, four heavy nails clung to it, like magic.

He went into the house and I thought he was going to ask her right away. It turned out he was just going in to wash his hands, he was finished for the day. He didn't ask until later that night, after he fixed a leaky faucet for Aunt Teresa. Meanwhile, I sat patiently out by the framework of the shed talking about spearfishing to the block of wood.

■   ■   ■

In order to go spearfishing on a Saturday night, and be awake to attend church the next morning, I had to go to bed in the late afternoon. There was nothing so oppressive and itchy as lying in bed with the shades drawn on daylight while my aunts and uncles roamed the house, cracking jokes and fixing sandwiches.

At one point I heard Anne ask her mother, "Where's Michael?"

"He had to go to bed early tonight."

"Why? What did he do? Was he bad?"

"He and your father are going spearfishing for those ugly carp tonight."

"He is? Can I go, too?"

"No, honey. The two of us will stay at home. We'll be the Carp Queens."

"I'd rather be Rosemary's Baby." Anne stomped off.

At some point near dusk, Tommy—not Uncle Tom—came into my room. He was seventeen and had a suede coat with fringe, which I envied. He lived in the top of Uncle Tom's house in a room with its own bathroom, and he had a boa constrictor for a pet, which lived in the bathtub. The snake had once bitten Uncle Tom. It hadn't even drawn blood, but had somehow broken its own jaw. All my aunts and uncles thought that it was very funny to see a snake with a cast on its head. That was what I knew about Tom.

He came in to get a paper bag he'd put under my bed. "Hey, Mike," he said. "Hey, little man. Hear you're going spearing tonight with the old man."

I nodded from my pillow. "Good man," he said. "It's an ugly job, but somebody's got to do it."

He secretly smoked cigars behind his parents' backs, and I could smell the tobacco in the fringe of his coat. "Don't you ever go spearfishing?" I asked.

"With the old man? You're joking. Any chance to keep away from him, I take. You be the son for him, he's been looking for a decent son for quite the time." Then he left.

I looked up at the Sacred Heart, and traced with my eye the networked pattern of the crown of thorns. It was like a frame, like my uncle's unfinished shed, a frame that constricted the Heart or maybe held it up, like scaffolding. I drifted off, wondering what Tommy had in that paper sack, and why he hid it in my grandmother's house, under the bed.

It took a long time to fall asleep, but the time passing in my sleep seemed instantaneous. Before I knew it, hours had passed, and Uncle Tom came in and found the light switch next to the praying-hands night-light. He said in a low voice, "Listen! Listen! The cat's a-pissing!" He flicked the light switch off and on and Chester jumped on the bed and licked my face. I didn't know what was happening.

■ ■ ■

As we drove over dirt roads in the night, Uncle Tom told me all about spearfishing. "That's how the Indians used to fish. Nowadays, only the Indians get to do it, we can only spear carp." The road was winding, and I could see the road kill loom, like live animals. Though they were dead, I seemed to see them awakening when we came up to their bodies. Sometimes the headlights showed wildflowers growing where they shouldn't in the gravel. I thought, He could leave me here if he wanted to, and I'd never find my way back.

"I hope it doesn't rain when we're spearing," I said.

"It's better to fish in the rain."

"Why?"

"I don't know, it is. Maybe the fish get confused about what's air and what's water, so they swim closer to us."

"Doesn't nighttime take care of that?"

Uncle Tom didn't answer, but swerved to avoid a dead and substantial lump of raccoon in the road.

■ ■ ■

Uncle Tom and I trolled quietly over the huge shallow lake, on whose shores the Carp Carnival had taken place. Far across the water, we could see the lanterns over the prows of other spearing boats. Uncle Tom had cut a wide plank, and on top of that, he had welded and bolted four Coleman lanterns, which shone directly into the water at the front of the boat.

Those lanterns were magic. I had stared as he fitted sexy lace bags, like tiny ladies' stockings, over little pipes in the lanterns. I thought they would burn up right away, but they glowed, and made a sound like the blow of a dentist's air gun.

I could stand in the front and lean over a bar Uncle Tom had constructed in an M shape. It was wrapped in cheap padding and then thick black duct tape. In some places the tape had buckled into sharp fins, which poked my skin. When I leaned over and looked into the suddenly illuminated water, it felt like flying.

From the stern, Uncle Tom called to me, "Do you know what? It's tomorrow now. It became tomorrow just a minute ago." I could only see his face and neck and hands in the dim light. His ears stuck out like mine, we had the same kind of ears. "Seen any carp yet?" he asked.

"No, just weeds."

"It's too deep here, we'll go to a sandy place. You keep watching." He steered to the left. The boat was creeping along, so that when the first big fish loomed up, it was as if it swam toward us, and might rise out of the water and attack with its whiskered mouth. Its eyes were fixed on the magic lanterns. Then the boat passed over and I wondered if the carp might get caught in the motor blades. I scrambled back to where Uncle Tom was. "I saw him. He was right there and he didn't move. We could have gotten him."

"How big?" My uncle cut the motor, and put oars in the oarlocks. "You've got a big job to do now, Michael," he said in his serious voice. "You've got to row the boat while I spear the carp."

"But I want to see. Can't I watch?"

"When I get right on him, you can watch." He showed me how to row evenly and said it was perfect. I couldn't move the boat too fast, because he wanted it to glide slowly upon his prey. "Whatever you do, don't splash. Paddle evenly. You must be silent, or you'll scare the carp away."

The night was simple; the stars were covered with clouds and the only thing I could see was the black water near the oars. Beyond Uncle Tom, there was nothing. I could see him standing, leaning over his homemade support bar, looking into the water like it was a crystal ball. In his hand, he held the spear he had made with a small pitchfork. He had put barbs on each of the three prongs, and attached it to a longer stick. The stick had a rope tied to the end of it. The rope was attached to the boat, in case he speared into deep water. He looked like he was guarding something in the lantern light.

"Listen! Listen!" Uncle Tom whispered urgently. Then, in a room-temperature voice, "We have to turn around, we're getting into deeper water. Pretty soon we'll be near a drop-off. Come and see what I mean."

I rested the oars on the edge of the boat and balanced my way up to where he stood vigil. He was right. I could see the upcoming abyss, the sandy floor suddenly giving way. "They won't go deep," he said. "They stay where the food is. They like the shallows."

"If I was a carp, I'd stay here. That way I could get the food and run for it if spears came." Then I said, "Look," and pointed. The fish was as dark as the drop-off, like a huge eel-shaped stain of the same color in the sand.

"Oh, my God," he said.

"Can I spear it? I saw it."

"No, I need to show you how. You have to understand that the fish is not where you think it is. The water—oh, my God." He stopped explaining and raised the spear up over his shoulder. The boat slowly moved toward the drop-off.

And then my uncle threw his spear. He threw it far beyond the target, I thought, and as I watched it break the water I was already groaning at the bad throw, the loss. But somehow he hit the carp; it was Uncle Tom's biggest secret that night, to be so wrong and end up being right.

The carp, pierced through, began to swim down into the depths. The rope, coiled in the bottom of the boat, slithered out and down. Uncle Tom tumbled backward, and grabbed the rope. He was laughing. "I heard you sigh, you thought I missed him, didn't you?" The thrashing fish was actually pulling us over the drop-off.

I stared into the upcoming dark. "Where is he taking us?" I asked.

"Straight to hell," Uncle Tom said. He pulled on the rope like a crazy man, heaving the carp up. I was impressed and terrified.

He managed to pull the thrashing fish up into the boat, onto the newspapers spread on the bottom. It had been speared by two of the prongs, almost lengthwise. My uncle grabbed the end of his spear and put his boot against the carp and pulled. I could hardly see its wounds. Such a small head, what could it be thinking? Its ugly gills strained out like mad red muscled wings. One deep eye looked down into the newspaper, ink to ink. The other looked at me, no matter where I stood.

Uncle Tom was whooping. "Look at that! Look at that!" He slapped me on the back. "First night out, Mike. You've got the knack. You're my good-luck charm. Let's ask your ma if I can adopt you. Mike, this is a winning fish. This is *the best carp.*"

It was fat, it was long, and its eyes were not dried up. It would have beat any carp hanging on the line that August. "Too bad it's too late for the carnival," I said.

"Yes, too bad." We were done so quickly with our business that we didn't know what to do. He said, "Run, run, get the gun," and then, "Aw shoot, he's all done." The boat drifted along the edge of the drop-off. "It's too bad, because this is not just the winning fish, it's a record-breaking fish." We sat in the boat and watched the carp die.

"Michael, I have an idea," Uncle Tom said, after idly recoiling his slippery rope. "But it will be a secret. Nobody can know but us, do you promise?"

I looked over the side of the boat so I wouldn't have to answer him. We were floating on the deepest part of the lake. Above and below me was the night, cool and easy like sleep.

∙ ∙ ∙

Back at my grandmother's house, Uncle Tom let me carry the bulky slimy fish over my shoulder up to the side of the house. It was almost too big for me to carry. First I tried to carry it by the head, slipping one hand under the prickly gills into its head, but I was afraid it would tear away, with all its weight pulling it downward. So I held its tail and its head draped behind my back. Uncle Tom stopped to turn the porch light on, which drew moths. The shed cast shadows like a huge rib cage.

"I've never done anything like this before, but I think the best thing to do is wet him down real good before we wrap him up." He ran hose water and soaked the carp. I went to the car again and brought back the extra newspapers. Then my uncle began to wrap the fish around and around with sections of newsprint. At first the newspapers got wet and stuck to the fish. When he wrapped it in another layer, the wetness made it possible to see the words from the page underneath. Finally, he wrapped the head and covered the carp's eye. I stepped back into the dark, away from the outside porch light.

It took him forever. When he was done, he produced a measuring tape from his pocket and measured the carp. "Over forty inches," he said, and whistled low. I wondered why he didn't get the exact measurement, if it was a record breaker. Then the two of us carried the fish into the house, through the kitchen, and down the narrow stairs into the basement.

That was when Chester started barking. He had not heard us come in the door, but the basement door squeaked and startled him. "Head him off," said Uncle Tom, "or he'll wake the whole house up."

I picked Chester up and brought him into the basement with us. I closed the door behind so he couldn't get back out. Chester put his nose up in the air and sniffed the carp, and wagged his crooked tail like a scythe.

Uncle Tom lifted the lid of the big freezer. There was a layer of steaks and hamburger and chickens and frozen vegetables. He carefully took out all of the packages and put the carp in at the bottom. It was so long that the tail bent up the side. Then he replaced all of the meat and vegetables, burying the fish. "Now he's in the tomb," he said. "We'll raise him up next August, and win something good."

"What if somebody finds it before then?"

"Listen, listen," Uncle Tom said, and picked up a package of rump roast. There was a date written on it in Magic Marker. It was two years old. "Not a word, Michael. Can you keep a secret for a year? Especially from my kids. Anne is a loudmouth. And Tom, don't even talk to me about Tom."

"You think?"

"They're wild kids. I can't keep track of them, they're just wild." I thought of Tommy and his boa constrictor.

I looked into the freezer one more time. "What will we name it?"

"Name it?"

"For the Carp Carnival."

"It's already got a name." I went to bed near dawn wondering what secret name Uncle Tom had given the carp.

∎　∎　∎

Aunt Teresa waited until ten o'clock before she sent Anne in to wake me up. Mass was at noon and she could wait no longer. I woke to find myself pinned beneath the sheets and blankets, snug at my shoulders. Anne's knees held me down. Her lips disappeared as she made one of her meanest faces. I could see the tendons in her wrists straining to keep me there.

"Last night, somebody turned on Grandma's porch light, and I could see it from our house. It woke me up," she said. "Now I'm waking you up, to tell you that." Then she sat back and her mean face broke, like a fever breaks. "We're all waiting for you in the living room. Hurry!" She leaned forward. "Or I'll tell."

I did not ask, "Tell what?"

I was so tired I came into the living room in pajamas and lay facedown on the couch with my hands under the cushions, feeling the coolness there. The texture of the couch was rough as burlap. Its pattern pressed into my skin. I dozed.

"Michael," Aunt Teresa said. "Wake up, or you won't be ready for church. I've got your clothes waiting in your room." She had on her summer dress and her hair was sprayed in a perfect shape.

Uncle Tom walked in with coffee. "Maybe he ought to sleep instead. We were out pretty late." He was not ready himself.

"That's just dandy," Aunt Teresa said. "I knew he shouldn't go with you. If he misses, he'll have to go to Confession, before he can take Communion again." She was putting on her new white gloves. "And *you'll* take him."

I sat up quickly. "I'm awake." I went back to my room, and when I woke up it was midafternoon. Everybody was back from mass. I came into the kitchen just in time for dinner, a ham and scalloped potatoes. All the aunts and uncles and cousins were there. Anne and Tom were talking secretly over the food. They came to me and wanted to know what we had caught the night before. "Nothing," I said.

"Bull," said Anne.

"Tell," said Tom. They reminded me of a wicked prince and princess who'd been disinherited by their father, the king. I was the hapless new heir to the throne.

．　　．　　．

In the middle of the following week, at colorless midday, I was relegated to the backyard while my grandmother's "stories" were on. I was trying to figure out how to climb an invariably wet willow tree with many branches, but even the lowest one was out of my reach.

Tom drove up the driveway in his own car. He was drawing on one of his cigars, and he thinned and hid his lips to blow out the smoke. He was wearing his fringed suede coat, even though it was very hot and the cicadas screamed like electrocution. "Hey, little man. Want to take a ride?"

I said I wasn't sure, but he opened up the passenger door and I got in. The radio station was playing music that always made my parents switch channels. Tom kept saying, "This is a really good song, do you know this song?" He said he was learning to play electric guitar.

"Are you going to be a rock star?" I asked.

"Sure. But first I'm going to Vietnam and kick some butt."

"When?"

"As soon as I graduate. I need somebody to take care of my snake while I kick butt in 'Nam. How about you?"

Nothing was impossible to me, I always had an answer then. Immediately I began to dream of taking care of the snake and wearing the fringed suede jacket. I wondered if Vietnam was down south, near Florida. Tom drove the car all over town while I stayed quiet, thinking about how I could convince my parents that I could take care of the snake.

"So," Tom said, "did you see any decent carp last night?"

"No, not many. I *saw* some," I explained, "but we didn't catch him."

"Annie says you and the old man were up to no good."

"Anne is retarded."

"It comes from your folks," Tom said, and just then, he drove up into my grandmother's driveway. "Well, gotta book." He reached across and opened the door for me, and the little fringes dangled over my nose. I got out and he pulled out of the driveway. The shape of his skid marks on the street looked like a perfect question mark.

I was still standing looking after him when Anne appeared on the porch. "You went off with Tom? I'm telling Aunt Teresa!" and she tore into the house. I chased her up the porch stairs, through the kitchen to my soft room. She stood protected by the bed.

"I'll kill you," I said.

"Ugh, I'm so scared. I think I feel faint, I'm so scared."

"You ought to be," I dared.

"It's okay, I'll just tell her later." Her arms were crossed, and her left foot was twisted in on the same line with the angling of her head. "Unless. Unless you tell me what you and my old man were doing late at night."

"He's not your old man, he's your *dad*," I said. I couldn't believe that she was as wrapped up in the secret as I was. I had thought about the carp all the time, too, but no matter how much I dreamed of the fish, like a greasy villain, under my uncle's boot, Anne had thought more. Only Anne could think about its terribleness more than me.

"Now tell me, Michael. What was that wrapped up in all that newspaper. Was that a body? Did my old man kill somebody?"

"You mean you don't know?" She didn't know.

"Sure I know."

I am not sure why I wanted to let her know. Maybe to break the power of the carp and Uncle Tom so I wouldn't dream of it anymore. Maybe so that Tom would like me, and let me take care of his boa constrictor. "Then do you want to see?"

"You mean you still have it? Where is it?"

"If I show you, you have to swear not to tell anybody. Swear."

"I swear. Where is it?"

"Where's Aunt Teresa?"

"In the living room with Grandma, watching their story."

I led her to the basement. The air came up from the doorway, damp. Anne whimpered, "Oh God, you buried it in the basement. Oh God."

I led her to the freezer. There was a bare light bulb on one long cord. When I clicked it on, it swung to and fro, making our shadows bend in circles. "There's another light over by the water heater. Turn that on, too," Anne said.

"You're scared, aren't you?" I said, grinning. I felt that I looked like Uncle Tom. I could make a hammer pick up nails, I could make the lantern wicks out of ladies' stockings. I could scare Anne to death.

"Bullshit," she said. "Let's see it."

Slowly, I opened the refrigerator lid. Then I grabbed the rump roast and tossed it to her. "Think fast!" I stage-whispered. She squealed, put out her hands, and the roast bounced away from her.

"You bastard," she said.

She looked like she was going to leave, so I promised I wouldn't do it again. She helped me move all of the meat and vegetables. We made a pile of them on the floor. In the freezer, I could see where the tail ran up the side, frozen in a hook shape. "There," I said.

"There what?"

"Don't you see him?"

"That's not a body. That's too small for a body. You're full of it."

"Sure it is. Do you know whose body it is?" I whispered this time. "It's Rosemary's Baby, with tiny cloven hooves."

"It is? No, it's not. You're full of it."

"Uncle Tom stole him from the Carp Carnival."

"He did not. I'm going to get Tommy."

"He already left."

"That's not Rosemary's Baby."

I leaned over and began to unwrap its head. The newspaper was stiff, wet, and frosted. I unwrapped the eye and one of the slimy mustaches first. The eye looked right at us, through a glaze of frozen slime. Anne screamed and then started crying.

"Shut up, Anne, shut up. Aunt Teresa will hear you and we'll get arrested." But she wouldn't stop wailing. Then I said, "Anne, it's not Rosemary's Baby, it's a fish. It's a carp."

Somehow, that made sense to her. I pulled the fish out and it was stiff in a curl in my arms, but easier to carry than in its wet state. When I unwrapped the tail, she started helping me unwrap the rest of it. By the time we were finished, I almost forgot that she had been upset. She had her regular face on again, a wedge of control.

"Why would you save something stupid like this?" she said.

"For the Carp Carnival. We're coming back next year and we'll thaw it out and win the prize for the best carp." I tried to wrap it up again, but most of the papers were torn away. "Stay here while I get something to wrap it up again," I said. "Guard the fish."

When I came back, she was gone, and so was the carp. The steaks and rump roasts were beginning to thaw, and they made a leaking rivulet of water, which ran to a little drain in the middle of the floor. I put them away before I went looking for Anne.

Tom's car pulled up while I searched near the unfinished shed. He got out and I ran up to him. "Have you seen Anne?" I gasped.

"She just called me. Said she got something I had to see."

"Oh, no," I said.

"Oh, no? Oh, no what, little man?"

"She's got my carp."

Anne ran up the driveway from her house. She was carrying the fish wrapped in papers. She was covered with fish gunk. She jumped into Tom's car and shouted out the window, "Come on, get away from that little jerk."

"That thing will stink up my car," Tom said. "Not cool, not cool."

We both went to the car. She cradled the carp like a baby. Tom said, "Anne, is this Mike's carp? Are you stealing Mike's carp?"

"Finders keepers, losers weepers, let's go," she said. Then she told him about our plans for the Carp Carnival.

Tom shook his head in admiration. "The old man, he's a sly dog. Cheats like hell."

"You promised to keep a secret," I said to Anne. "You're going to burn in such a great big hell, I hope your eyes melt out."

"Don't worry about it, little man. I can keep a secret. And I'll take care of Anne." He put the half-smoked cigar in his mouth and went to light it. "But you know, I don't think it's going to work. You can't bring a fish back to life. Look at that thing."

It did look bad. All over its body was an inch-deep layer of slime, that oozed from its insides, too, as it thawed. I said, "Sure we can. I'm sure it will work."

Then Tom made a face like his cigar gave him a big idea. "Get in the car," he said.

All along the road, Anne kept screaming, "Hurry up, it's super cold and it's starting to drip on me." It didn't smell, though. It didn't have a smell.

I thought, Aunt Teresa will wonder what's happened to

me, but by then we had reached the wide shallow lake in Tom's car.

.   .   .

When we got into the boat, Tom did not make us wear life preservers the way Uncle Tom did. He rigged up a line behind the boat and hooked the fish to it. "We'll troll him and see if that will thaw him out. We'll get all that shit out of him while we're at it. Then we'll see if the old man's scheme will work."

"Don't tell," I chanted. "Promise not to tell."

"Don't worry about it, kid." He started the motor. I looked into the bottom of the boat. There was gas on the bilge water and it made swirly rainbows. Tom threw the fish out behind and we started through the water.

The carp kept swinging out to the right because its tail was frozen in the curve. After a few minutes, Tom slowed the boat and pulled the fish in. It was still hard and the slime seemed to be coming forever. "Hell," Tom said. "Once he quits oozing, there won't be anything left of him." He looked up at me. "So what's this guy's name?"

"I don't know," I said.

"Let's call him the Old Man." He threw the fish out and trolled it some more. Anne sat in the front—she'd lost interest in the whole thing. She was trying to wash the gunk off of her shorts. The fish was for Tom and me.

Tom checked on it again and it was half-warm and half-cold. And it was a skinnier fish. Tom showed me a dark spot near one of its fins. "Freezer burn," he said. I looked into the Old Man's eye, but it was so covered in slime that I couldn't tell if it was looking at me.

When Tom threw him back, it landed in a patch of weeds. We went almost halfway across the lake before we realized the carp had come loose from the string and we had lost it.

We searched for two hours, but we never found the Old Man.

.　　.　　.

"Hey, little man, just play dumb. It's not your prob. Either play dumb or tell him that when you checked on the carp, it was not in that freezer." We sat at my grandmother's kitchen table for a long time drinking lemonade, and Tom coached me for what to say to Uncle Tom. "Tell him it wasn't there, and you wouldn't dare ask Aunt Teresa where it was."

"Yeah, but I miss the carp." I stirred the lemonade listlessly, and propped my head up over the table on my arm.

"It's not a goddamn pet," he said. Anne was stirring in extra lemonade mix until she had a thick layer of it settled at the bottom of her clear glass. Tom pushed the canister of mix away from her, using the end of his spoon.

"A carp can be a pet if a snake can be a pet," Anne said to retaliate.

"Besides, he had a name—you gave it to him. We were a sure bet to win a prize," I said. "I think it was a magic fish. Even the way Uncle Tom caught it was magic. He aimed in the wrong place in the water and the carp just jumped right on his spear."

Tom took his spoon and stabbed into his lemonade. The handle of the spoon broke perfectly in two at the surface line of the lemonade. "That's not magic, little man," he said. "It's just the water."

Late-afternoon sun, the sunlight best for barbecuing, lit the kitchen. Uncle Tom came in the door. He still had his police uniform on from work, and Aunt Teresa had called him over to yell at Tom for taking me away from the house without telling her (that was the part of the blame Tom agreed to take). We were waiting for him.

"Hey, old man!" Tom said.

"Hey, old man!" Anne said. "How are you, old man?"

Uncle Tom pointed a finger at Anne. "*You* had better not call me that again, little lady, or I'll blister your behind so fast it will make your head swim."

Anne bunched her face up into a vexed fist. "How come he gets to?"

The pointed finger moved from Anne out the door, like Uncle Tom was directing traffic. "Get home—both of you. How would you like to be grounded for the rest of the summer?" They followed his finger out the door, Anne dragging her feet and Tom strutting, the fringe on his coat wagging in stylish curves.

Uncle Tom sat next to me at the kitchen table. He pondered the spoon in the glass of lemonade. "So," he said. "How is the Old Man?"

I bugged my eyes at him. "What do you mean?"

"I mean our best carp. The Old Man is the name of our carp, right? It's named after us, right?" Uncle Tom looked more comfortable in his police uniform.

"How did you know about that?"

"Know about what?"

"That we named him the Old Man."

"Who is 'we'?"

I couldn't lie in the moment in which a lie was most important to my salvation. He knew, I figured. I took him to the basement, down to the freezer and its emptiness. "What happened?" he asked.

I looked straight at him, reporting a crime to the officer. "He disappeared."

"Where?" Then he quickly stopped asking me: "I wonder where?" He was letting me off. "Did Anne do this to you?"

"To me?"

"Did Tom do it?"

"No! I'm sure he didn't do it. Anne maybe, but not Tom."

"Listen, listen. I think it's best not to mention this to any-
one," he said. "Not a soul. I'll take care of it." Why was he
worried? I wondered what he would take care of. So many
members of the family claimed they would "take care of it,"
but this usually amounted to silence, burying the evidence in
a deep freeze or at the bottom of a lake.

Many times after that, in my fuzzy stupors, I thought I
could see the carp trapped in the weeds. I dreamed that he
was still alive but dying, abandoned, flopping and snarled in
lily pads with a string parachuting from his mouth, sticky
with newspapers all over him. His eyes were lidless, he could
not close them, but I couldn't see the eye through the glaze
of his own slime.

■   ■   ■

A few days before I left my great-grandmother's house that
summer, Aunt Teresa took me to Confession because I had
missed church. I told Father O'Hara I had lied to my father,
that I swore, that I said mean things to Anne, and that I had
committed adultery. Then I told him about the carp. "Is it a
sin if we were going to cheat at the contest but then it didn't
happen, not because we didn't want to, but because we
couldn't?"

Father O'Hara didn't answer me for a minute. Then he
said, "Yes." Then he said, "Michael. You did not commit adultery. It's also a sin to say you did something when you
didn't."

CHAPTER 3

The Power of Prayer

A few months ago, I paid a visit on my aunts Charlene and Charlotta. Both their husbands died almost a month apart, and their children were grown like me, and they moved into one of their houses, consolidated the furniture, and grew to look more and more like each other. When I saw them, they had a Mantovani album on the old stereo. It was playing just loudly enough that I could identify the tune, but not loudly enough to catch the melody.

"You can turn that up, if you like, I can barely hear it," I said to Aunt Charlene.

"Oh, but we hear it just *fine*," she said. They both sat on a dromedarian divan, tiny and dollish and fat at opposite ends, their elbows uplifted to rest on the overstuffed arms, where they balanced coffee cups.

"Isn't it nice?" Aunt Charlotta said, and hummed a moment with the music so that I could make it out.

"Beer, Michael?" Aunt Charlene offered, gesturing toward the kitchen. For something to do, I took her up on it.

There they were, the twins, both wearing well-combed wigs, identical cat-eye glasses (they think those are the height of fashion, I realized at the time) and identical faces, feet in the same position. Not all of this x-equals-x stuff could be spontaneous, I thought. Which one decided, I wanted to know, that they should wear that particular coral lipstick color? Which decided that they should both pluck out their eyebrows and draw them back on?

The curtains in the room drew my attention. They were heavy and velvet with gold tasseled fringe. All of the furniture, like the sofa, was massive and made my aunts look shrunken. In the awkward moments before we had a long talk, I noticed the stumbling ticks of more than one clock in the house. It was the sound of heart murmur. Faulty hearts ended so many lives in the Kaiser family.

I tried to count the clocks surreptitiously, and came up with nine, but reminded myself that in the final tally, I could throw in wristwatches and an alarm clock, maybe even the oven timer.

What *was* the time? I wondered, having forgotten to change my own wristwatch during the flight back to Michigan. "What is the time?" I asked Aunt Charlene.

"Let's see"—one sister looked at the other—"have you changed them again?"

"Just this morning."

Aunt Charlene got up and began to walk around the room, tapping each clock with her forefinger. She pointed out to me two more I hadn't noticed. "Let's see ... this one says four-thirty, and this one says two-ten, and hell, Charlotta, you've got this one way back to noon. Cheat!" After a few minutes of calculating and of mystifying comments, she came up with, "Three-fifteen."

"I think you're right," said Aunt Charlotta. "Damn good, Charlene."

"I don't get it," I said, trying to be polite.

"We take turns changing the clocks on each other," said Aunt Charlene, and tapped her temple with the same forefinger she'd picked off clocks. "It keeps your mind nimble."

Every clock told a different time. Through the machinations of some secret mathematical formula agreed upon by my aunts, they challenged each other to a chronic game of chronological roulette. They were *not* hard of hearing. They were *not* going senile. They were *not* growing old. Theirs was a *folie à deux* of never-ending youth.

"It runs in the family, Michael, so watch the hell out," Aunt Charlotta said.

"What runs?"

"Senility. You saw your grandmother. Mad as a hatter." And then the three of us talked about my grandmother, dead some years. We talked until a cuckoo clock, one that I hadn't noticed in my tally, struck two o'clock. A small white wooden bird, tight as a wing nut, bobbed out twice. I told them it looked like it was time to go, as I had to visit a dozen other Kaisers in Monsalvat.

■   ■   ■

There were two reasons why, in the summer of my eleventh year, I was taken to my grandmother's house in Monsalvat, and heard the record from the top of the Empire State Building. One was strictly religious—the Pilgrim Virgin Statue was in my grandmother's house for the month of July. The Pilgrim Virgin Statue was a plaster statue, knee-high, adorned in a stiff velvet cape and a rubbery gold crown that came off the Virgin Mary's head and fit like a webbed ring on my index finger, and left flecks of glitter on me when I took it off. She was kept dust free by a clear plastic pocket, like a tea cozy, which fit snugly over Her head. The members of my grandmother's parish took turns having the Pilgrim Statue in their homes, having family over to say the rosary. It was the Kaisers' turn, and Aunt Teresa invited us to make our own pilgrimage north so that I could learn to say the rosary.

The other reason I went to Monsalvat for a weekend was

because my maternal grandparents, who lived in California, had come to Michigan to see my brother Hugh for the first time. I myself had only seen them once before, but they were the source of a hundred presents and postcards, so I thought I knew them well.

My grandfather was the war hero who fought with the marines in Asia at the end of World War II. He married young, just before he marched off to war, and when he got back, my mother was already born. My mother married my father at a young age, too, and so we were about one generation ahead of the other uncles' and aunts' families. The grandmother in Monsalvat was actually my great-grandmother, a distinction drilled into me while my immediate grandparents were visiting from California.

"Here he is, here he is," the tan golden-looking woman said, who was my new grandmother, Louise. She wore a heavy beige mohair sweater because she said she was cold in Michigan, she was so used to the California sun. I thought it was funny, because I was begging to run out barefoot in that liberating spring heat, which comforted me and afflicted my grandmother Louise.

"Hey, Dutchman! Ma, give him the stuff," my grandfather said. He looked like Uncle Tom, only less weather-beaten, and with a different part in his hair, with less hair oil. He wore reading glasses and cleaned them often with lilac-colored crinkly tissue paper.

"What stuff?" she asked him.

"You know, the money, the knife, that stuff we brought."

Gifts? I wondered. Money and a knife? My golden grandma got up and led me to her suitcase. There was a small auto trash bag with "Keep America Clean" and a California credit-union address printed on it. Inside, there were several items, all for me. There was a cardboard-thick hundred-dollar bill with the credit-union address on it, and my grandfather explained that if I put it in water, it would puff up like a sponge and I could use it in the bathtub. He was amused by this, and kept coming back to it over the weekend. The knife was actually a plastic jackknife with plastic blades and the different kinds of credit-union accounts I could have listed on each blade. There was a comb, a whistle, a little harmonica, and a rain bonnet in a plastic case, all with the credit-union name printed on them.

"What a bunch of crap," Anne said to me, once she saw the bag of gifts. "And why does he call you Dutchman? You're not Dutch. You're German, just like everybody else." She was helping herself to all of the objects, and passing them on to Tom, for inspection.

"No, he's not," said Tommy. He was looking at the disappointing knife, and looked just as disappointed as I was. "Mike's last name is Bellman, because Uncle Lewy is Irish."

"You mean he's not a goddamned Kaiser? Ha, that's a laugh."

"Shut up, Anne," Tom said. He looked like he was bored with my loot. "You're jealous."

She said she wasn't, but a few hours later the little harmonica was missing and I found the hundred-dollar-bill sponge abandoned, soaked and puffy, sitting on the edge of the sink in the bathroom next to my baby-blue room.

■　■　■

My grandfather made a career of the marines, and once my mother was out on her own, he and my grandmother Louise moved to Camp Pendleton near San Diego. Then he retired from the military and took a job working for a company that made airplanes. He was the first person I knew who had a worldview, who had opinions about the evils of other countries instead of the evils of the welfare queen down the street who was spotted at the butcher's buying filet mignon with food stamps. I came into the living room with my bag of

cheap gifts, and heard him say, "The Russians, they don't believe in God, it's in their *culture*, but you know, we could get
along fine with them, one-on-one. What *I* want to do is drop
a couple bombs on the French, those goddamned French."

He was talking to Tommy, who stood idly in the doorway,
wearing his fringed coat and his sunglasses, not committed to
the conversation and ready to walk out at any moment. My
golden grandmother, Louise, came up to him in her fuzzy
sweater and kissed him like she was a foreign movie star.
"Tommy! I hear you're going to be in the marines! Good for
you! Brave you!"

Tommy gave her a little hug. "Everybody loves me, now
I'm going to go shoot guns at people," he said, shrugging
himself free of her embrace.

"Are you scared?" she asked, straightening out the mohair.

"Nah. I figure I've got nothing better to do, so I might as
well go."

"You should be more excited! I'll bet you're scared. Come
on, admit it, you're scared."

My grandfather pulled her arm. "Let him go, Ma. He's got
the right attitude. Never trust the ones who're too eager,
Tommy. They're the nut cases. They'll shoot at anything."

He got quite an audience with ideas like that. Between my
grandmother Louise's photo albums and my grandfather's
worldview, they stole the family show. My grandmother had
brought, besides the sack of favors for me, a handful of eucalyptus pods, which smelled like cough drops and which was
the best gift they ever gave me. Along with the pods, though,
my golden grandmother had an exhaustive selection of photographs showing eucalyptus trees.

The entire photo album held endless rows of landscapes:
mountains, oceans, forests, all from faraway California. None
of the pictures had people in them. My golden grandmother
insisted that she liked her pictures to be *perfect* like this,

pretty and generic as postcards. By perfect, she meant peopleless. Here and there, I could make out a waving arm or my grandmother's shadow, phantoms. "Look at this, look at this, four generations!" my golden grandmother said, pulling out her omnipresent camera. "Let's get a picture of all of you." She forced my great-grandmother, my grandfather, my mother, and me onto the living-room couch and flashed out four pictures. I saw one of them months later, and we looked small and nondescript, except for smiles, hair color, and the flower print on my great-grandmother's dress. Far away like that, none of us looked old, flawed, or different, we looked as *perfect* as those California vistas.

"Now let's get one of you and little Hugh together," she said to me. That photo has always looked strangest of all to me, whenever I see it. Going to Monsalvat has always been, in my mind, something I did on my own. The age difference between me and my little brother was one reason. But there was also a sense that however little I didn't belong among these Kaisers, Hugh and my parents belonged even less. They were ghosts among those visits, watercolors on an oil landscape. The picture of me, sitting on the piano bench at Grandmother Kaiser's with Hugh on my lap, seems a false one. We are imposters.

In the same way, Anne's younger sisters and brothers and the other children belonging to my aunts and uncles were mostly invisible, in my memory. They were never so threatening or problematic as Anne or Tommy, so they are lost in the fuzz of their niceness, niceness being a terrible quality for those who wish to be a pungent memory to me.

My golden grandma, Louise, went on a shooting spree while my grandfather expounded on his worldview. All of this bothered Aunt Teresa, who was trying to get people to pray a scriptural rosary to the Pilgrim Virgin Mary. "John, could you take your act into the other room? We're trying to say a rosary in here." She had bought some candles and wanted to have a nice ceremony, where everybody took turns reading passages out of the New Testament and lighting another candle between sets of ten Hail Marys and one Our Father.

"I didn't know we were starting up a church, lady," he said. But his wife said that she wanted to say a rosary with his sisters and get to know the family a little better. "You want to be a goddamned Kaiser broad, like the rest of the them, Ma?" my grandfather declared.

"Kaiserbroad?" she said. "Is that the original spelling?" They all laughed at that one, it was turned into a story for years afterward. My grandmother pouted. "Well, I just thought. You know, the immigration people used to change names all the time when you came into this country. I just thought."

"Kaiserbroads. It sounds like a good name for our bowling team," said Aunt Charlene. "Do you bowl out there in California?"

"Hell no," said Aunt Charlotta. "When the weather's always nice, why would you stay inside? They don't bowl, they golf. They have Kaiserbroad Invitationals instead of Kaiserbroad Tournaments."

"Are you girls going to pray with me or what?" Aunt Teresa said, getting down on her knees and taking her cut-glass rosary out of a sky-blue fuzzy ring case. "The family that prays together stays together. Michael? Where's your rosary? Anne? Tom?"

Tommy pulled the sunglasses down and looked square into Aunt Teresa's eyes, shook his head warningly, and walked into the dining room. He had just graduated from high school and was soon headed for boot camp. In the meantime, as the day for boot camp approached, every minute was a last hurrah. He had let his hair grow very long. When Uncle Tom complained, Tommy defended himself by explaining that for the next three years, his hair would be shaved to his skull, so he wanted to enjoy himself while he could. With this argument, he was able to drink more beer and smoke his cigars in the open; before, he had done those things in secret.

"Once, he gave me a hard time about my seegars," Tommy told me about his father. "But I told him, hey, what happens if I get blown up over there? What if I die and I didn't enjoy myself just before I went? He didn't like that a bit, he didn't want to hear one word about my getting blown up. Now he lets me do anything." With that in mind, I watched every magical move he made, and remarked every moment of his control; smoking seegars didn't seem much compared with things he might have done with his boa constrictor, or his car.

It was all women, except for me, who were praying this rosary. My aunts, a couple of daughters of each of those aunts, my golden grandmother, and my mother made a semi-circle and threw throw pillows on the floor to kneel. Two of my cousins wouldn't sit still, and I think they were whispering jokes about me to each other. I waited for the congregation around the Pilgrim Statue to settle in and knelt at the periphery, a few feet away from the doorway into the dining room. At the big table, my grandfather had suffered my cousin Tommy to come up to him. I could hear both the ritual of the rosary and my grandfather talking, there in the borderlands, and I clasped my rosary in disguise.

"So you wanna be a jarhead," my grandfather was saying to Tommy as my aunts, the Kaiserbroads, and my grandmother, the honorary Kaiserbroad, recited the Apostles' Creed all together. I did not recite, but watched Aunt Teresa lighting the first candle. Chester came up and licked her hands, which he loved to do whenever she was working with them. She pushed her dog away from her.

"One of these days," said Aunt Charlene, "you're going to have to put that old dog to sleep. He's just a blind old coot."

"He's just fine," Aunt Teresa said, and lit another candle more gracefully this time. The room seemed like a holiday.

Tommy said, "Well, that's the plan, man." My great-grandmother, my grandfather, and Tommy sat around the table drinking lemonade. Somebody was mowing a lawn a few doors down. Anne, present a moment before, had gone somewhere.

"It's not the same kind of war," said my grandfather, under his breath, like he didn't want to wake somebody sleeping in the room. "Not the kind I fought in. 'Course, we had a lot of free time, and the war was almost over when I got there. It wasn't fair, the way we stomped on them."

Aunt Teresa was saying the first Hail Mary very loudly: "Blessed art thou among women and blessed is the fruit of thy womb, Jesus. Holy Mary, Mother of God, pray for us sinners, now, and at the hour of our death. Amen."

"Down there in the Philippines, you know," my grandfather said, "everybody's Catholic. Missionaries came in there and gave them all rosaries. All them Filipino women took them and put them around their necks. Like they was necklaces. And they don't wear shirts around there. They run around without any shirts on. The gals do. Then us GIs, we'd give them our extra T-shirts, and you know what they'd do? They'd cut holes in those good government-issue T-shirts, one for each boob, so they'd stick right out. You'd go down by the water, and you'd see these gals washing clothes on the bank, slapping their clothes against the rocks, and their rosaries around their necks and the boobs hanging out of our GI T-shirts, and these little kids, no bigger than Hughy over there, scamper along from gal to gal, sucking on their boobs. They looked like skinny rats, and they'd take their turns on all of them, like every one of them was their mama."

How could I pay attention to the prayers with words like that? I listened with the same kind of unavoidable terror with which I had seen photographs of natives in *National Geographic*, those women covered with mud and tattoos, living strangely happy lives without a God that asked for articulated and incessant prayers. And so, since my grandfather was not saying prayers and was talking about these shirtless women on the rocks, he was as much a wild native savage as the Filipino women.

Tommy had taken off his sunglasses and his fringed coat. I tried hard to concentrate on the prayers, but the words blended together with what he was telling them. Aunt Charlotta said, "The Joyful Mysteries. The Angel Gabriel was sent from God."

"So they were nice folks?" Tommy said. He was writing figures into the sweating lemonade glass. "They didn't want to kill you guys for coming around and blowing things up?"

"Hell, they loved us. We had money, and T-shirts. We could get taken real easy, we were gullible Americans. Talk to any of those Orientals, they'd want to make a deal with you. They'd smile at you and you'd want to buy something from them and they'd name a price and you'd haggle with them. It's a different *culture*, you see. It's not who's right or wrong, there, it's who doesn't lose his cool. So you stand around arguing and smiling and bowing to each other until you make a price, say, over a wristwatch, and you finally get the wristwatch and the little Oriental guy gets his money, and you find out after he's gone that he's taken all the guts out of the watch, it's empty. They loved us GIs."

Tommy was doing anything to look like he was not interested in what my grandfather had to say. He reached behind to his coat hanging off the back of the chair and stuck his hands in the pockets, like he was still wearing the coat. He leaned back in the chair, so it rested on its two back legs, like the chair was part of him, and the whole mass might walk out on my grandfather at any minute. He said, "Geez, Uncle Johnny, were you that stupid?"

"Hell, you'll be that stupid. They've got a million cons there, they con you because it's their *culture* to con you. Someday you'll see what I mean. Someday you'll find out how stupid you are, too."

Here was the man who had sent all of those foreign stamps to my grandmother. Here he was, inviting my cousin Tommy to leave the family, sending him away, to risk death and come back with his own stories.

Aunt Charlene got up to get a glass of water; she whispered that her throat was dry from reading out loud as she passed me. But she sat down with Tommy and my grandfather and did not return to our rosary.

"What the hell are you telling this kid?" I heard her say to my grandfather, but she kept quiet as he continued his savage stories. And while Aunt Charlotta led us through three more joyful mysteries, I was thinking of those women with rosaries around their necks, kneeling at the waterside, looking to the Virgin Mary in the high blue Asian skies, the two holes in the soft white fabric, and their brown breasts dipping out of them, as they did in *National Geographic*, the little boys like my brother Hugh flicking hot sand behind their skinny, flailing legs. I wondered if they were so terrible, after all.

And what was Tommy thinking about when my grandfather told him his own litany of stories?

"You want to hear how I got fleeced?" my grandfather started up again. "I was getting something, something nice for Ma, to take back as a souvenir. I didn't have much money, only the sorry excuse they called a paycheck, but I saw these moccasins, these slippers. They were all leather and this guy had hand-tooled designs into them, real nice, little designs with beads and rocks, the way the gals like them. I had to get them. I asked the guy how much, he says, not for sale." My grandfather turned his face into an arrow shape, the eyebrows gashing downward to a focused point on his two bucked front teeth, when he imitated the Chinese man: "nah fo say-oh." "He said 'not for sale'? I says, why do you have them out if they're not for sale? He says, 'Sam-poh.' Sample? I says, sample for what? For what you don't got? I want these, name your price. He says, 'Twenty dollah.' Now that was a hell of a lot for then. Hell of a lot for now. So I dickered with him, back and forth, arguing, smiling, bowing. Get him down to about fifteen dollars, but I'm broke after that. I'll have to live on coffee for the rest of the week. But I've got me a deal. I figure Ma will never walk out on me if I give her these puppies. I get back to camp and put these swanky slippers under my cot, and next day it starts to get cold.

"It snowed. They turned up those little gas heaters in our big tents, and we start smelling something, something bad. It's coming from Kaiser's bunk, they're saying. They start sniffing around my cot, and they pull up those moccasins. Pee-you, they all start yelling, these things smell like piss. Like piss. You know why? That old shyster soaked the leather for those moccasins in horse piss so the leather would soften up. They do that! It's another *culture*. So here I was with these useless pissy moccasins." He stopped and drank lemonade, and stayed quiet.

"So," Tommy said. He was looking at the ground as if he were paying more attention to our prayers than my grandfather. He took his time before he said, "Did you give them to her?"

"Sure I did. A gift is a gift, they still looked nice. Why throw nice things out?" He looked for approval from his wife, Grandma Louise, tucked away at arm's length behind the table. "We kept them outside in the garage, hoping they'd air out after a while. Then mice got to them, or dry rot, I don't remember."

Tommy leaned forward. "But did you get hurt in the war?"

Aunt Charlotta announced, "The Sorrowful Mysteries. The agony in the garden." It was my turn to read from the Bible they passed around. I read, "Then Jesus went with them to a place called Gethsemane, and He began to experience sorrow and distress."

While I read, my grandfather got up and waded through

the room of kneeling women and headed for the stairway. Tommy waited patiently with my great-grandmother for him to return. She said to Tommy, "I thought he was dead when he went to those places. We didn't hear anything from him because he didn't like to write letters much. Not even to me. Not even to his wife."

Tommy said, "I will write you letters." It was funny, I noticed, how people, when they wanted to sound reverent, didn't contract words: not "I'll write you letters," but "I will write often."

"Write in big print," she said, and tapped her eyeglasses on the lenses, one for each, like she was anointing them.

Tom fumbled in his fringed pocket of the coat hanging on the back of his chair, and pulled out a half-smoked cigar. He turned it around in his hand, then caught himself and put it back into the pocket. My great-grandmother pushed a blue glass ashtray toward him and smiled. He smiled back and pulled the cigar out and lit it. He said, "You're a cool lady." She thanked him, and sipped lemonade.

My grandfather did not come down until the Glorious Mysteries, and by then, the cigar smoke filled the room like an incense of burning tea. It smelled like autumn again; it reminded me of the carp. My grandfather carried handfuls of medals and souvenirs, and nearly dropped them. I immediately recognized them from the trunk in the attic. Aunt Charlotta got up from her prayer and helped him carry the things in. She, also, did not return.

"Look at this stuff. I haven't seen this stuff in years," he said to Tom. He laid out the medals one at a time, and they sounded like silverware, as if the table were being set for dinner. He was explaining each one as he went along. I held out the bead of my rosary to see how many Hail Marys were left. I was suffocating with boredom. Like wedges of time on the face of a clock, I saw the groups of beads as lengths of time. This many beads meant this much time, I calculated. I wanted to see the medals, the souvenirs.

"This one is for marksmanship. This one is for bravery, and this"—he placed it gingerly before Tom with two fat Teutonic fingers—"is the Purple Heart."

Tom raised his eyes. "Where were you hit?"

"All over hell," he said. "But look at this." He laid out several vaguely tattered pieces of cloth. One was a white headband, and from where I sat, I could make out a perfect red circle in the center. "I got the bastards back."

I couldn't see enough, and there were seven Hail Marys left. "I picked this off the Jap I killed, took his gun, too, took everything in his pocket. The spoils of war!" Some coins jangled down on the table. "Yen," he said.

Tom ran his fingers over the piece of cloth, he was as intent on it as Aunt Teresa was on the statue and candles before her. "So," he said. He looked disgusted, full of loathing, like he'd just swallowed a worm. "You killed the guy?"

"Yep."

"So, this is blood?" Tom's disgust changed into something else. He looked like he might cry, or explode, or laugh.

"No, *this* is a headband." My grandfather tried to joke around with him. "It's got blood on it."

"You shot him in the head?"

"Yep." I openly craned my neck to see him point to one of the medals. Aunt Teresa glared at me, I didn't dare leave. "This one is for marksmanship. Someday, you'll have your own souvenirs, medals, and yen—what kind of money do they use in Vietnam?"

Tom got up. I could tell by the way he put his sunglasses on that he had had enough. It must be a very bloody headband, I imagined, to make Tommy lose his cool. "They don't have money," Tommy said. "They trade. They barter. It's a different *culture.*" And he walked out the back, through the kitchen.

My grandfather turned to his mother. "What's crawled up his ass and died?" I listened to him like he was the noble savage again, using forbidden words.

She said, "John. He's scared. You think you're a big help, but you scared the tar out of him, bringing those things in here." It must have been a very bloody headband.

"May the Divine Assistance remain always with us. And may the souls of the faithful departed, through the mercy of God, rest in peace. Amen." The rosary prayer had calmed my aunts and fidgety cousins with its candles and chanting, but with that last amen, Aunt Teresa immediately rose from her kneeling. "Good God, John," she said, "couldn't you show some respect? You talked all the way through the rosary. You'd better watch out, because She's in this room, watching you right now." I looked at the Pilgrim Statue of Mary, and thought of Santa Claus.

"Teresa, I didn't fly way the hell from California to watch you on your knees." He walked out to the kitchen. I heard him fix himself a sandwich. Tommy did not come back.

I went up to the table decorated with the shiny medals, coins, and souvenirs. The Purple Heart was valentine-shaped, not shaped like the Sacred Heart. The money had square holes in it. And the headband, which I was sure would be soaked in blood as red as the rising sun printed in the center, was only like a trickle on one edge. It was dried brown like a coffee stain. I was disappointed. It could have been just a spill. I said to the headband, "How did this happen?"

■　　■　　■

That evening, at the dinner table, Tommy did not show up, even though it was a special dinner, like a holiday, with the younger cousins sitting at the kitchen table and the aunts and uncles and parents sitting at the main table, in honor of my grandfather's visit. It was also in honor of Tommy going to boot camp, which was still a month away, but the last chance to toast him with this big a gathering. A nicked-up wooden leaf was added to the main dining room table to accommodate my parents and golden grandparents that day. The tablecloth didn't hang over the end; it was hiked up like a woman's skirt. Tommy's chair was left empty in case he showed up.

I had a seat in the kitchen, but close to the doorway, so I could hear most of what was said by the grown-ups. Those places in between, not in one room or the other, suited me.

Nobody seemed worried that Tommy was not there. His troublemaking reputation was looked upon fondly that day. In fact, they were all drinking a lot of beer and telling funny stories about the different kinds of trouble he'd gotten into his entire life.

"Hell," said Aunt Charlotta, "I remember his kindergarten class did a big pageant. Each kid sang a song about what he wanted to be when they grew up. Tommy borrowed Jimmy's police uniform, and hell, you know how big that was, and sang about being a policeman. All through the song, Tommy stood there zipping his fly up and down to the music. Ha!" She drank a long gulp from her beer bottle. "Scared the hell out of that nun playing the piano for him."

"Charlotta," said Aunt Teresa. She made eyes in the direction of the Pilgrim Statue of Mary, within eyeshot of the dinner table.

"Hell," said Aunt Charlene, "I remember the day when Kennedy was shot and he thought they said Kenny was shot. Kenny was his best friend in school and happened to be out of school with a cold for the day. He said he kept seeing his teachers crying, so he thought it must be true, his best friend was dead. So he went to all of the kids in school and told them Kenny was dead. We come to find out, Kenny's home watching the stories on television with a head cold."

Suddenly, Anne got up from our kitchen table. She squeezed past me into the dining room and asked, "Since Tommy won't come, can I sit in here with you guys? I don't want to sit at the baby table." They let her sit at the empty table setting, between Aunt Charlene and Aunt Charlotta. "So," said Aunt Charlene, "do you want to grow up and be a Kaiserbroad like us?"

"God forbid," said Uncle Tom.

"No, she doesn't, do you?" said Aunt Teresa. "You want to grow up and be a good example, don't you? Nothing like your brother. I don't know why you glorify that kid's antics, he's been a heartache from the word go. Sits in the dining room smoking a cigar instead of praying so he'll live through the next three years."

"Oh, hell, let him go, I would've gotten out of it, too, if I knew what I was in for, with your scriptural rosary jazz. Takes forever," said Aunt Charlotta, brave with beer. "Where was Anne while we were all praying the rosary?"

"Yes, where were you?" said Uncle Tom.

Anne kept eating. "I was selling magazine subscriptions," she said.

"See," said Aunt Teresa. "She was working."

"That's good," said Uncle Jimmy. "Are you raising money for your church youth group?" Anne said no. "For Girl Scouts? For the choir? Then what for?"

Anne drew her head back as if Uncle Jimmy's face was a too-bright light bulb and said, "For *me*, so I can buy something for me."

"Much better than Tommy," said Aunt Charlene, out of the side of her mouth.

"Tommy won't even show up at a dinner in his honor," said Aunt Teresa.

My great-grandmother leaned forward so everybody at the table could suddenly see her, and said to Aunt Teresa, "You were always a perfect girl." All eyes went to her end of the table. Aunt Teresa wiped her mouth and went into the living room to extinguish the votive candles, and I wondered how perfect she had been.

"Where could he possibly be?" said my golden grandmother.

"He went to boot camp," said Anne, piling food on her new plate.

"Boot camp?" said Uncle Tom. "Boot camp isn't for another month."

She shrugged. "I saw him pack that big army duffel bag you gave him. He said he was headed for boot camp."

"Anne. Why didn't you tell us?"

"Because he said he was going to tell you himself. He said he'd write."

Uncle Tom looked at my grandfather. "What did you tell him?"

My great-grandmother said, "He said he killed somebody and took their stuff."

"I was exaggerating to make a point!"

"Well, if you were exaggerating, then you must have really wanted him to listen to you. It must have been real important that he believe you." My great-grandmother kept eating from a spoon while she talked. I couldn't see all of her from my corner, just the spoon moving to her mouth. Everybody looked nervous when she talked.

"Well, it was," my grandfather said, and had his hands in the air like he surrendered.

"Well," she said, "it worked."

. . .

That night, I went to my blue chalky second bedroom and listened to the Kaiserbroads talking. I could see them through a crack in the door. There had been no sign of Tommy, and they were wondering where he'd gone. They drank coffee and passed a tall bottle around, which they poured into the coffee now and then.

They stayed up very late and played cards and talked low, and it sounded like prayer. They were telling stories again, but none of them laughed. They were very uptight. I waited until they turned out the kitchen light, and the bright line was replaced with darkness like a draft under the doorframe.

I went into the living room by the light of praying-hands night-lights. I carefully removed the dustcover and took the crown off of the Virgin Mary. Looking at her painted face, as sweet as a cartoon girl, I wondered whether, if I wished hard enough, she might come to life and give me a secret message, like I'd heard so many others had been witness to. I imagined so hard that for a moment I swore I saw her wink, although even then I knew better. I knew she was just a statue, as inanimate as the bedpost or the banister.

But years ago, the headband had had blood on it, the red was once wet, even if my grandfather had exaggerated. And at some point, the Virgin Mary had lived and breathed. And at some point, the words captured on the old record from the top of the Empire State Building were live words, vibrating in windy air. Why couldn't all of these things be fresh and real again? If once, then why not forever?

I did not think that thought again until years later, when my great-grandmother died, and I peered into the open casket at her, and swore she winked, the way the Pilgrim Virgin Statue did.

That night, I took the crown from the statue and wore it to bed on my finger.

CHAPTER 4

Burning Furnace of Charity, Abyss of All Virtues

At school, there were certain people who had long-standing reputations for being crybabies or creeps or burnouts, and yet somehow were able to make use of that ingenious witchcraft which I will call self-invention. For example, there was a girl named Sally who had a reputation for not washing. She smelled like body odor and her clothes were dirty and too small for her. After six years of school, she came back one year washed and wardrobed, and we were all convinced that "BO Sally" was long gone, and this Sally was a new Sally. She became a pommerette in high school and dated a track star, and nobody seemed to remember that she smelled like body odor and wore dirty clothes throughout grade school.

My cousin Tommy never truly reinvented himself, but added layers to his reputation with all of the objects with which he adorned his life. His cigar, his car, his fringed suede coat, and then the guitar and the boa constrictor and even the sunglasses (which he left behind when he dodged the draft, and which his sister Anne adopted), they all added up to make a bigger legend of himself; he changed with each addition. He was like steel: we learned in science that steel picks up hot and cold temperatures and exaggerates them (I recalled trying to rest my back against the freezing bottom of my great-grandmother's steel claw-footed bathtub). Sunglasses, innately cool, were even more cool when Tom wore them, he amplified their coolness, like steel. He amplified trouble to his family. Secretly, to me, he amplified goodness. Even his running away from the draft was an enhancement of his character.

But I remained the same. The summer Tom ran away, I was beginning junior high school. They asked us to preregister, and I decided it was my first chance to reincarnate myself from that absorbed strange boy into a chaotic, junior version of Tommy. I had no fringed coat or sunglasses, but I wore the loud dashiki with colors as quick as pinwheels, which I bought at the Monsalvat County Carp Carnival and Petunia Festival, to the junior high school for registration. The only other preregistering classmate was Joe Shipley, the class clown who blew out the fuses in a whole wing of the school by sticking a blade of his art-class scissors into a wall socket, and whose parents punished his misbehavior not with groundings or spankings, but by shaving his head. I was writing my name and address on several cards in the school office and he sat down next to me. His hair was a bur of black thistledown.

"Hey, Bellman, cool shirt. You're a real wild man, ain't you, Bellman." He laughed all the way out of the building. Objects spoke to me but never for me. I went home and put on the heaviest of corduroys and plaid shirts and brown sweaters to fit in like the furniture. I felt dishonest in the dashiki and never wore it again.

On the Fourth of July weekend, we went to Monsalvat for a barbecue. I expected many dealings with Anne, unbridled by Tommy's absence. But she, too, had invented a new self, one no more accessible to me than her old self. One of Anne's favorite pastimes used to be chasing Chester around the limited boundaries of the house with a jack-in-the-box, cranking out its "Pop Goes the Weasel" song on a breakneck jag, right up to the *pop!* point: "The monkey thought it was all in fun—" Chester would walk up to her, thinking she had desisted, and she would turn the key forward and it would spring out *pop!* into Chester's face. He would run whining for some corner. She would follow relentlessly, holding it like a war drum under one arm and stirring out the song with the other hand.

But lately, Anne had lost interest. She had taken to being a good girl. She sat in chairs reading books and being quiet. Since Tom's disappearance, she knew that she was more favored by her parents and that behaving well would only deepen their belief in her—dinner conversation was filled with compliments for Anne. There were no vicious words for Tommy's draft-dodging run for cover, only an abysmal silence. No one even uttered his name.

"I knew she'd come around," said Aunt Teresa. "I had a whole shelf of my Young Lady's Library and I said, Anne, you should give these a try, I think you'll like them. I told her to try a horse book, because all girls go horse crazy at her age. She picked up *Black Beauty*, and she's had her nose in books ever since."

The volumes of Aunt Teresa's Young Lady's Library were kept on shelves above the hutch in a glass cabinet, like antiques. Each one had a dustcover that a younger version of Aunt Teresa had made out of brown paper bags. In black Magic Marker, in the hand of somebody thinking they were writing in fancy lettering, the words "Young Lady's Li Brary" ran down the spine, finished with a John Hancock flourish. Now Anne Teresa Kaiser was opening them up one by one and indulging in Louisa May Alcott, Laura Ingalls Wilder, and Sylvia Ashton Warner. Chester would come up and ask to be petted or tormented, and Anne would not look up from her paper-sack-covered book.

Then he would wander over to me. I'd pet him reluctantly. Chester was getting very old. He was blind, his eyes spooked by cataracts, like a demon dog I had seen in an afternoon movie. The worst part of his getting old was what Aunt Teresa called his "incontinence." He couldn't help himself anymore, and made wet piles anywhere his body's spirit willed it. I saw it happen only once, the Saturday morning before he died. He scared me, partly because I was in the kitchen, alone with him and Aunt Teresa. Chester moved his head around and started to squat; he looked embarrassed, heartbroken. He was in pain—he looked beyond me with his murky marble eyes and let out a loud unearthly moan, a sound as weird as a cat in heat, and his low hind legs trembled. "No, Chester, no," Aunt Teresa said, and fell to her knees. She grasped Chester around his belly, her apron bunching ladylike around her bare legs, and she tried to clamp Chester's mouth shut, to stifle the cry.

"What in the *hell* is going on out there?" Aunt Charlene called. She was trying to put on her cat-eye glasses, the armatures of which were bound together by the same kind of beaded string as a rosary. "Jesus, Teresa, see what I mean? That dog is in pain. You've got to let the old dog go. You're being cruel."

For the last few months Aunt Teresa had depended upon Uncle Tom like a knight-errant, to fend off these attacks. But by that weekend, even he insisted that Chester had to be put out of his misery. In fact, he began to take the lead in the arguments to do him in, and wanted to have the end of Chester's misery be the highlight our Fourth of July celebration. As he and my fat uncle Jimmy set up the grill near the porch, Uncle Jimmy and Uncle Tom argued about which way to end the misery was the best.

The Kaiserbroads and their husbands were all arranged on the wraparound porch in rockers, swings, and chaise longues. On my grandmother's porch, in the doorway, she'd made permanent, deep marks marking the height of her six children as they grew up—girls on the left, boys on the right. They read "Tom, aged 5, 3′4″," and "Charlene and Charlotta, aged 10, 4′8″," all the way up like a piano keyboard. There was a passage that chronicled my grandfather's horrific growth spurt, measured by the month, collapsed for me in a moment of terror as I watched it move up the doorframe. I had just learned about growth spurts in health class, and I knew I was soon doomed to it. What else have I inherited? I asked the doorway.

Along the walls of the porch, all the way around the wraparound, about a foot off the ground, blind Chester had been using his nose to find his way to the door, bumping into the walls with his wet snout, so that dust collected in the moisture from his nose dried in a perfect line one foot above the floor, all around the perimeter. And three feet up, in another perfect parallel line, were the scuff marks of chairs against the paint.

"You're a real he-man, Tom, bringing out your gun," said big Uncle Jimmy, stacking charcoal briquets into a pyramid.

"It's the easiest way, it won't hurt for more than a second. You got a better idea?" Uncle Tom said. He was squirting starter fluid on the briquets. He kept squirting until Uncle Jimmy knocked the can out of the line of the charcoal and it squirted on the grass. Uncle Tom knocked him back.

Aunt Teresa came out onto the porch with a bowl of unshelled peas. "Charlene, could I have my chair back, I have to shell these peas, and it's hard to work inside on such a hot day. Jimmy, are you drinking beer? For God's sake, it's still morning. What are you reading there, Anne?"

"*National Velvet.* It's about a girl who cuts her hair and wears pants because she wants to run the steeplechase with a Thoroughbred horse, and only boys can."

"That's right," said Aunt Teresa. She leaned over and petted Chester.

"That dog smells like death warmed over," said Aunt Charlene. She was drinking a beer, too, and helping my great-grandmother into her own rocker in the shade.

I watched Chester. When Aunt Teresa stopped petting him and returned to shelling peas, Chester banged his zigzag tail against her leg and nudged my great-grandmother's slack knuckly fingers. It was very hot, and he was sweating with his tongue. I thought, He must not know how long he's been petted, he's got no sense of time, just the change of the sun and moon, and not even that anymore, just a dark-and-light through the milk-and-water glaze of his cataracts.

I suppose he had endless expectations, though, as Anne was expected to chase him eternally, and Aunt Teresa was expected to smell like dust and hairspray, and Uncle Tom was always mistaken for the smell of another kind of animal.

The two old neighbor ladies, Philly and Millie, who I figured had lost their husbands and combined their households the way I would later see Aunt Charlene and Aunt Charlotta do, came over to join us. They brought more beer and Millie plugged in a portable radio and tried unsuccessfully to tune in a baseball game. They were friendly, I liked them. More than once, Philly had helped me get Wiffle balls off the roof and Frisbees out of the trees. They were even nice to Anne. They even liked Chester. They were friendly with Aunt Teresa, but Aunt Teresa was always short with them.

"Will the kids be going down to the fireworks tonight?" Philly asked. "They said they've bought the most they've ever been able to afford, it oughta be spectacular."

"Yes," Aunt Teresa said, and went back into the house for nothing at all, fidgeting. Philly and Millie had fun turning my little brother Hugh upside down until he screamed with laughter.

Uncle Jimmy had lit a match and the whole bowl of the barbecue pit ignited into a bonfire. The extra lighter fluid took a long time to burn off. I looked over at Anne. She was watching the fireball, and I wanted to see her fight the desire to go near it, to see her toes clench tight to her flip-flops, to see her hide her need. But she went back to her book, unperturbed.

"What are you reading there, Anne?" said Aunt Charlene.

"*Girl of the Limberlost*. It's about a girl who catches moths and sells them to pay her way through school. It takes place in the Upper Peninsula."

"Good," Aunt Charlene said.

"Ain't there a bar up at the lake called the Limberlost?" Aunt Charlotta asked.

I looked at Anne, but she kept her nose down in the book. Was I the only person to hear her give two different answers?

"What a blaze!" said Uncle Tom. "Do you know where the word 'barbecue' comes from, Michael?"

I said I didn't. "It's from the Portuguese. It means 'stinking meat.' I read that in *Reader's Digest*. See, I can read, too," said Uncle Tom to Anne.

"Bull. That's bull," said Uncle Jimmy, waving Uncle Tom away as if he smelled. "It's a Haitian word. It means 'cooking meat.' Why would the Portuguese eat stinking meat?"

"Have you got a dictionary, Mr. Know-it-all? Have you?"

Uncle Jimmy grabbed the lid of the barbecue and fit it over the fire. "This thing will burn forever unless we douse it." Smoke streamed out of the three air holes in the lid's domed surface.

"What did you do to the fire?" Uncle Tom roared. "You put it out! It's got to breathe, it needs oxygen." Uncle Tom took the lid off the smoking barbecue. Immediately, another ball of fire ignited and both Uncle Tom and Uncle Jimmy fell back. "What the hell!"

Both of them had a slightly helmet-shaped head of hair where the ends had singed and melted. After they got mad at each other for a minute, they went around to everybody on the porch so that we could feel their eyebrows. Uncle Tom leaned forward and I pinched his eyebrow with thumb and forefinger. It felt crunchy. Aunt Mary took him in to see if he had any burns, they both returned, and she rubbed suntan lotion on his forehead. "That feels real good, Mary," he said, and grabbed her hand to kiss it. Besides growth spurts, I had learned a whole lot of other things in health class that spring. I spent a lot of time looking at married people with children and trying to imagine them in bed. Aunt Mary and Uncle Tom? Fat Uncle Jimmy and his poor dead wife whom he always talked to in the air?

"You're not going to shoot the dog, you ape, I forbid it," said Uncle Jimmy. Aunt Charlene and Aunt Charlotta, with pink aprons and huge metal spatulas, were trying to take over the barbecue. Whenever Uncle Tom stopped to drink his beer, Charlene grabbed the spatula and flipped the burgers and Charlotta split buns and laid them upside down like clams to toast on the grill.

Both of my parents stayed near the Kaiserbroad aunts, listening to every story and baiting them to tell more. My mother passed my brother Hugh to my father, and after a few minutes, he would pass him back. They never left the porch, comfortable to prattle in the shade.

All the while my aunts cooked, they were picking on Uncle Tom, who was trying to be the know-it-all. The ribbing turned into an argument between the twin sisters. They each accused the other of being more gullible to his fount of facts, gleaned, I guess, from alarmist grocery-store tabloids and *Reader's Digest*.

"You," said Aunt Charlene, "were the one who believed him when he said that we were having bad weather more often because the Apollo rockets were pushing the moon out of its orbit."

"You," said Aunt Charlotta, "were the one who bought his

whole story about all his army buddies dying of cancer at the same time from some mysterious chemical warfare."

Uncle Tom ignored them and continued to work with a sort of ferocity. Grabbing the spatula back and losing it again and again. "Jimmy, you take over here, and I'll take care of Chester." He stormed to the unfinished shed, the roof covered with plywood but without shingles, a huge padlock on the door that only he had the key to. He pulled out a big wheelbarrow and a bag of cement and began the task of making concrete. "Michael," he said to me, "I need your help. Get Anne to help you dig a hole in the flower bed." All of these plans seemed diabolical to me.

My great-grandmother, years ago, was a dozen-time winner in the Monsalvat County Carp Carnival and Petunia Festival. She grew a yardful of wilty petunias of different colors, along with roses, tulips, snapdragons, and violets which bloomed in arranged patterns, and were the pride of the family. For another dozen years, though, she had been too old to grow flowers, and what was once a well-tended garden in the middle of the backyard, framed by bricks, was now overgrown with weeds and briars. Even though the perennial petunias had disappeared, I could see an insidious geometry of beautiful patterns in the remaining tulips, irises, and roses, if I stood far away, outside the garden, even in Philly and Millie's yard. Now Uncle Tom wanted me to dig a grave there.

I did not want to help him with that project. I had seen the pain Chester was in, but I didn't have the heart to kill him. I thought about the things that Chester could still do. He could feel the rare cool breeze on his underbelly. And he could smell: hamburgers beginning to sizzle and drip on the grill, mice nesting under the porch, the woody-oily odor of Aunt Mary's camphor rub, the perfumy flowers, the odor like ether and meat of the neighbor's trellis of gardenias. All those foul and delicious smells were part of another standard of things that were good and things that were bad. They were smells that only Chester could discern, and I didn't want to take that away from him.

"I forbid it," Uncle Jimmy said.

"What?" said Uncle Tom. He drank back half his can of beer and it seemed to make him feel cooler in the cloudless heat. He had the hose out and was filling the wheelbarrow full of cement mix with water. He started using his thumb to make the hose spray in a wide arc, so Uncle Jimmy had to keep his distance. Uncle Jimmy danced around the flower bed. "You're stepping on the damn hose," Uncle Tom said, and the sprayed water made a rainbow.

"Don't change the subject. I'm not leaving until you say that you're not going to shoot Chester."

"I won't argue with you. You can't make me do anything I don't want, you never could, no matter how much of a boss you've tried to be."

"How come you've suddenly got something against the old dog?"

Uncle Tom turned to me. "Come look, quick. Look at this." I leaned over a tall weed. I didn't see what he was pointing at, but when my eyes caught it, I pulled away. There was a praying mantis bent over the stalk, its head skewed at a quizzical angle. "Looks like your aunt Teresa, don't it?"

Had Uncle Tom reinvented himself, too? Uncle Tom had been Aunt Teresa's best friend all along, and now made fun of her. The praying mantis did look like her. He had been forever protecting old Chester, and now he wanted to do him in. Uncle Tom said, "Nasty monsters. Did you know that the female praying mantis will call the male to mate, all prettied up with her long leggy arms and million sparkling eyes. He's a fool. A fool for love. He gets on her, and she starts eating his head while he mates with her. She eats and eats, so he doesn't have to think about it anymore, until they're done, and he's gone, eaten alive. That's a woman for you." My eyes bulged. I ran away to find Anne, wondering if this were another of my uncle's skewed facts, or the truth about women when they mated.

Anne was still sitting on the porch with her girl book, but she had stopped reading to talk to my grandmother. "Where are you going? Do you need some help?" Anne asking somebody whether they needed help? She had really changed, I thought despairingly. This wasn't just a good mood, she was changed.

"It's a little too hot out here for me," my grandmother said, using the railing for support. "I'll be sitting in the kitchen and enjoying the sun through the window, if anybody needs me." She stopped again and looked at Anne like she was from another planet. "What's that you're reading?"

Anne held the page up to her. Like Chester, my grandmother had cataracts. "*Little Women*. It doesn't have any horses in it, but it's good."

"It used to be my favorite," said my grandmother, letting the screen door slap behind her. I could see her sitting at the table, looking through the window onto her garden.

"Hello, Michael," Anne said, and smiled. Her hair was so blond.

I grabbed the sack-wrapped book from her hands. "What are you really reading?" I said, and ran down the steps away from her, trying to study the page and also keep away from Anne, who was desperately trying to grab it away from me while moaning, "Give it to me, please."

The title on the first page was *The Nurse and Her Stud*. I read, "I wrapped my lips around his throbbing member and began to nibble at the head of it. He was stiff as a board." Stiff as a board? Was that a good thing? "Then I took his hard prick into my wet snatch and rode him like a wild horse. He begged me to stop, he said he was coming, the sensation was too good, he yelled, but I wanted all of him."

I was thunderstruck. This was nothing like my health textbook. This was like a foreign language. In my health textbook, intercourse consisted of a sperm from the penis reaching the egg located somewhere beyond the vagina. Other than that clinical description of intercourse, and my own wild surmises, which extended to imagining married people making love, this was my first introduction to sex. Many of the phrases were indecipherable (stiff as a board? wet snatch?), but I figured out the gist, and stood staring.

"Michael, give her back the book," I heard my mother yell. My temporary paralysis was long enough for Anne to grab the book away from me. I couldn't have fought her off, my arms were as heavy as dumbbells, the heat of the day was like a darkness. There were a thousand secret and terrible worlds.

Nobody was apt to get up with the baking sun to face. Anyway, Anne did not want their attention any more than I did. Everybody wanted to be like furniture that day.

"Don't tell," Anne whispered, pleaded.

I looked at her. "You have to help me dig a hole. Your old man said to help me."

She did not argue with me, she welcomed the chance to talk to me more. She begged me again and again not to tell. I was not interested in her fears, I was too enveloped in another of my stupors, pondering the page I'd read. What rotten things people do, and call it joy, I thought. I thought of it the same way I thought coffee had a terrible taste. But after mechanically digging with a shovel for a few minutes, listening to Anne drone on, "Please, come on, Michael, don't say anything," I realized that I wanted to read more.

"I'll say anything I feel like saying. Give me the book or I will say something."

I smiled at her. That made her furious, and she began to pogo-stick on the rungs of the shovel head with force, until it disappeared into the ground and brought up clods of earth and roses, still upright in their earth; they fell on their sides when she pushed them off the shovel.

My uncles were having a squabble of their own. They were both yelling at each other as quietly as they could, because they didn't want any of my aunts to come over and take sides. Uncle Jimmy was still trying to convince Uncle Tom not to kill Chester. "Look. We'll take him to a vet on Sunday and they'll put him to sleep."

"Costs too much." He came over and started helping us dig, he kept moving with some furious agenda. He seemed to enjoy the sweating.

"Well, at least take him to the dump to shoot him—you can't shoot a dog in the *suburbs*."

"It costs twenty-five bucks to get a dump sticker. You got twenty-five bucks?"

Aunt Teresa came around and served us all hamburgers. She was wearing long shorts, the heat had forced her to, and she looked uncomfortable in them. She had arranged the hamburgers with a handful of ridged potato chips and some of the overcooked peas she'd spent the morning shelling. She passed a paper plate to Uncle Tom, he barely had it in his hand before letting go. It nearly fell to the ground. Uncle Tom yelled out, "If you're looking for sympathy, you'll find it in the dictionary, between shit and syphilis."

Aunt Teresa turned around and said, "Not in front of the children, Thomas. Put your shirt on when you eat."

We stopped shoveling to eat. Everything tasted like lighter fluid. Anne sat, like a servant, next to me. I ate at a leisurely pace, savoring the bad taste. It was a relief, I thought, to know that she had not changed. I had no intentions of telling on her, I wanted to be the exclusive purveyor of her secret self.

"Daddy, will you get me another pop?" Anne asked, trying to break the bond between the two of us.

"You shouldn't have guzzled the one you had. You'll make yourself sick in this sun." But he got up to get it, because he wanted another beer himself.

"Come on, Michael," she hissed, once he was gone.

"Come on, what?"

"What are you going to do?" I could count her expressions like the stages of death: anger, denial, fear, depression, acceptance.

"I don't know, I have to think about it," I said blithely.

Then we both stood up. Aunt Charlene or Aunt Mary had screamed. There was a moan, then a short hiccup of laughter. We ran up onto the porch.

Old Chester had died on his own. He had lain down under Aunt Mary's lounge chair and she'd been petting him now and then. When she offered him a piece of her hamburger, he did not take it. He'd been dead, perhaps for an hour. "A modern miracle," Uncle Tom said. "Now I won't have to shoot him."

"You poisoned him with something," Aunt Teresa said, pointing at his shed.

"Poison, hell." Uncle Tom threw out his hands like he was diving. "The burger probably killed him."

Aunt Mary had the willies. She was shaking all over, which looked odd in the tense heat, and had to lie down to calm herself. Aunt Charlotta rested a cold washrag on her forehead. Aunt Mary joked nervously about maybe getting Chester's fleas and diseases. "The second he kicked off, I'll bet his fleas jumped ship, and crawled right up my hand." Everybody laughed and it made her feel better, but she scratched her scalp self-consciously. I heard her fingernails scrape the skin beneath her hair.

Anne and I returned to our shoveling. After all, Chester still needed to be buried.

"Poor Chester," I said, to make conversation. Anne agreed with me, and then I turned on her. "Don't play Miss Goody-two-shoes around me, you liar. You didn't care about Chester, you tortured Chester."

"You're the one who shut his tail in the door. At least I didn't mangle Chester." She was beginning to right herself again, and I knew she would start lashing out soon like a cornered animal.

Suddenly, something occurred to me.

"You know what I think? I think you probably did that," I said. "I don't remember ever shutting Chester's tail in the door. I'll bet you did it and told Aunt Teresa I did." At first, I was saying this to pick a fight, but as the sentence came forth I knew it was a *fact*.

She dropped her shovel and lunged at me. We rolled in the hole we'd dug, and she bit me on the arm. I pulled her blond hair. I could hear our parents yelling toward us and I restrained her arms, threatening to claw my face, and said in the strain, "I won't have to tell them anything about *The Nurse and Her Stud*. Look at you, all dirty and fighting. You're no good girl. Good girls don't fight."

She dropped her arms and sank back breathlessly in the dirt.

"Knock it off, you two," said my mother. But Uncle Tom said he would take care of us, and everybody else went back to the porch, where the sun would not get to them. Uncle Tom did not take care of us, he went to the shed to work on other things, as focused as a mad scientist.

Anne and I rested in the dirt. "God, I hate you," she said.

"Me too," I said.

"The only reason I hate you is because you just happen to know everything. Otherwise, I wouldn't even care about you. I'd ignore you."

"I know," I said. "I know more about you than anybody else. Except for Grandma, maybe." Then I took her arm where it was scraped by the dirt. "Feel better?" I asked in baby talk.

"Yes," she said. "When you see a hearse go by, you may be the next to die," Anne sang in a merry, galumphing voice, "Do you know that song?" She shoveled some more, and I resumed, too, although our hole was deep enough.

We would have talked more, but Aunt Mary, who, upon her own recovery, had spent the day as a nurse (which was funny, because Aunt Charlene was the RN in the family, but always said "It's my day off" when anybody had a pain), came with a bottle of Merthiolate and pulled Anne out of our hole. She made frantic gestures for Anne to clean herself up, and bade me do the same as soon as I finished helping Uncle Tom bury Chester.

Chester was wrapped in an old tarp that used to cover Uncle Tom's boat. He pulled it out of the unfinished shed and wrapped the dog in it. He tied the package up with coils of twine, and when he finished, Chester looked like a folded flag. I shoveled dirt on.

"Not yet," Uncle Tom said, and pulled the shovel out of my hand to prove his unreadiness.

I wondered if we were going to say a prayer or something, the whole family gathered around the hole in my great-grandmother's gone-to-seed flower garden, but then I saw that Uncle Tom had no intention of drawing any attention to our deeds. Suddenly, it became clear to me why he was interested in putting Chester out of his misery: in a burlap sack, he carried a weight over his shoulder that was not potatoes, not fertilizer, but something whole and wobbly. When he threw it in, the sack formed over the shape of dead Chester.

I never saw Tommy's boa constrictor, never got a clear view of it. But the burlap sack outlined the shape of it as much as everything in the world formed around it. Like the absent Tommy, his name never mentioned and his body far away, the boa constrictor made the entire landscape deny itself into existence; the space it left in the world was a perfect hole in the universe in the exact shape of it.

Immediately, my uncle began to scoop some shovelsful of dirt, which formed over the mound. Then he brought over his wheelbarrow and started mixing the quicklime and cement with his bare hands. He didn't notice that the quicklime had rubbed off the skin of his fingertips until drops of blood collected on the soupy surface of the wet concrete. He pulled his hands out and gray and red streaks ran down to his elbows. "Mary!" he shouted.

Poor burned and bloodied Uncle Tom, he'd done more damage to himself than the boa constrictor was able to do by taking a swipe at him. The next morning, Aunt Mary would tell everybody the funny story of how Uncle Tom, his fingertips bandaged like erasers on pencils, was incapable of unbuttoning his shirt or tying his shoes, and slept spread-eagled on the bed at night like he'd been crucified, and we all laughed and watched him try to eat a bowl of cereal. Uncle Jimmy said, "Now he can commit any crime he wants, he doesn't have any fingerprints!"

Uncle Jimmy was the one who poured the cement into the hole, and he never noticed the extra package he buried there. I think I was the only one who saw it. When Anne made a cross out of ice-cream sticks and drew a long dog crucified on the cross, I was tempted to erect a second cross, but the act might have called attention to the second burial.

That night it cooled off with merciful breezes, and Anne and I and a handful of cousins were allowed to stay up late to watch the fireworks over Clear Lake where we had speared the carp. While we waited for the big show we lit sparklers and threw them into the lawn. They landed deep in the grass and looked like magic, illuminated places. We had to stop throwing when Anne accidentally threw one on the roof and everybody was worried it would set fire to the house. "That would be a perfect end to this lethal holiday," said morose Aunt Teresa.

Uncle Tom, bandaged and helpless, sat next to her and

consoled her, explaining over and over how Chester was happier now, he was in heaven. Aunt Teresa, however, refused to be cheered. She fed Uncle Tom beer. "The pope says dogs don't have souls," she said. "There's no heaven for dogs."

Although the family stayed up late and everybody had gone to bed, I wasn't tired. I sat up in bed reading a real book from the Young Lady's Li Brary, *Little House in the Big Woods*. I prepared for the time somebody would ask me what it was about: "It's about this girl who grows up on the frontier. She has a corncob for a doll and has to eat bark." I read until very late under the light of the praying-hands nightlight. My room being near the kitchen, I heard somebody step through the screen door because it whacked shut on its spring. I slunk out to look through the screen. From the kitchen, anybody could see everything that happened in the garden.

It was my great-grandmother. She was wearing her crushed-velvet housecoat. The air was room temperature, so there was no difference from the inside and outside of the house. My great-grandmother was smoking a cigar. She was standing over the mound of dirt in her ragged flower bed.

The moon was full and shone on her hair, and she had let it down like an old princess undone for the night. She pulled her housecoat tight, and sat down in the grass, and put the cigar out with the dewy grass. It was so quiet, I could hear the fizzling as it was doused. Then she ground the cigar into the fresh dirt.

That is when I joined her. "It's me," I said as I let the door whack shut so she wouldn't be frightened. I noticed that from where she sat, the porch was illuminated. With the lines made by the furniture, the marks on the pillars showing the heights of my aunts and uncles, and the trail of dust left by Chester's nose, the house reminded me of an old aquarium where the water had evaporated little by little, leaving lines of scum and algae where water and sea life used to be.

She picked up a dead rose bush. "These can be replanted," she said. "The roots are stronger than the flowers."

I told her I would spend all day tomorrow planting them on the grave. "Where did you get the cigar?"

"You saw that, did you? Well, you don't have to tell anybody about that. They're illegal, you know."

"Illegal?"

"They're Havana cigars. From Cuba. Communists. You can get them in Canada, but you can't get them here. I have some old friends in retirement down in Florida, and they send them to me from there, brought in by Cubans."

"Wow," I said. We sat quiet for a little while, and I picked up a spade and dug for her. "So. Are you sad about Chester?"

"Oh, yes."

"Did you remember when he was a puppy?"

"I remember when everybody was little. Can you believe I can remember when your aunt Teresa was little? I can't believe I remember that." We laughed. "She was a good girl then, she used to read those horse books and I couldn't get her to do any of her chores."

"Good girls don't do their chores?" I asked.

"You'd be surprised what good people will do," she said.

"Like Tommy," I dared.

"Yes."

All the time, I kept digging and started putting irises and tulips into the ground. Some had withered in the heat during the day, but still it seemed worth replanting them. They had lasted twelve years without any help. "Do you know where he is?" I asked.

"He writes to me, and I write to him," she said. So many people with secret second lives, I thought, and with that thought, I connected the cigars she smoked with Tommy, sending the Havana stogies from somewhere in Canada.

From Anne I learned another thing, how to be wily, and energetic, and do twice as many things in the same amount of time—one good thing, like read from the Young Lady's Li Brary in private while reading *The Nurse and Her Stud* in broad daylight. Duplicity attracted me. I learned from her that perhaps I could not invent a new me, a Michael Bellman who could wear a dashiki, but I could be two Michael Bellmans, one that blended in with the furniture, and another that had a silent, secret, and wild life.

Someday, I thought, Tommy's going to write a letter and Aunt Teresa will pull the mail from the mailbox and recognize his handwriting. Someday Tommy's need for somebody to know about his secret life will be his downfall.

One of the tulip blooms fell off its stalk. I held it between my thumb and forefinger and simply enjoyed feeling its waxy, fleshy feel. I handed it to my great-grandmother and she put it next to her face. "Does it look good there?" she said, and I thought about how she was once young, too. "Does it compliment my eyes? Does it show how gray blue my eyes are, like lead pipe?"

I couldn't really tell in the dark, but I remembered them from daylight. "As gray blue as my favorite color," I said. She dropped the flower.

"You're quite a flirt," she said.

We stood there as if we were surrounded, not on the outside of the garden but in the middle. I thought, Without this house all around us, without the frames of lawns and fences, and without the filmy shadows the droopy tulips made under the front porch light, the two of us might be nothing, or in nothing, and if we didn't have all these things crowding around the shape of us, we might as well be dogs, innocent, staring at flowers, not knowing the names for them, and just sniffing.

CHAPTER 5

A Prodigal Son

Unlike most people, I did not get it into my head to try running away from home until I was almost thirteen. There was always some fond object to ensnare me, something in the lawn, a snail shell, for instance, down deep in the web of quack grass that grew over these small objects. I would hunch down and set it free, not with force, but with careful dexterity, and then explore it for hours. Now I decided that not even mysteries in the grass could bind me to my home.

It was time to move on.

I had a place to go (Toronto) and a very sensible idea: I would get a job. That is why I brought my Sunday sport coat, vest, tie, and shoes.

And I would not sneak. I explained to my mother, in her kitchen, that it was time to go and that I would get a job, probably something simple like shelving books in a library, and find a place to live.

My mother was making meatballs, rolling the waxy meat with her hand against the surface of the counter. She stopped to listen to me, her head a little to one side, looking at me as if I were still a child. She nodded and nodded, but then, as I was about to walk out the door, she reached out her greasy hand. "Wait a minute, wait a minute." I turned to her. "Where do you think you're going with that nice suit?"

"I need it to get a good interview for a job."

"You can't take that."

"I can't?"

"Oh, no."

"Oh, no?"

"Oh, no. That's for the new boy we'll be getting after you're gone."

"The new boy?"

"The replacement."

■   ■   ■

I did not run away until many years later. But I still continued to dream about going to Toronto; it was the city I knew the most about. Detroit did not count, it was too horrible. Even comedians on television used Detroit violence as a joke. "Take him to Detroit!" the comedian said, dressed as a Mandarin emperor committing a treacherous Mongol spy to death.

Toronto is the place where Tommy lived after he ran away from the Vietnam War. They found him through his letters to my great-grandmother, and one weekend, in the springtime of the year after we buried Chester, my uncle Tom methodically drove out on a Friday night and returned on a Sunday afternoon with my wayward cousin. I was not there, which is why I imagine it so strongly: Uncle Tom driving for twelve hours there and back wearing his police uniform, bursting into my great-grandmother's home, where the Kaiserbroads and their families were gathered around the television. I imagine Tom with a leash around his neck, cowed, forlorn, like a captured ape.

Then Uncle Tom did the strangest thing. He refused to let

Tommy live in the house again. Since he had run away, he came back to Monsalvat and found himself up for trial and without money. And nobody would give a draft dodger a job. It was my great-grandmother who let him stay in the big house with her and Aunt Teresa. He moved all of his stuff into my chalky blue room, the one where I always stayed during my visits. Aunt Teresa did not like the arrangement.

I remember sitting at the kitchen table listening to my uncle Jimmy and aunt Teresa talking. They were brother and sister, but she was skinny like the broom she was sweeping the kitchen with and he was the Fattest Man in the World. Once, Uncle Jim had grabbed Anne around the neck and pressed her, in a headlock, into his sweaty, blubbery thigh, and gurgled out, "WHO'S THE FATTEST MAN IN THE WORLD!" It was a command, not a question, and required Anne's salute. But even Anne was not sure how to deal with this one, and she peeped out, in a little lilt of sweet questioning, looking up, trying to appease him, "Uncle Jimmy?"

"That's right, and don't fergit it, none-a-yuh!" and that was how Uncle Jimmy became the Fattest Man in the World. He was always putting on acts like this, the tough-guy fat-guy, the guy who threatened to shoot Uncle Tom if Uncle Tom shot Chester, he was always asking for the glory of a fat-guy reputation, but it was never as good as he guessed it would be, and he wasn't really that frightening.

While Aunt Teresa swept he was heating up two Pop-Tarts in the toaster, one for him, one for me. He haunted my great-grandmother's house often. I think he was sometimes lonely. He talked about Tommy. "Don't that beat all? The kid runs off and gets himself caught in the most obvious place, the dummy."

"You sound like you wanted him to get away," said Aunt Teresa. "You sound like you're actually rooting for him. The boy committed a crime." She was savagely sweeping dirt out from under the refrigerator. "He ran away from the war. In my book, that's as good as suicide. It's like suicide because he didn't go off and kill just one Vietnamese, he made the whole world go away, he killed the whole world because he didn't like his situation. He killed his *family*, for God's sake, he ran away from his family. That's suicide, and it's a mortal sin."

"Oh, get off it, Teresa. Or I'll have you sent over to fight in the jungles. I'll bet the communists would run away if you start praying at them." He shook the salt part of the salt-and-pepper praying hands at her, making dog commands at her: "Sic 'em! Sic 'em!"

But Aunt Teresa's opinion was the prevailing one.

Tom, by now, was without his boa constrictor and his fringed coat, but he had grown his blond hair even longer and grew what beard he could, which amounted to a little light tuft on the tip of his chin. He looked like Jesus in the big painting, with the vaguely Middle Eastern, drugged eyes and Sacred Heart on his chest. He was beautiful, like a boy and girl put together. I think that is another reason why most of the family, even his parents, were mad at him. We are not a handsome or beautiful family, and Tom was by far the best. I was beginning to look at my own face in the mirror more. There, I saw my chin, which is my mother's, like a piece of wood, or my cheeks, which pushed out too much. I was beginning to hate the way I looked, how flawed I was next to the perfectness of Tommy.

Two months after he started living in my grandmother's house, I went up to Monsalvat for a week of my summer vacation. I found that Aunt Teresa had enslaved him. Tommy replaced Uncle Tom around the house as the odd-jobs man, which helped him earn his room and board. He had gone to court by then, and the court told him that he was off the hook as long as he went to the junior college full-time and got an education, and also did some extra citizenship work. He was

required, he told me, to write weekly essays on the importance of being an American citizen. I was expecting him to
tell me he cheated, copied the essays out of the book or
slipped in terrible sentences every once in a while to see if
anybody really read them. But I think he was beaten down,
and went through the motions of writing boring paragraphs
about the history of the flag, the constitution, and Benedict
Arnold.

One afternoon, he came into the kitchen, where I sat ar-
ranging toast crumbs. He was sweaty and grassy from mowing the lawn. He made a pitcher of frozen lemonade and he
took it into the bedroom. I followed, and we sat Indian style
on the hardwood floor, which was cool in the hot day. Tommy
lit one of five small stubs he had left of what used to be
grand Havana cigars, and desperately enjoyed it for a minute
before dousing it. He was only wearing a pair of cutoff
shorts, and I watched him. There were ropy veins near his
wrists, and the muscles on each of his calves were divided
neatly into two defined mounds, like strange extra vital
organs in his body. They were shaped like every piece of pol-
ished doweled furniture I had ever spoken to.

I wanted to touch his wooden calves, with the small cork-
screws of hair blurring the sharp lines of them. He sat down
on the floor in his room, once mine, and put the pitcher between the two of us. The pitcher and he exaggerated the
coolness in the heat. There were no glasses, so we took turns
drinking from the lip of the pitcher. I noticed that he never
once wiped off my backwash—since he had no sleeves—and
so I didn't either. Tom pulled the cold cigar out of his mouth
and looked at it like it was a jewel. He leaned forward, and
over the pungent tobacco, I smelled fresh-mown grass.
He said, winking three times during the sentence, "A pretty
girl is like a melody, little man," and then he whispered his
thrilling secret, "but a good cigar is a *smoke*." He took

a long drink from the lemonade, and I looked under his arms.

He pulled several of the books from his nightstand onto the floor. They were thick and pictureless. I said, "How do you remember all this? It looks real boring."

"This stuff ain't so bad, you know?" He pulled the fattest book toward him, the wobbly spine bending back as he flipped it open. "You got to exercise your brain like you exercise your body, or it'll get flabby like Uncle Jimmy. You want your brain to look like Uncle Jimmy? Here, look at these. These are the first ten amendments of the constitution. Now, sooner or later, little man, the big man is going to want you to know these. So if you help me memorize them, maybe you'll learn something."

He put the cigar down. I picked it up and held it to one eye like a periscope. I could smell the burning tobacco leaves mixing with the staleness of the house, lemony furniture wax, and Aunt Theresa's hairspray.

He said, "Look here, number one. The freedoms. Freedom of speech, freedom of assembly, freedom of religion. Number two. Right to bear arms. Do you know how to remember them? You remember their initials, and you make a sentence out of the letters, a funny sentence that you can't forget."

I knew about mnemonics, about how the names of the Great Lakes that fit like a mitten around Michigan spelled out the word "HOMES" (Huron, Ontario, Michigan, Erie, Superior), and that the order of flats on a musical staff made up the sentence "Boys Eat At Diners Girls Can't Find."

"Like this," Tom said. "Freedom, F. Arms, A." He took out a pencil and wrote in the margin of the book: FATSASJBPS, for Troops quartering, Search warrants, and the rest. "Look. Here's a sentence you'll never forget, it's all about the Fattest Man in the World."

"How?" I asked.

"FATS AS Jimmy's Butt is Positively Stupendous. Hah!"
We both laughed our heads off, and then Tom started pushing
me over. I pulled away and ran from the room. He didn't
chase me, but he yelled, "Remember what I said about a
pretty girl. And remember what I said about a good cigar."

■   ■   ■

I spent the week playing with various cousins in groups of
threes and fours. Having a lot of cousins made for excellent
baseball, volleyball, and kickball teams, and frustrating badminton, croquet, and bowling. None of the Kaisers were good
at taking turns. They loved to rush the net or cream the guy
with the ball. More than once I would be winning at checkers
and one cousin or another would upset the board and send
the plastic red and black disks flying. One of our favorite
games had been Jarts, weighted oversized darts that were to
be thrown like horseshoes at a target hoop across the lawn.
The point would embed itself in the dirt. Aunt Teresa took
them away from us, though, because David, Anne and Tommy's youngest brother, threw a Jart without waiting his turn,
and the point embedded itself in his best friend's bare calf. I
can call up the sight even now, the Jart stuck in like some
strange weapon, a skinny trail of very thick maroon blood
running down that boy's ankle and into his shoe. Aunt
Charlene had two sons who were younger than me, and we
tried to build a tree fort, but Aunt Charlotta's son Eddie and
his sister Kathleen tore it down when we went in for lunch
one afternoon.

But I preferred hanging around with Tommy, which forced
me to make a choice: I could either be with him, or with everybody else. There must have been hissed admonitions
among my great-aunts and uncles to all my cousins-once-
removed that whatever they do to make the summertime

pass, they were *not* to spend time with Tommy. Opting for games with Tommy, I was faced with the choice of playing nonteam sports or badminton, which bored us quickly. We took a perverse pleasure in playing all the games that were least likely for two to play—war and crazy eights (who *cared* if the direction of discard was reversed?), any of the Parker Brothers board games (*Clue* made me fascinatingly miserable). When we played baseball, we faked it by sending out endless "ghosties" on the bases as we returned again and again to reinvent ourselves under a teamful of pseudonyms. Anne was the only one who would play with us, but three is worse than two if you're playing ghost baseball.

"You and Mike against me," said Tom, grabbing Anne by the shoulders and placing her next to me.

"No *way*, I don't play with babies," she said. "I'll be on both teams."

Tom put the baseball bat out and explained that this was the way we would see which team went to bat first: the captains would wrap their fists round the fat end of the bat and take turns working our way hand over hand up the length. Whoever had room left to grip the wooden nubbin at the base won his team the chance to bat first. Anne was furious that she was not chosen as captain. "That's what you get," Tom said, "for not being on Mike's team."

The two of us grabbed the base of the bat together. The edge of my hand nested comfortably on top of his. I could feel his sweaty palm and a heat like a furnace. I was hot, but like steel, he was hotter. He looked down at the bat as we moved our fists higher and higher on the length of it. I was looking only at him. He could not look at me looking at him, I realized, when he was so intent upon being first at bat. I wished, as he accidentally gripped part of my fist when grabbing a higher place on the neck of the bat, that Anne was not watching. His wrists pulsed with those ropy veins as we frantically grabbed upward; it would soon be over. I suppose I ought to have been hoping that my hands would grab the top, that I would win, but I wasn't even thinking about that.

Then, when there was no room left but the handle, it was my turn to move my hand and I grabbed triumphantly at the toadstool cap. And then, Tommy slipped the bat between his legs and made a mock moaning sound. He made believe that the bat was part of him, and I grabbed him there. I was supposed to let go, but I didn't, I looked at him fiercely and held tight to the end.

"Ha-ha." Anne thought it was hysterical. "What are you hanging on to down there, Michael? Ha."

Finally, he let go. "All right, little man. If you want to be first so bad, it's all yours," he said.

I let go. Tommy took the bat. "You let go, you lose. My team goes to bat first."

But he went out to pitch and field and Anne went to bat with me, and we only stopped after we had hit about thirteen home runs and Tommy had struck neither of us out.

We won out of boredom, and Anne cheered herself into a frenzy. I was still not interested in victory or defeat, but continued to think about what Tommy had done with the bat. It had been a year, that summer, since I had learned about sexual intercourse from health class and the book that Anne was secretly reading, and since then, I could think of nothing else. My whole year had been charged with moments like the one with the baseball bat: Kenny Gordon with condoms in his wallet, Tammy Jennings writing her boyfriend's name in ballpoint pen on her jeans, noticing that Doug Emry was only fourteen years old and actually had hair on his chest, sneaking looks at *Playboy* at the drugstore, Steve Sheets going up to the blackboard to do math problems with a boner, and Darcy Cope misunderstanding the health book and thinking that every time a guy got a boner, he had an orgasm. I remember when Darcy read in the text that boys going through puberty had twelve to fourteen spontaneous erections each day, she squealed out loud in the middle of class.

■   ■   ■

Tommy taught me drinking games, too. He'd smuggle a bottle of beer into the light blue bedroom at night and we'd sit with the door closed. He'd pour two glasses and explain how to play quarters.

"Here's how it works, little man." He was wearing only shorts again, to show his mahogany-smooth liver-shaped calves. I noticed for the first time that he had an appendix scar. I felt instantly sorry for him, wondering what he looked like when he suffered physical pain. "It's like tiddlywinks. We take turns bouncing this quarter off the floor and into the glass. If I get my quarter in, I get to choose somebody who has to take a drink. If I don't get my quarter in, I have to take a drink. Same goes for you."

It was another game for more than two people, joyless without somebody to gang up on and get drunk. But it was one of the first times I had a chance to get drunk, and so I was baffled by the object of "quarters"—if I lost the game, and got drunk, I got what I really wanted—I would win by losing. I made a point of missing every time, and got to drink the lion's share of the beer.

Tommy figured me out soon enough and the two of us got silly drinking gulps of beer and bouncing the quarter in the opposite direction of the glasses. At some point he pulled out one of his dwindling cigars and lit up. He looked like a philosopher, or somebody reckoning the runs and errors on the scoreboard at a baseball game. "You know what we'd do if Chester was still around, little man?" he asked. "I'd be asleep in my bed and my old man would bring Chester over to our house and put him on the bed. He'd have these two heavy flashlights, those kind that only a cop can get, and a bottle of Aunt Teresa's ammonia he'd swiped while he was here getting Chester. That Bo-Peep ammonia." He stopped to drag in on the cigar, and the coal turned red, there was a real fire smoldering in the tip. "He'd shine that flashlight in my eyes and let Chester lick my face until I got pissed. Then the old man would say, 'Let's go.'"

"Go where?" I whispered.

"It wouldn't be until after we got on the road that I would wake up to figure out we were out searching again. Chester would put his ratty paws on the dashboard, then down on the seat, then up again, as antsy as the old man can get, if he could only show how antsy he is. The old man has got permanent ants in the pants. This whole damn family has them."

While he said all that he was putting his lanky arms up and down on the bed, imitating the way Chester got excited.

"So," I coaxed, "what were you searching for?"

"We'd drive out to the Long Drive golf course, and it would be pitch-black. Dark as a hole in the ground. We'd walk over the greens and the fairways, and the old man would tell me jokes about how God and Moses and Jesus would play golf, and Moses would part the water traps." Tommy took the rest of the beer for himself, he must have figured I'd had enough. "All along, he'd pour a little of Aunt Teresa's ammonia into the grass. And you know what would happen?"

He leaned forward and hung one of his long dog-paw arms over my shoulder until I almost fell over. "What?" I begged.

He put one of his fat-farmer fingers through an "okay" sign he made with the thumb and index finger of his other hand and shouted, "Night crawlers! Night crawlers as thick as my fingers, wiggling there. Worms, the biggest ones you ever saw, little man. We'd grab them, but they had this real strong grip, you know? And I'd pull until they came loose, but sometimes they broke in half. When we were done, you'd shine that cop flashlight into the coffee can and it was slimy and brown. The whole can would squirm."

"Gross, man," I said. I was trying to use "man" at the end of my sentences as often as Tommy.

"Then you know what we would do?"

"Fish?"

"Sometimes. But first we'd put them in Aunt Teresa's refrigerator when we got back, and she'd come down in the morning to make breakfast, and there they'd be. She'd come running over to our house and yell the old man up and down and we'd laugh and I swear it was funny as hell." We laughed ourselves. Then the room was silent, like the joke backfired.

Then I offered, "Let's go now!"

Tom's eyes got big for a split second, but then he threw the little button of cigar into the wastebasket and climbed up on the bed. "No man, I'm all tired. I'm all ready to hit the sack. I got to study the ten amendments." He looked at the door like he was escorting me out of it. Usually, I was the one who stayed in that room. I was staying in another empty room across the hall, which had no praying hands in it but which had piles of braided palm fronds from years and years of Palm Sundays, stacked on a dresser.

The next morning, I fished his cigar butt out of his wastebasket and saved it, wrapped in a paper towel. It was still damp where he had put it to his mouth.

■　■　■

"Hey, it's the Fattest Man in the World! Good morning, Fattest Man in the World. How did you sleep, Fattest Man in the World?" Since that moment when she was scared by Uncle Jim, when he had her in that headlock, Anne had recovered herself. Now she claimed her revenge. She called my uncle that name as much as she could, often in public places where people outside of the family could hear her.

"Your dad's going to come over later," Uncle Jimmy said to Anne, "and I'm gonna tell him who's the brattiest girl in the world."

She thought that was funny, and laughed him off. It was the Saturday morning after Tommy had given me beer and told me the story of worm hunting with Chester and his father. It seemed that a lot of the family converged on my great-grandmother's house. I came in woozy and found Anne already finished with one bowl of cereal and starting on a pile of white toast.

Nowadays I am afraid of all those things I used to eat in Monsalvat, not just beer and fish but iceberg lettuce, canned food, white sugar, white bread, white toast. I wore polyester for years, not knowing any better, rubbing against it. I am sure that my bones are made of some of those artificial fibers now. Dacron runs in my blood. What cotton fibers there might have been in the twist of the twill soon washed out of the clothes I wore in those days, and what was left were those stiff-weaved plastics.

I felt it then, began to hate the way I looked. I would sit in the bathroom and feel my face in places where there were lumps along the jaw, polyps of petroleum by-products, fat deposits. No matter how many nice sweaters I wear now, how many all spinach-leaf salads I make, nothing can undo the parts of myself that were made of preservatives I consumed at Aunt Teresa's kitchen table. No doubt I will keep, pickled in my own grave for ten years after I die; I've got a shelf life from all the chemicals I ate in Monsalvat, Michigan.

I put two Pop-Tarts into the toaster.

Anne shoveled a spoonful of presweetened cereal into her mouth before she talked. "Michael, are you coming with me and Aunt Teresa to church? We're confessing." She proceeded to pull the free prize out of the cereal box, a ball that glowed in the dark. After she pulled out her hand, the cereal inside was crushed and the sides of the cardboard box were warped.

"Nope, Tom and I are doing something."

"What are you gonna do?"

"I don't know. Pull weeds. Catch earthworms."

"Why do you hang around Tommy so much?"

"Because I like him."

"Ugh. That's fairy nice. Lezbee friends. Homo you don't." She chanted.

I looked around to see if Uncle Jimmy or Aunt Teresa heard. I was always hearing swear words out of Anne's mouth first, and I knew, if only vaguely, that she was saying something terrible. "Tom likes me, too."

"He doesn't like you. You're just the only person in this whole family who will talk to him."

"Well, I'd rather spend time with Tom than I would with you, any day."

Her eyes blazed like the tip of Tom's cigar, and she stormed out of the kitchen, her cereal unfinished.

Tommy came in soon after. He did not look like he had drunk anything the night before. He had showered and combed his hair into a raceway pattern back over his ears. He ate two pieces of Anne's abandoned toast and drank coffee while Uncle Jimmy and Aunt Teresa made more food and cleaned up. Nobody said good morning to Tommy. Nobody said anything for a while.

Finally Tommy dared to say something to me. "So, little man. How about you and me taking the boat out fishing? Catch us a mess of perch and have us a fish feast tonight."

Aunt Teresa turned from her sink and grabbed it from behind for support. "Oh, no, you don't," she said. "You've got work to do. I've got a list here of about twenty things you didn't get done this week, and this house is going to fall apart if you don't take care of them. This is not a charity institution."

"Oh Teresa," said Uncle Jimmy, with the weakness only huge people can show. "Let the kid fish, for God's sake."

She walked over and slapped down a crumpled list that she pulled from her apron pocket as some kind of proof. I couldn't see the words from where I stood, but the list looked like a chain, a rosary of penance, weeding, washing, hoeing, on and on. "And if you know what's good for you," she said to me, in a tone barely nicer than she had said things to Tommy, "you'll come to Confession with Anne and me."

She must have seen how much time I was spending with him and wanted it to stop. I was punishing him by being near him. It struck me as an awful thing that in order to do the best thing for the person I liked the most, I had to ignore him.

Tommy didn't even bother to finish his coffee. If he was lucky, he muttered, he'd get them finished before dark, just in time to study the amendments of the constitution. I noticed that whenever he was around Aunt Teresa, his shoulders became less broad, and he talked more about the constitution and law and order.

There was a curious catechism taught to me in Monsalvat. It was about what was punishment and what was reward. Aunt Teresa ran the house on rules that seemed arbitrary, where punishment was reward and vice versa, where running away from certain death in war was suicide, where neglecting Tommy was benign, and hiding the sordid ends of fairy tales made them go away. She got these rules from the Bible. When she got sulky, she read the fire-and-brimstone passages over and over. She especially loved the book of Leviticus, with all the tough rules. No red clothes. No eel eating, no cloven-footed animals, no laying down with the same sex, no wearing shoes in the house, no leaving things on her kitchen table. These were the laws that governed the Kaisers.

I went to Confession that day, and for the rest of the vacation I stayed away from Tommy, but when I got home from Monsalvat, I found an empty cigar box and kept the cigar butt wrapped in the same tattered paper towels, under the bed, and every night, in bed, I violently imagined that we were detectives together, two brothers, both with a bad rap from the law, and we were on a dangerous case, trying to make it up to the government for crimes we didn't commit. I imagined one scene where thugs caused a huge I beam to hit me in the chin, disfiguring me but actually making me look better, and less like my mother, and Tommy leaned over me in his shorts and took a long time washing my bloody chin and bandaging it, touching my bleeding mouth with his fingers. I imagined that part over and over.

CHAPTER 6

Other Devotions

Knowing how much Tommy liked letter writing, I wrote him a letter the fall after I spent summer vacation with him in Monsalvat. In the letter, I asked him how he was doing in school. I asked about the family and about Anne, and then I told him I thought school was boring but that I didn't want my brain to look like Uncle Jimmy. When I signed it, I put, "P.S. It's Positively Stupendous!" He didn't write a letter, but only sent a postcard back, and he'd scrawled, "Little Man, It's Positively Swelling! Tommy." The exclamation point was dotted with an "o" shape, which was the sort of thing girls did in my junior high school.

It was impossible for me to keep my mother from seeing the postcard. She said, "What's positively smelling?"

I laughed very hard but shook my head. "Positively *swelling*."

"Tommy who?" she pressed.

"Tommy my cousin."

She walked out of the room without saying anything, not even correcting me by saying, "Cousin once removed," as she usually did. I wondered if there was any way to make her say Tom's name out loud. Perhaps here is a reason why my parents seem so shadowy in this whole situation: they always followed suit after the Kaiser family. Whatever rules they laid down, my mother and then my father followed. If Aunt Teresa issued an edict, a vow of silence around Tommy, my parents honored it. Even with the Kaiser source of power one hundred miles away most of the time, my parents were more distant, less authoritarian, to me.

Tommy was the first adult who took an interest in what I said straightaway, and with whom I got into a kind of trouble together, and not apart, like I had with his sister Anne. I spent the fall and early winter trying to unravel the one clue he had given to me in the summer, about how he thought of me, when he told me that a pretty girl was like a melody.

But I decided not to write to him again. I had the cigar in the cigar box under the bed, and I placed alongside it the postcard with his handwriting, which I studied every day.

■ ■ ■

We drove up to Monsalvat two days after Christmas, which was a relief from my enslavement to the new holiday gifts (I felt required to play with new toys and wear new clothes in an intense manner). I had bought my grandmother some perfume that came in a dove-shaped decanter, and I gave Aunt Teresa a tissue-box cover I'd made in shop class. I had saved up enough money to buy Tommy a box of very good cigars. I had to have a friend's father take me to a tobacconist, insisting that I needed the cigars as a Christmas gift for my father. I went into the store with him, which was full of glass cookie jars full of loose tobacco with strange names on red labels: "Serbian Blend," "Chocolate Mix," "Red Man No. 4." There was an ivory pipe in a glass case carved to look like a dragon claw holding a bowl, and I dreamed of buying it one day. The store also sold chess sets and silver fountain pens, all signs of distinction that I had never before linked with my cousin Tommy.

The first evening, I sneaked into the blue room, and begging him not to tell my parents about the gift, I handed him the box of cigars. He slapped me on the back and said, "Ace! Ace! Little man, I promise you'll get a puff or two off these buggers."

Anne brought over a couple of her own Christmas presents. She was starting to get makeup and girls' things for gifts, but the most interesting thing she got that Christmas was a big picture of Jesus, the kind that looked like Tommy. It was a 3-D picture, and if I looked at it crossways, it suddenly turned into an impression of the famous Shroud of Turin. The outline of the 3-D picture of Jesus was made to match the outline of the ghostly outline on the shroud, his eyes shut and his mouth looking toothless and forlorn.

"Did you know that the image made on the Shroud of Turin was caused by an incredible source of heat and light that lasted a skillionth of a second, like the light of an atom bomb?" Anne asked. I could tell she had memorized it out of a book—she always looked down at the ground when she was lying and up at the sky when she was remembering.

"Don't you think the picture of the live Jesus looks like your brother?" I asked.

She narrowed her pinched-up eyes at me. She didn't look at all like Tom. "I think that it may be a sin to say something like that," she said. "Jesus didn't look like *any*body, you dink. Jesus looked like *God*." She spent several minutes moving the picture a little to the left and a little to the right so that Jesus blinked his eyes open and shut, and all I could see were his eyes.

. . .

This was the long airless week after Christmas, when Uncle Tom might go outside in the snow wondering what he ought to be doing. Even in Monsalvat, he stood like a symbol of the rest of the family that traditionally spent New Year's Eve together and didn't quite know how to make the time pass. The few stray cousins who did not live in Monsalvat, like us, brought campers with paraffin heaters in them, and parked them around my great-grandmother's house. The campers all smelled like candles in the cold outside. My parents didn't own a camper, so they stayed at Uncle Tom and Aunt Mary's—in Tom's old room—but I asked to stay in my regular light blue room. Actually, Tom asked for me.

"Is it okay, Aunt Teresa, if the little man and I share my room? There's enough room for two." My aunt, torn between common sense and punishment, let me stay. It solved an accommodation problem. I also think my grandmother put in a good word, or a sidelong look.

In the evening, Tommy and I went to bed at the same time. The room smelled like tobacco and all the old smells of dust and mothballs of that room. Other than the tobacco smell, and the book on citizenship, there was nothing Tom had done to my old room in seven months. Tom stripped down to his underwear quickly and hopped between the sheets. I was wearing flannel pajamas, which were plain plaid, luckily, and did not have embarrassing airplanes or ducks. "Do you always wear underwear to bed?" I asked him.

"They're not underwear, they're *briefs*." He picked up the same old book on American citizenship from which he had read me the constitutional amendments. He was studying hard because he had a big exam at the beginning of the year, and if he failed, he would have to go back and face the courts again.

"What did they do to you in the courts?" I asked him. I climbed into the bed.

"They yelled at me. They said I ought to be ashamed." He put the book down and I could see his wrists where they flexed to grip the book. They were strong, not nearly as skinny as mine. He had made them that way by spending any stray moments making chords on an old electric guitar without an amplifier. Aunt Teresa had forbidden him to play the guitar in the house with an amplifier, so when he played, only a puny melody emerged. I thought it sounded crippled. He said, "I wish more people would yell at me. Then I would know exactly everything I ought to be ashamed about."

"Don't you know?"

"Yeah, sure, I get the general idea, but I figured I'd pay my dues and they'd stop making me feel ashamed. I figure if I go to Confession enough times, Aunt Teresa won't be so pissed off. But I must've done something else, and nobody's telling me. Even my old lady won't talk to me." I thought of weak Aunt Mary, strong enough to resist Tommy.

"Why didn't you go to Vietnam when you were supposed to?" I asked.

"Well, see, little man, here's the thing." I expected him to say that my grandfather's war stories had scared him, but he seemed to have been waiting for somebody to ask him this question for a long time. "When I think of dying," he said, "I think of getting a massive heart attack like the Fattest Man in the World is going to get, or my lungs collapsing, or if I'm going to die violent like in a cop show, I'll get shot in the heart or maybe the liver. But never in the head. I always thought that my head would come out of it in one piece. Just before I was getting ready to go for my training, I saw this picture of a guy who was in the war. He had his head blown off."

He put himself under the sheet until only his head was showing, and made a stark, eyes-wide face like he was dead. "No way, José," he said. "The only way I could stand my brain failing me is because my heart let me down. I couldn't, I just *couldn't stand* the idea of my head going away." He rolled over and put the book on the night table, and turned out the lamp. In the grainy glow of the praying-hands nightlight, I could see a sheen of light and oil on his bare arms and neck.

I lay there thinking about how I agreed with Tom, although I didn't quite understand what he meant. I couldn't stand my head going away, either. In those days, there were only two kinds of pain I dealt with: physical and mental. Mental pain was more tolerable than physical pain. I have always had a low pain threshold. I hated scraped elbows and stuffy noses, and still do. And usually, by concentrating mentally on bodily pain, even magnifying it, I would cloud it, to help me explain it away. The mental always saved me from the physical. But I would *never* want the physical to alleviate a mental pain—never, for the sake of the pain of boredom, heartache, or depression, would I scrape my elbow or catch a cold.

I rolled over and asked one more question. "Tom?" He made a noise. "Do you have a record?"

"A record?"

"Yeah, like a police record. Do you have a file? Do they watch what you're doing?"

He made a laugh into his pillow. "I guess so. My old man probably updates it every day down at headquarters."

"I've got a record, too, you know," I assured him. He laughed, but he didn't challenge me.

I did have a record. All the things, the wooden bedposts and the mirrors and the banisters and teacups in my great-grandmother's house were witness to me, and knew everything I did. The body of Chester, buried out there in the flower bed, knew what I'd done, and the speared carp lost in the lake, they were my confessors, far more than police or priests could ever be. They were the everlasting mute witnesses.

I waited a long time into the night to make sure he was asleep. At some point he must have been having a nightmare, a falling dream, because he suddenly jolted around as if he were catching himself. I reached under the covers for his arm to calm him. I was sorry I couldn't help him in the place where the dream was. But I was also pleased to be able to touch his skin. He had a shell of heat around him. My fingertips knew when they were close to his body. I touched it and pulled away again, scared. Then I reached again, and pulled away again. Then I realized that only the bedposts, only the night-light and the citizenship book were witnesses, and that this secret thing I did could not be put on Tommy's record, only on mine. I rolled closer to him and let my cheek press against his wide back. His back was like the surface of a big animal, a wall pressing back at my own pressing.

In the morning, he got up early to get the shower first, and I looked all around the starched white sheets for little whorls of his hair that might have come off. I felt for a trace of his body's heat and imagined I'd felt it. His hair was too light to find, but I saw the impression of his face in his pillow, almost as clear as the image of Jesus on Anne's Shroud of Turin picture, and just as sad. I pressed my own face into it, I hid my self in his outline.

■ ■ ■

When I went into the kitchen, I found a handful of cousins practicing their poems for the New Year's Witch. One of my cousins, David, and his best friend, who had been wounded the summer before with the lawn dart, were interrupting each other as they tried to recite. Anne was bossing them around. I walked through without stopping and she said, "What are you looking for?"

"Nothing. Tommy. He's helping me memorize my poems for the witch."

"Tom's too old for the New Year's Witch. And so are you," she said.

"I'm not either. She came up to you last year. How come boys are too old for the witch before girls are? I'll bet you're all ready if she comes up to you this year."

Every New Year's Eve, just before midnight, my great-grandmother's house was visited by the New Year's Witch, a stranger wrapped in raggedy bedspreads, huge and veiled and carrying a gnarled old stick. The only part of her face that showed was a long crooked nose that was wrapped in strips of white bandage. This was a family tradition, indigenous only to that household. Whenever I told my friends at home about it, they were either jealous or thought it was weird. She would come to each child in the house, prod threateningly with a stick, and screech "Whee! Whee! Whee!" which was her way of demanding a poem to be recited. If it was a satisfactory poem, there was a bag of candy for a reward. This year, I wanted to impress the witch with a long poem I'd worked on for many months, "The Jumblies": "Far and few, far and few, are the lands where the Jumblies live; their heads are green and their hands are blue, and they went to sea in a sieve."

I could not find Tom anywhere. The house was full of relatives, but they were gray, inert, flopped in chairs looking at the television or napping with the newspaper steepled over their chests or putting together a jigsaw puzzle of an ugly lighthouse. They were best represented by my aunts Charlene and Charlotta's husbands, who always seemed so inert anyway, compared with the Kaiserbroad energy. Did the Kaisers marry dull people in order to underline their own colors? I thought of the sleeping town in Sleeping Beauty, and I was looking for the one person who was awake and full of life. I waited for him to dart down a hall.

I asked people if they'd seen Tom, but everybody denied knowing where he was. Even my grandmother didn't know, but she suggested looking in our bedroom. I had looked there a dozen times, but this time, after her advice, I found him sitting on the bed, reading the citizenship book.

"You're always reading that thing, aren't you?" I complained.

"It's important," he said. He was wearing a sweatshirt with a long rip from the collar to his shoulder.

"Don't you want to do anything else?" I asked. "You could hear me memorize my poem for the New Year's Witch. 'Far and few, far and few are the lands where the Jumblies live—' "

"I've got my own memorizing to do," he said.

"Come on, you've memorized enough. Come on, you know it—FATS AS Jimmy's Butt is Positively Swelling." He kept reading.

I sat on the bed staring at him, but he wouldn't look up from his book. I was distressed, because I had turned down a dozen other activities, hoping Tommy would be available. He didn't budge.

I left the room and had to listen to my little cousin Joe, Aunt Charlotta's youngest son, entertain Aunt Charlene and Aunt Charlotta by reciting for the millionth time his New Year's Witch poem. A few weeks before Christmas vacation, he had been part of the kindergarten pageant, where each kid was a letter of the alphabet. They wore white garbage bags that had been decorated with construction-paper cutouts of their assigned letter, anthropomorphized, so that Miss R was a ravishing red rockette, Mrs. O a roly-poly orange octopus. My cousin Joe was Mr. M, and although the pageant had been over for weeks, he still wore his garbage bag around the house shouting his rhyme, "Mr. M can munch and munch/Meat sandwiches make a marvelous lunch." Aunt Charlene squealed with laughter and said, "Say it again, can you say it again?" I thought of her story of Tommy zipping his fly up and down in his father's oversized police outfit singing "Mr. Policeman."

I wandered away, wondering how to get Tom to tell me why he was so sullen. Then I came up with an idea.

I would write a letter to him. If all he wanted to do was read, and he liked letters, I would write him a letter and put it in a place where only he could find it.

In a drawer full of yellowed clear tape, empty envelopes

with addresses on them, pens, a broken ruler, and a packet of little gummed labels with my grandmother's address on them and Aunt Teresa's name, I found a stationery pad. It had no lines, but there was a darkly lined piece that could be put under the clean sheet so that I would write in straight lines.

I took the paper down into the basement, and leaned over the big treasure-chest freezer where the carp had been frozen. I'd seen pictures of people trying to write an important letter and they always had a dozen wads of paper thrown on the floor all around their feet, because they were frustrated. They didn't know what to say. My problem was the reverse. I knew what to say, I had too many things to say. After two hours, I had written a stack of letters, and all of them were different. One letter yelled at Tom for not paying attention. One said I was sorry for getting in his way. One told my life story. One had a fantasy plan, not far off from my dreams of being bad-boy detectives, to get the family to like him again. One said how many times I thought about him over the summer. Another said that Aunt Teresa was bad news.

I didn't know which letter would be the best to give. They were all true in one way or another, but not one of them told the whole story. There was a terrible moment when I thought that what I wanted to do the most was write him a church hymn, because hymns sounded so happy about sorrow and passion. Instead, I decided to take parts of some of the letters and make it a single letter which would contain all the up-and-down feelings in it, and he would get the idea. Rather than a short, elegant church hymn, I was prone to the Kaiser family way of glutting the letter with a clutter of all things— like my great-grandmother's living room, with its porcelain and photographs and postage stamps. The letter was a mish-mash of the abundance of the world.

I crafted a long letter and made sure that each of the sentences from each of the letters was a sentence about Tom and not about me, because I didn't want him to think I was only thinking of myself. And I didn't want him to think that anything was wrong, so it was cheerful. In the end, I did not sign it, in case anybody found it and got the wrong idea. Nobody could pin it to me, if I didn't sign it.

Then I took an envelope, the kind with a smeary pattern on the inside that made it confidential enough to put checks in, and I wrote out Tom's name, and the whole address of my grandmother's house. I waited in the kitchen until he left the room to answer Aunt Teresa's call, and when he did, I slipped the envelope into the citizenship book. I had the same exact feeling of terror and joy that I had while trying to touch him in the bed the night before.

Now all I had to do was wait. To do something with myself, I went out into the living room, and went up to the terra-cotta manger scene that was spread out on top of the television. After Christmas day, nobody paid much attention to the crèche. There was a small flame-shaped red light bulb burning behind the stable. It put me in a strange mood. I imagined the simultaneous birth of the baby Jesus and the eruption of a volcano. I picked up the plaster infant. Its hands were splayed out baby style and one was nearly nicked clean off, like a premonition of the infant's own future.

I sat down on the couch and ran my fingers over the piece, looking for all of the molesting flaws in the hand-painted plaster. I allowed myself to say words to it. Tom was right again: even in crucifixion, Jesus was thinking. His brains failed because his lungs failed.

Suddenly, I realized that across the room, my great-grandmother and Uncle Tom were arguing, and they were arguing about Tommy. "Ma, you've been giving that kid money again, haven't you?"

"That's none of your business."

"I saw a box of expensive cigars in his room. If you keep letting him freeload, you're never going to get rid of him."

"He's no problem to me."

"That's not what Teresa says. Teresa says he steals money out of her purse. She says you give him hundreds of dollars and he spends it on crap."

"You tell Teresa that if she keeps lying she'll get sores on her tongue. He uses that money to pay for his tuition. He can't get a loan because of his record. He doesn't get help from you or your hypochondriac wife."

"He ought to be earning that money."

"He does! He's a regular handyman around here. Lord knows you never come over here anymore. We could all blow up before you'd get around to fixing the stove."

I could see Anne coming down the hall toward the living room. She was carrying a book and her blinky Jesus. Even from far away, I thought the eyes on Jesus looked straight at me. Uncle Tom saw Anne and called her over to him. "Come here a minute, Annie."

She skipped the rest of the way in. "What do you want? I want to memorize my poem for the New Year's Witch." She sat down on the arm of my great-grandmother's chair and put the thick book in her lap, expecting her help.

"Don't you think you're a little bit old for that?" her father said. "The witch is for the kids. You'll look silly standing up there."

"I'm not too old! What about Michael? He's old, too, and he gets to say a poem." She looked at me, now trying to hide behind the brittle browning Christmas tree, and looked at me like I was the one who said she was too old.

"Michael is not as old as you. Girls who get makeup for Christmas don't get to say a poem to the witch."

"That's not fair!"

"That's called growing up," my uncle said to her. "Now tell me something. Have you seen what your brother does all day in this house?"

Anne had shut down. She pulled the book up out of my

grandmother's lap and squeezed it close, her lipsticked mouth chewing on the cover. She was miserable. "I don't know."

"Just tell me what you see him do. Does he drink in his room? Does he steal?"

"I don't know! *God.* I'm not his mom. All I see him do is read."

"I wonder what the hell he reads. You couldn't get the kid to pick up a book when he was in high school. I wonder what gets him so interested in reading now," my uncle said. He put both of his hands on his belt, as if his gun and club were there as usual.

Anne offered, "He plays that stupid guitar that doesn't make any noise. Maybe he steals. I'll bet he could steal."

I stood up with the baby Jesus figurine in my fist. "He doesn't steal. I bought him those cigars. I'll bet anything he doesn't steal."

Uncle Tom smiled and Anne glared at me some more. She said, "What's that in your hand, Michael?" I looked down at my hand with everybody else, and opened it up. "Ha!" she said. "You're trying to steal the Jesus. How can anybody believe somebody who tries to steal the baby Jesus?"

I felt dirty. I put it back and walked away.

■　　■　　■

It was after dinner when I got the better idea. I was worried that even though I'd placed the letter in Tommy's citizenship book, he might not know exactly who wrote it, since I hadn't signed it. I decided that if I moved it under the passage about the first ten amendments, he'd be sure to know and it would mean more.

But when I went to our room, and looked in the book, the letter was gone. A sound, a note, came into my head, long and sustained. He must have found it and read it already. I thought back over dinner, and wondered if he had made any significant looks at me across the table. But I had spent most of the meal thrilling to the fact that he would soon get the letter. Would he hate me or like me? I wondered. He must see how important it was, if I went so far as to write him a letter. He must see that. He must see that my brain was razor sharp, not flabby like the Fattest Man in the World. When he had risen from the dinner table, I recalled, he turned his head to one side, showing those tendons and chords in his smooth neck, and I decided then that one way or another, he had not found the letter yet.

But when I found the letter gone after dinner, I decided that he found it. When I asked Aunt Teresa where Tommy went, she said that he was over at his father's house getting a good talking to.

"Is he in trouble?" I asked. He couldn't be in too much trouble, if Uncle Tom was actually speaking to him. The gradations of hatred put "a good talking to" closer to love than stone silence was (Tommy might have a better time with my own conversation pieces, the banisters and bedposts and teapots).

Aunt Teresa was washing a mountain of dishes, which she insisted nobody could help her with. "You bet your boots."

"Why? What did he do?"

She shook soapsuds off of her hands and waggled her head, without looking at me. "Someday he won't be getting into trouble, and he won't be getting so many other people into trouble."

. . .

Although nobody said anything formal about everybody being present on New Year's Eve, the entire family floated into the living room as if hypnotized. I thought of those summer Sundays years ago when I was the one floating in a timeless world among these people. Now my feet were on the ground, I measured out the draining minutes of the old year by the countdown on the television. I was the only one awake among sleepwalkers.

Aunt Teresa made soup and sliced leftover gristly turkey for sandwiches. It was like a mockery of a holiday. My father worked with her, in the kitchen, mixing endless batches of whiskey sours for my uncles. The Fattest Man in the World drank four of them in an hour and said he didn't feel good, so he was going home to sleep it off; he'd try to stop by at midnight. When he was drunk like this, he would often look up to the ceiling and declaim to his dead wife, the aunt I never met, and that is how he left the house, saying her name as if she had left the bathtub water on too long and made it overflow.

I watched my father working down the hall, and I thought he looked desperate not to turn into the black-and-white in-laws like my aunts' husbands. He and my mother, though, always seemed drab and tiny—even faceless—in the house full of big people.

Once again I was pushed up against the Christmas tree and I crushed a bulb, which I hid in my pants pocket. When I leaned against the branches, the needles poked me and then fell off like brittle flakes.

My grandmother sat in her overstuffed chair. Her face looked posed, her mouth hinged on two wrinkles on either side of her chin; but through her cat-eye glasses, her eyes were wet and alert and gleaming. I was thumbing the baby Jesus figurine again, and she pointed to me and beckoned me over.

"I won't break it, I promise," I said, sitting on the arm of her chair.

"Don't worry about that. Do you know how many times that thing's been broken and glued back together? Look here. And here." She was pointing to hairline fractures in the surface of the baby Jesus, which I had never seen before. "This little guy has been through the ringer," she said.

"Who broke him?" I asked.

"Lots of people. Nobody remembers after a while. It's boring here, isn't it? I'm bored."

I said I was, too.

"The only person who could liven this group up, besides you, Michael, is gone."

"He's not coming?"

"No. He's being punished. Your Uncle Tom said he found something in his room. Tom said he had something. They found evidence against him."

"Evidence?"

"Not drugs. Tommy doesn't smoke drugs. Just cigars. But I'll tell you, take it from me, they're not *just* cigars. Those things pack a wallop. When I smoked those nice Havana cigars, I could arrange petunias for a week, I felt so darn *creative*, if I wasn't so darn *high*."

Evidence. I thought about the letter. He never read the letter, somebody else had read it. Like Uncle Tom. When I thought of that, I had only the terrible feeling, only part of that feeling I had when I was trying to touch Tom's skin that night, without any of the heart-racing part. Where I had had one tremendous feeling, the feeling I had tried to convey in my letter, I now had only a piece of the feeling, like one of the small, incompletely drafted letters I had started with. I felt incomplete as well, distracted and unsatisfied.

I looked over at my uncle Tom. He had his eyes glued to the television, his whiskey sour balanced way down on his knee, far away from his mouth. But when he took a drink, his eyes darted over at me from behind the safe warp of his drinking glass, just for a moment. It might as well have been a million glances. I imagined him reading my private letter, and then I imagined him reading it out loud, to all of them.

If he knew, who else knew? Aunt Mary? My great-grandmother? Aunt Teresa? The Fattest Man in the World? Anne? No, not Anne! My parents? I looked at my grandmother's eyes. They stayed wet and dark behind the thick lenses as always, and I didn't think she knew, or at least she didn't see the harm I'd done. I ran to the kitchen. My father kept working, revving the blender full of slush and liquor, a palpable noise that seemed to comfort him. The kitchen seemed as big as the house, and he was on the other side of it from me. Aunt Teresa was singing and not looking at me. It meant she knew, as well.

I wondered if I was ruined. If all those people knew, and knew all through dinner, why hadn't they said anything? When I ran through dinner again, I remembered that hardly anybody spoke to me except to ask for plates to be passed. But Uncle Jimmy—the Fattest Man—and my grandmother had been exceptionally attentive to me, and even talked about adult things. They had asked me if I knew what I was going to be when I got out of school, if I had thought about it.

Aunt Teresa and my father remained silent, and I despaired. I went back into the living room, dreading the dropped eyes and pretenses. I looked for Anne, but she had not arrived yet, she was still home with her mother. I knew she would be in a bad mood, knowing that the New Year's Witch would pass her over on this night.

I sat near the decaying tree again, and nobody spoke to me, not Aunt Charlene or Aunt Charlotta or any of the other adults. I did not want to be playing board games with my cousins. Suddenly, I was gray and inert and asleep and they were all alive. I watched them all and waited for every one of them to sneak a look at me. I caught them all.

Finally, I decided to slip back through the halls to the bedroom. I noticed that the book of American citizenship was gone. So were his shoes, the cigars, and the ampless guitar.

They were punishing him for what I had done, because he made me be that way. He made me write a letter to him, they must have thought of it that way. He was gone, and he had left me nothing to help me replace him—that was what I thought at the time, that I was to be the new Tommy, the son Uncle Tom always wanted, and now even more like the Prodigal Son. I returned to the living room and gazed at the lights of the Christmas tree splayed on the ceiling.

Half an hour before midnight, the door opened and Anne came in, scampered up, and sat next to me. I said hello to her, but she didn't say hello back. She kept smiling and smiling at me. Then she whispered into my ear, "Where's your boyfriend?" and laughed and ran out of the room. She didn't know the odd comfort that was, how I could always count on her to open up her mouth in this sea of silence.

Just then, the New Year's Witch came down from the attic, down the long steep stairs that creaked as she descended. I wondered if, and then I hoped that the witch was actually Tommy in disguise, that there was an outside chance, and I would recognize the shape of his shoulders through the raggedy bedspreads, the way I had recognized the shape of his boa constrictor in the flower-garden grave. I would see the hairs on his bare hand as he reached into the basket. I knew I would recognize even the way he moved with all of those robes.

But the New Year's Witch was too big to be Tommy. The New Year's Witch was the Fattest Witch in the World. It couldn't be anybody else. When the witch made the trademark "Whee! Whee! Whee!" noise, it sounded like a piglet, and it resonated in my uncle's big throat. One by one, he came up to the kids in the family, and they recited a poem, tormented but gleeful for all that attention.

I half watched my cousin Joe announce that "Mr. M can munch and munch," but I was invisible in my thoughts, and made invisible by all the thoughts around me. Anne was sitting tall on the piano bench, hoping to be noticed, hoping that there was an outside chance that the witch would relent and see her as subject to the rules of the game. But the witch passed her by, poking Anne away once with the walking stick. Anne narrowed her eyes. I could see that she was clumsily wearing some of the makeup she got for Christmas. I was trying to hide away from Anne's attention, but I also half wanted my chance; I thought that if I said my long poem, they might forget the letter they had read and which they would not talk to me about. I now knew what Tommy was talking about when he said that they were punishing him with the silence.

Most of the poems my cousins were reciting were talked-out versions of pop-song lyrics, the cheaters. I saw the Fattest Witch in the World hand out huge lunch sacks full of candy, one for each cousin. He moved on and poked my eight-year-old cousin Kathleen, sitting next to me, who seemed to be making something up off the top of her head. The adults were laughing from relief and whiskey sours.

Then the New Year's Witch skipped me. He walked right past me like I did not exist, and I wondered if he couldn't see well through all the folds of those bedspreads. I let him finish the last two kids, and waited for him to come looking for me, but he headed toward the attic again.

I jumped out and blocked his way. I thought that my body might fail, I couldn't feel anything, but my head was still working, and I was no longer gray and inert. I put my hand on the base of the banister and barely reached the other wall, so that the witch could not go past without running me down. I stared him down desperately. I focused on the nose that was made out of cloth wrapped into a bent knot. It had come loose, and if the witch stayed too much longer, the nose would fall off on the floor. He knew that, and was desperately trying to get around me.

I yelled out, "Listen! Listen! The cat's a-pissin'! Where?

Where? Under the chair! Run! Run! Get a gun! Aw, shoot, he's all done!"

Everybody was looking at me. I could see the lights on the tree blink behind the witch. The Fattest Man in the World looked straight at me, but I couldn't see what kind of expression he had. I wondered if perhaps it was not Uncle Jimmy. I wondered if Tommy's saying "A good cigar is a smoke" didn't mean what I thought it meant. "That was my poem!" I said.

The New Year's Witch shrugged and opened up his basket. I looked in; it was empty.

I let him by. I let my hands slap to my pants and sat on the piano bench. People started talking again and the aunts, uncles, and cousins started reminiscing over the poems they'd recited. I saw my cousin Joe engrossed in his enormous bag of candy.

Aunt Charlotta came up to me and said, "You're a little old for the New Year's Witch, don't you think? Come on now. You don't believe in Santa Claus, do you?" The New Year's Witch trudged up the last of the stairs and disappeared dramatically into the attic with a slam of the door, thereby assuring that no cousin of mine, under the age of ten, would go to the attic or Aunt Teresa's room unescorted. That was the last time I ever saw the New Year's Witch, as spectator or participant.

A few minutes before midnight, Uncle Jimmy, the Fattest Man in the World, came through the front door miraculously recuperated and carrying six bottles of pink champagne. He popped one open and it sprayed sticky foam all over the manger scene and the television.

Uncle Jimmy shrugged at me and lifted his eyebrows until fatty ridges formed in his forehead. He poured some champagne into all my aunts' and uncles' and parents' glasses, and then he poured two small glasses, one for Anne, pouting and chewing the lipstick off of her lips, and one for me. When he handed my glass over, he said, "Sorry about that, kid."

After I had drunk some of the champagne, Aunt Charlene came to me and talked about how hard Anne was taking it, not being poked by the witch with a sharp stick. She had no idea, she said, it would be so hard on the two of us.

Feeling a little giddy, I went outside the house without a coat, and looked at the house. I remembered the Fourth of July evening, a year and a half ago, and once again, the house looked like an aquarium full of strange undulating light, from the Christmas tree and the television. I could see them all drinking and moving and celebrating, but like fish, they might die out in the cold air, where I stood. Amphibious me.

I was looking around for footprints leading in any direction, in the snow, and only found the ladder from the attic window to the ground, the only means of escape for the New Year's Witch.

PART II

LEAVING THE HOUSE

I have always been impressed by those hundreds of stories Aunt Teresa and my grandmother had in books, with their mythic illustrations and postures. Even today, having gone away from that place, having met all these adult fears and wonders, I am a bit terrified and adoring of each old story, little girls treading on loaves, drinking bottles marked "drink me"; little boys turning into gingerbread and little boys who were wood and wanted to be flesh, but were swallowed by whales instead.

Monstro, the terrible whale, big and blue and worst of all, real. There were hundreds of real whales swimming in the world at least as big as Monstro, legless teardrop-shaped bulks, their obscene fleshy blowholes and huge expanses of meaty sides were walls of living matter full of blood and muscle.

And the eye. In the storybooks, the whale is *en passant*, just a huge portion of the whale wall and the eye, screwed up with anger, but with a cornea, retina, white, pupil. No sign of the other eye, so far away from this one that spies me from the page. A huge monstrous eye in Monstro, terrible because it was like my *own* eye. I was not afraid of the whale. I was afraid of the whale's big eye.

It's the familiar in the strange that terrifies me. I was not afraid of my nose growing if I lied, or of being changed into gingerbread; I was afraid of the way I would have been a regular boy in a world that could change boys to gingerbread, and wood to flesh.

It's the familiar in the strange that terrifies me. And every day, all the familiar things become more and more strange to me.

CHAPTER 7

In a World of Women

The summer I got my driver's license was the summer four guys in my high school killed themselves for their girlfriends and the summer I started running around with Marsha. Marsha was beautiful in a plain way, like the responsorial psalm portion of mass. Her eyes were raccooned with insomnia but her skin was light and her hair long. She would come to school having washed her hair in the morning, and it would stay wet through second period (third, if it froze in winter on the way to school), then dry a shade lighter, like paint.

Marsha was a year older than me, the same age as my cousin Anne, and she complained that her high-school-graduation photo wasn't *dreamy* enough. I suppose she meant that she was not looking far enough into space (the future), and that she was not airbrushed into an idealistic glaze (perfection). I remember the photo, though I've lost it: she looks straight into the camera, a little disappointed.

Marsha always destroyed library books with neglect, or lost them. She never returned the surviving ones on time. "Ha-ha, guess I'm a bad socialist," she said, digging in her purse to pay the steep overdue fine, and I'd go home and read up on socialism, to find out what she meant. My sense of humor, and my wish to skewer enemies with killing logic were the two motivating factors to expand my vocabulary.

There were two big reasons why I was excited by Marsha. One was that Aunt Teresa, while pretending to like Marsha, secretly and obviously hated her. She would talk abstractedly about morbidly distracted young ladies, because she had caught Marsha more than once talking to me about dying while pacing the perimeters of a room. Aunt Teresa forbade phone calls in her Monsalvat house after ten P.M., in order not to disturb my grandmother. That was a house rule created only after Marsha called for me one evening at midnight, to tell me she missed me. Her voice at midnight over the phone was as soothing as the praying-hands night-light.

It took Aunt Teresa three years to tell me she didn't like Marsha, after Marsha had gone far away to marry a foreigner with bad teeth, and even then, Aunt Teresa blabbed it to me tipsily, at Anne's wedding, the liquor doing all the talking. "I'm so glad you won't be marrying that Marsha." She seemed to lob her drunken words with her hands, like scoopsful of mud. "She was self-absorbed and morbid."

But in those days when my driver's license was new, Aunt Teresa treated Marsha like this girl was my personal salvation. When I asked if Marsha could join me on a road trip to Monsalvat for Labor Day weekend, Aunt Teresa went through the motions of a scandalized mother.

"I don't think it's a good idea," she said. "I can just see you two off doing something in your great-grandmother's home and she would walk in on you and die of a heart attack."

She secretly loved that, I think. It was easy, or easier, for her to imagine my interest in de-skirting Marsha than a hundred other things I did each time I visited, things that mystified her. It was easy for her to imagine a growing boy begging for the taste of what is achingly, shamefully required.

I, on the other hand, had built up an imagination like bodybuilders develop biceps, as if I had lived spread-eagled on a storytelling bench press, and overdeveloped only those particular muscles to a disproportionate size. My imagination made my mind top-heavy, apelike. Because the things that required the most imagination to me were the things that were supposed to come most naturally—like de-skirting Marsha.

People wonder why these certain kinds of men, in later years, left to their own devices, get into all sorts of strange game playing: leather, bondage, drag. It is all a kind of alien paraphernalia of an already wild affectation, it's all showmanship, an act, a ritual. Of course we dream up these fringe games—after all, we played the most bizarre one right at the start. The most mind-warping thing I ever did, the most my imagination ever bench-pressed, was kissing Marsha on the lips.

Marsha and I drove to Monsalvat in a pale blue car with an AM radio and no air-conditioning. When I drove too fast on the freeway, the auto's body would tremble.

We stopped, for the car's sake and for Marsha's, at every possible roadside attraction. All of the produce stands were brimming over with late harvests: strawberries, cherries, corn, apples, rhubarb, squash, and watermelon. The way people eat these things are the way so many other things are done there: by binging. Marsha bought two pints of cherries, and systematically ate every one, getting no real pleasure from any of them except for that last one. That pleasure came from the thought that there, we ate them while they lasted, we ate them before they went bad.

Some stands gave away the squash for free.

The plenty along the road was our torture. I knew that Aunt Teresa would have five pies cooling on the kitchen counter, which had to be eaten, for there wouldn't be anything like it for another year. She made strange, desperate concoctions of strawberries and rhubarb, blackberries and apples, invented with her own grim and fierce ecstasy, eaten in the same spirit.

Then there was the dark problem of sweet corn. Farmers vied to bring their customers the freshest ears; some grew their cornfields right to the edge of the road, and when we asked them for a dozen, they'd pick them off the stalks and tell us, "Quick! Boil them now or they'll lose their freshness." Some even set up barbecue pits fitted with boiling washtubs of water, and dropped the corn in for us, to be eaten on the spot.

As I drove with Marsha, she showed me things I had long ago forgotten about. She made this old stretch of road seem strange. "Look at that." She pointed to the huge Christmas-ornament-shaped billboard that said, VISIT FRANKENBRON-ER'S! WHERE IT'S CHRISTMAS EVERY DAY! "Look at that. The Christmas ornament that ate New York." I never thought of the sign as menacing, but as a marker, fifty miles away from Monsalvat. When we drove back, I'd look at the seamy backside of the ornament shape, recognize the structure that held it together, another marker, a hundred miles away from home.

Marsha wanted to buy a dozen donuts and a jug of cider, but I passed the mill. She saw a hitchhiker but I drove by without slowing. Marsha pouted for twenty miles.

Then she had to go to the bathroom, so I pulled into a rest stop. I had to go, too, so I stepped into the men's room and up to a urinal next to a man who had a beer gut and a hunting jacket. There was an orange license tag in a clear plastic pocket safety-pinned to his back. He looked at me and I smiled back. I was going to ask him what he hunted, ducks, deer, carp? He turned to me, his pants still undone. He didn't smile now. It was so big.

I got out fast, feeling the frustration I felt when I thought of a hundred comebacks to a putdown. (What good was my expanded vocabulary if I expended it on "I should have said's" within my own silent fantasy bench press?) I got into the car and started the engine, hoping Marsha would come out soon. She didn't return for five minutes.

So she also didn't see when the hunter came out and approached my car, didn't feel the lyelike juices piping through my stomach and intestines as he came closer, and for what?

But he got into the pickup truck parked next to me. He wanted to leave faster than I did. He stared at me the way Marsha stared out of her high-school-graduation photo—not dreamily, just disappointedly. Along the cab of his truck were a half-dozen stickers, aligning the driver with the National Rifle Association, Smith & Wesson, and Ducks Unlimited.

He was long gone by the time Marsha crawled in on her side of the car, sighing. "You guys are lucky. Girls have to stand in line because other girls take so long in the bathroom. They have to unzip their dresses or fix something or fuss with something. Guys never fuss."

There's a secret world in every place, even along the road, I thought, a sneaky place that overlaps the other. When we got to Monsalvat, I found out that not only had Aunt Teresa baked the five pies, but she had panicked because we took so long to get there, and she had called my mother and the highway patrol had been alerted and prepared to find two bloody bodies in a pale blue car, covered with donuts and sticky cider.

■　　■　　■

"So you're not Catholic?" Aunt Teresa asked Marsha. They both had their sleeves rolled up and were pulling the stem and pith from strawberries, soaking in the right-hand sink. Some of the strawberries floated and some sank to the bottom, and I wondered why that was. I was sitting with my grandmother, peeling and coring apples for applesauce. My grandmother was looking through a huge three-ringed album full of yellowed recipe cards, looking for her secret recipe for applesauce.

"No, but I know a lot about dogma," Marsha said, and laughed at herself.

"Oh, you do, do you?" Aunt Teresa turned to wink at me. She was going to ask the Trick Question, the question she always asked at this point. "So do you know what the Immaculate Conception is?"

"Sure. That's the part where Mary had Jesus without doing it."

"No!" Aunt Teresa raised her hands out of the water, splattering all of us. "That's just it! It's not about Mary having Jesus without doing it. It's about Mary's parents having Mary without doing it."

Aunt Teresa's triumph coincided with my grandmother's finding her secret recipe. She tore it loose from four corners of yellowed transparent tape. I watched how her hand, all tendons supporting tented sheets of bullfrog-spotted skin, trembled. The secret ingredient to the recipe was rum.

Then Anne stomped in. I had not seen her since the previous spring, and she seemed puffy and sullen. Morbid and self-absorbed. She didn't bother regarding me, but immediately appraised Marsha. She said, "So this is the girlfriend."

"Grab a knife, Anne," Aunt Teresa said, "and give us a hand. There's a bushel of tomatoes to do after this. I can smell them going rotten even now."

"Can't. I'm going over to Philly and Millie's. They said they have some books for me." Anne took a strawberry and never stopped, heading out the other door. My grandmother's house was situated between Uncle Tom's house and the two old women who had come to that Fourth of July barbecue years before—Millie and Philly—who lived on the other side. The path was shorter if Anne used the trail through the house to the next yard.

"What's her problem?" I asked.

"She's very preoccupied," my great-grandmother said.

Aunt Teresa went to work pithing strawberries again, grimly, as if they were going bad right there in her hands. "I only *wish* she was preoccupied," she said. "If she was very preoccupied, she wouldn't have any problems."

"Idle hands are the devil's workshop," Marsha said.

"You said a mouthful," Aunt Teresa said, popping a strawberry into her mouth.

"She should know," I muttered, and Marsha stuck her tongue out at me. All during these pronouncements, Marsha worked steadily, though. To each strawberry, she ventriloquized a voice for it as she was gutting it, in a stage whisper, saying, "Don't cut me. No! No!" and when she dropped it into the colander at her side, trimmed and scrubbed, she said, quietly, "Boink," as if that were the cartoony sound a strawberry made when it landed.

That was the other thing that excited me about Marsha. She was an animist. All the things in the world were alive and speaking, active, and sometimes they even revolted against her. While I found comfort in speaking to the banister and praying over statues of the Virgin Mary, objects were speaking to her. They had names and personalities, not cute names like pets, but sexy ones, females like Valerie for a low-cut dress and Pauline for a coffee cup, males like Rod for a broom and Rick for the hood of the pale blue car. She was gleeful for the way they lived, not morbid at all, even for the things that were threatening, and might cause harm.

I confessed to her, once, that I had actually stepped on the tines of a rake and the handle clobbered me in the head.

"Sometimes, I think I do things like that on purpose, subconsciously."

"Oh, no," she said, as if I, or anybody in the world never did anything clumsy, "Oh, no, it's just that these things like to do things *to you* on purpose."

■　　■　　■

Philly and Millie were a little older than Aunt Teresa. Philly was short for "Philadelphia," which is where she was from. She was always working on the yard, wearing her overalls and riding a lawn mower in a tightening circle and caulking up holes in the log cabin they lived in. For all of this yard work, there was a thick hedge of Queen Anne's lace, goldenrod, and thistles, the smell of which reminded me of the boring summer I spent years ago. Millie wore housedresses and a sunbonnet when she was outside, but usually stayed inside.

When Anne came back from their house, she was carrying a copy of *Our Bodies, Ourselves*. Aunt Teresa turned away from the sink and put her fist at her waist, the paring knife pointed from the hip at Anne. "What sort of crap are those women unloading on you now?"

"This isn't crap," Anne said. "It's science." She sat next to us apple corers at the table and flipped through graphics of fallopian tubes and ovaries. These books, and the teachers of the books, tried their best to make sex dry and merely scientific, but even my ugly biology teacher's demonstration of the ovulating female womb—holding out his arms with a tennis ball in each hand and letting one bounce away like a descending ovum—was exciting. The word itself, "sex," was exciting, the ideas behind it easily slipped out and inflated rapidly like a life raft in the compartment of a downed plane, or fell like overripe fruit from the tree of that word. Consume it fast, I thought, before it goes bad.

I craned my neck to look into the book.

Anne said, "I don't know why you don't like Philly and Millie. They only do nice things for you. They gave you all those apples, they gave me this book. Sometimes Philly even mows your side yard."

"Oh-ho-ho, don't let your father hear you say that," Aunt Teresa said, into the hollowed recess of a larger strawberry. "Those gals are always having Tom over to fix something, in-*clud*ing that junked-out lawn mower."

"Oh, get over it," Anne said. "Like he never helps you around here. They're helpless old widows just like you."

Aunt Teresa turned with the paring knife aimed from the hip again. "They are *not* widows. Those two never married. I married. I'm a widow. They are not widows. Those women are *tough*."

I suddenly understood something that was right in front of my eyes for years, the way Marsha made me notice the Frankenbroner's sign. "Tough" was Aunt Teresa's way of saying a woman was not interested in men. Philly and Millie were a nice couple, happily settled in their misplaced log cabin, pretending to be happily married.

My great-grandmother said, "They sure give us nice apples."

■   ■   ■

"Would you like to meet Philly and Millie?" I asked Marsha while we sat on the wraparound porch drinking apple cider and eating pie.

"Are they relatives, too?"

"Nope, they're the only ones on the block who aren't Kaiserbroads." I was afraid and hopeful that those tough women might think it strange for me to come by and intro- duce Marsha, but Anne was right, Philly and Millie were always extra nice to me, and Philly had given me half a tackle box full of artificial lures years back, when I took a brief interest in fishing—with Tommy.

I thought it would be a good idea to bring them over some of the applesauce we had made with the apples they gave my grandmother. I took a jar, displayed on a patchwork of kitchen towels on the big table.

We knocked on the cabin door and Millie answered. She was barefoot wearing a flowery dress. I noticed that her toenails were painted candy-apple red. "Michael! How good it is to see you. We never see you enough. Philly said she saw you drive in. I can't believe you're driving now. Next thing, you'll be shaving."

"I already do shave."

"Stop it, you're breaking my heart. What's that? Applesauce?" I handed it to her. She did not even hide the fact that she had two dozen of her own canned apple sauce in the pantry: I watched her put my proffered jar next to all the rest. "Who's your friend?" She buttonholed Marsha, literally.

I introduced her, and while I did, Millie led us into another section of the cabin, which was the living-room part. The place was cozy and full of stuff, not the kind of stuff that my grandmother kept around, but necessary stuff, pots and pans and furniture, but cluttered, if necessarily cluttered. Marsha was putting her hand on every possible thing, and making birdy sounds. Philly was lounging in a chair in a plaid shirt and jeans, and at first we didn't see her there among all the things.

"Philly, look, it's Michael. And he's brought his little friend, Marsha."

"Mike!" Philly said, getting up from her complicated easy chair. Behind her was a huge framed photograph. It was probably a painting but it seemed like a photo, one of two naked women listening to a man playing a Middle Eastern stringed instrument to them, all snug on a big skin rug. The women were beautiful, and the cracks of their buttocks showed as well as the poured-honey outlines of their breasts. Their eyes made them look like science fiction, painted with odd shades. The man was also naked, except for a turban on his head, and he had a triangle of chest hair, which didn't seem quite real and made me realize that this was a painting and not a photo. Otherwise, I would have never known for sure. The painting looked strange in this rustic cabin, with the log walls showing and the pots and pans on pegs not more than a few feet away. It was almost elegant. I kept staring at it while Philly talked to me.

"That's enough of that, Mike," Philly said. "They're pretty ladies, but there are other pretty ladies in this very room. So let's pay attention to them."

I ought to have been embarrassed when Philly reproached me, but I wasn't, she was being chummy. Aunt Teresa had an easy-listening record in the living room, called *Whipped Cream and Other Delights*, and on its cover was a naked woman covered in whipped cream. She held a rose in one uncreamed hand and had a dollop of the stuff on the tip of her other hand, which she was tasting provocatively while smiling toward the camera. When I looked at that for long periods, Aunt Teresa would come in and say, "That's enough of that, Michael," as if there were a certain amount of time in which it was appropriate to leer at the woman on the album, and beyond which time it was dirty. I always felt dirty when she came in to tell me my time was up.

Philly and Millie offered us pie and asked us all the right questions. They asked how my grandmother was doing. They wanted to know whether Anne was having any trouble. "She's preoccupied," I said, agreeing that something must be up. Marsha kept getting up and examining things, and the two women let her.

"Do you think she's having boy problems?" Millie asked. "She wanted to know whether I missed boys. She came over today and asked whether it would be all right to live without any boys around her."

Philly said, "She likes boys too much to live without them."

Marsha shrugged. "Maybe she's pregnant."

Millie gasped. "No. You don't think? Do you suppose? No." I watched the question pose itself and fade and return again to her, her nail-polished fingers a fence over her mouth.

"That's a rumor," said Philly. "We don't know that, so let's just dismiss it like the rumor it is. People get hurt over rumors." I wondered what rumors had hurt her, them. Still, she looked in a congratulatory way over at Marsha for thinking it up.

"Your aunt Teresa is very hard on her," Millie said in a low tone.

"She was always strict," Philly said.

"She's got her opinions," I said. "She's got house rules."

"Mike," Philly said, "do you have a mind for mechanical things?" and led me into the kitchen, leaving Millie with Marsha talking about *Our Bodies, Ourselves*, which happened to be one of Marsha's favorite books.

I didn't have a mind for mechanical things, and Philly found that out right away. "Your mind's more artistic, I can tell," she said, and smiled like it meant a lot more. But she had me help her stack some firewood in the back anyway.

"Have you heard any about Tommy?" she asked me nonchalantly.

"Nothing," I said, wondering how much she knew.

"He's one of those kids who always gets into trouble because he can't lie," she said. "He tells the truth and he gets punished for it."

"And I always tell lies and I never get in trouble, no matter how hard I try," I half joked.

"I know all about that one," Philly said, and winked. "As long as you follow your aunt Teresa's rules, you'll never get into trouble." We worked a little more on the woodpile, and she said, as if I had missed a whole middle portion of our conversation but came out on the other end in the same place where she was, "I don't think we'll ever see Tommy again."

When we finished and came back around the front of the house, we found Millie and Marsha outside, on their hands and knees in the sandy section of the overgrown hedge. Millie was showing Marsha ant lions, mysterious splayed anemone-shaped bugs deep in the cone of a volcano of sand. Ants would slide down the dunes and the ant lion would close on them like a bear trap, and feed.

Millie had found an ant, and dropped it into the sand pit. Marsha was providing the horrible sound effects of ant, lion, and struggle. Millie looked up at us. "There you two are. Look at this. Violence! All sorts of brutal things going on around here. We live dodging thunderbolts. Look at this! Open spaces in the arrow of south-flying geese where one's been shot down up there. Dead fish belly-up on the lakes down there. And look at this. Violence!" She pointed into the ant trap.

"Help! Help!" Marsha narrated for us.

■   ■   ■

Aunt Teresa was parboiling tomatoes and slipping the skins from them in two or three knife slits and one firm hocus-pocus motion of the hand over the fruit. Marsha and I were playing war with a deck of cards, the game I played with Tommy that often lasted forever. Anne stomped into the house and let the screen door bang. Two hornets got in with her, attracted to the sugar of jelly pectin and rotting tomato skins.

"Has anybody seen my book?"

"Which book?" Marsha asked.

"*Our Bodies, Ourselves*," Anne said.

Aunt Teresa never stopped stripping the tomatoes. "I sent it back around to Philly and Millie. That book is smut. It will only give you ideas."

"It doesn't give you ideas," Anne said. "It's science."

"Don't tell me that," Aunt Teresa said. "I read that whole chapter about sexual pleasure. Don't tell me that was science."

"There's a whole chapter about birth control, did you read that?"

"If you know about birth control, you're liable to experiment with it. Your father doesn't buy rifles to look at them. He buys them so he can run around with his Ducks Unlimited buddies and get drunk and shoot each other up."

Marsha put down her cards. "Ducks Unlimited? What's that?"

Anne said, "It's a bunch of guys who raise ducks in preserves so that there are lots of ducks."

"That's sweet," said Marsha.

"So that they can set them loose in the woods and shoot them."

"That's awful," said Marsha.

"That's boys for you," Anne finished.

I said, "There are girls in Ducks Unlimited." By then, Anne was dodging one of the hornets flying at her fingertips. She was squealing for help.

Marsha watched Anne try to protect herself behind kitchen chairs. She spoke for the hornet. "Yum, yum, get a load of her, she's a *sweet* young thing!" Anne glared at her, then swatted the hornet dead with a newspaper.

■　■　■

"No, I do *not* want you following me to the drugstore, fathead. Haven't you got enough womanly attention from the chick who talks to herself?"

"She doesn't talk to herself, she's just narrating."

"She sounds like my little brother playing with his army men."

"Come on, I'll drive you to the drugstore."

"No, Michael, just let me borrow your car. I won't scratch it."

"Not unless you tell me what you're going for. Are you going to buy birth-control devices? Or is it too late for that?"

"No, I am not pregnant, no thanks to creeps like you."

"Come on, I'll take you. I'll stay in the front of the store and you can do your business without me looking. I won't tell anybody. It'll be done before anybody wakes up."

"You'll tell the babbling girl. And she'll blab it to the kitchen appliances and then everybody will know."

But Anne said all right, finally, and since Marsha was sleeping in and I'd already had breakfast, I took my cousin to the drugstore. We were quiet in the car until we got to the end of the road. I looked over at Anne's profile, concerned and bird-shaped. She said, "No, I haven't heard from Tommy, so don't ask."

"Why did you think I was going to ask?"

"Because you were, weren't you? I knew the same way I knew you thought I was pregnant."

"Philly and Millie could've told you that."

"It wouldn't bother Philly and Millie if I was, so I would've *told* them. It's only gossip if somebody thinks it's bad. Only people with dirty minds would think it was bad."

"I wouldn't think it was bad."

"No, but you're a pervert. You'd be happy if anybody was a pervert like you are. You and every other boy."

"You know other guys who are perverts?"

"My boyfriend, for one. I don't see what the big deal is. I let him check out the stuff to see if it was any big deal. Even if he had three times as much fun as I did, he won't bother touching me ever again."

I said, "Oh." Then I said, "Marsha told me the same thing. She said she couldn't stand it the first time."

"First time? I'll be damned if I do that again. I'm never going near another boy again."

"So why are we going to the drugstore?"

"Shut up."

"If you've got the stuff around, it will only give you ideas."

"Shut up."

Anne went down the long aisles to the back of the store. I think they build all drugstores long and narrow, like a corridor on purpose. There were three women in white lab coats and glasses like Aunt Charlene's, and they looked at me carefully, daring me to follow Anne back, with her, presumably, to shoplift several packages of condoms. I believed in the secret world of women, then, believed that these women knew Anne would swipe condoms but that this sort of activity was built into the budget of every drugstore, they were made available to be stolen for the sake of other women.

I stood near the greeting cards and magazines. The magazines were fanned along the shelves by subject matter, left to right: gardening, food, fashion, crossword puzzles, motorcycles, guns, comic books, *Playboys*. Whose value system? Perhaps there was another secret plan of the women behind the counter to make the *Playboys* temptingly close to the comic books.

I picked up a *MAD* magazine, slid it over the *Playboy* so that I could look at the pictures in the *Playboy* without any of the lab-coated ladies seeing. I learned this trick from Anne and her Young Lady's Li Brary. The girls in the magazine were photographed to look just the way Marsha wanted to look in her graduation photo—perfect and futuristic, airbrushed into unreality, staring into space. None of them looked disappointed, but there seemed to be a layer of oil, or frost between me and the pretty ladies. I kept looking up to see if anybody was watching me. I read three cryptic party jokes. Another reason I wanted to expand my vocabulary was to understand more sexy jokes.

On one of my nervous pigeonlike glances around the store, I saw the thing that made the lye plumb through my esophagus into my stomach, and come up to the base of my skull like a spray: *Play*girl. The magazine was like a revelation, like a crucifix between the antlers of a deer. *Playgirl.* Playgirl? Could there be such a thing? Recklessly, I pushed the *Playboy* aside and nested the *Playgirl* between the pages of *MAD.* It fell open at the centerfold.

He was not airbrushed. He sat on the edge of the bed, mustachioed and muscled. It was so big. I studied every part of him. His naked feet, hairless, seemed vulnerable. The hair under his arms was curiously straight, like a Japanese girl's. Except for the mustache, he was close-shaven until his chin glowed semiblue. The room he sat in seemed foreign even to him, and might as well have faded away along with the three women behind the drugstore counter. Within the secret world of women were the two of us, tight-knit, no oily or frosty film between us. Neither of us was disappointed.

"Hey, Michael, checking out the *Playboy*s?" Anne slipped up behind me.

I have, since, always believed in the genius of desire. I know that I had the ability to kill, to kill Anne or anybody, to stab many times, right there in the drugstore, to stab and run my hands through ribbons of flesh and grip it here and there, with the desire and the need to protect my desire.

"Hey, Michael, show me your favorite model. Do you like 'em mousy brown like the babbler? Or blond? Guys sure treat blondes differently. Do you like big tits? Most girls stuff them, you know. Take it from me. Anything to keep you guys interested. So show me, which one do you like best?"

Somehow, I would have to get the *Playgirl* back on the shelf without her seeing it. I turned to her. "None of them."

"Oh, yeah, you're that guy who says you can put a bag over her face and any of them will do the trick. I know that one, too."

I realized that at that moment, my salvation would be compassion. I said, "Anne, were you forced to do something you didn't want to do? Is your boyfriend that big a jerk? Not all guys are like that."

"That's a laugh. If even *you* are a pervert, where am I going to find one that's not? Uncle Jimmy? Maybe I'll marry the Fattest Man in the World."

"Four guys in my school killed themselves for their girlfriends this summer. Would you like your boyfriend to kill himself for you?"

"They didn't kill themselves for their girlfriends. They just got the idea from whichever one started it. It's a fad. And the one who started it was probably an accident."

Still, I wanted to say, an idea is an idea. Just because something was fashionable didn't mean it wasn't important. But all the time we were talking, I was slipping the magazine back into the rack. Anne was running her hand along the *Vogue*s and *Cosmopolitan*s, pulling one out and looking at the clothing models, showing me one now and then. "Isn't she pretty?" She didn't ask me if she was my favorite, because she had her fancy clothes on. I agreed that some were pretty. I wondered why I couldn't look at a handsome model and say, "Isn't he handsome?" without making a mess.

While she thumbed through the fashion magazines I had set to the task of deftly detaching the centerfold of the *Playgirl*, the pages closed but my finger divining the center of the magazine, and pulling just slightly, feeling the page pull away from the single flimsy staple like taffy. Then I folded the centerfold in half, then quarters, down into the rack so that it was as small as a love note passed in class. I shoved it into my pocket, next to the car keys.

This I did, as well, due to the genius of desire. I didn't get any ideas from other sources, no book showed me how to do that, no television show, no pervert leading me astray. I knew that this was what had to be done to take home the object of my desire.

And I also knew that it had to be a secret thing, that simultaneously with the clarification of my urgings came the knowledge that it was something to be guilty for, that to Aunt Teresa, even to Anne, it was *wrong*. Maybe everybody had a dirty mind. Otherwise, how could anybody know that some things are wrong?

In the car on the way back, I listened to Anne complain about her boyfriend some more. At times she would almost wail, but then she would pull back and blame all men, especially me, for being perverts. I could feel the edge of the eighths-folded centerfold dig into my inner thigh where it rested in my pocket.

Anne pulled out the condoms she swiped. They had names like "Feel Free" and "Morning Glory." They came in packets that might fit tea bags. I said, "Morning Glory sounds like peppermint-and-lemon tea." Anne laughed and we spent the rest of the ride making up different flavors for the different condoms.

■　　■　　■

When we got back to the house, everybody was up. Fruit flies swarmed ineffectually over the kitchen garbage can full of tomato skins. The second hornet from the day before was caught in a glutinized pool of grape jelly. I asked Aunt Teresa where Marsha was.

"I thought she was with you."

I went out to look on the porch, and from there I could see Philly in her overalls, pulling up clods of dirt near Millie's flower bed. She stopped to wave. I went over to her. "Have you seen my friend Marsha?"

"Sure, she's inside drinking tea with Millie. Do you want me to get her?" I told her no, she could take her time. When I went back into my great-grandmother's house and told everybody to stop looking for her, because she was over at Philly and Millie's, Aunt Teresa, serving my great-grandmother two frosted Pop-Tarts, lost her patience.

"What could she possibly *see* in those women? What do you kids see in those tough women? I don't understand. Why can't you stay in your own yard? Why do I have to watch you every minute?"

My great-grandmother swallowed a bite of her Pop-Tart. "What are you afraid of, Teresa? That they'll change her? Or are you afraid that *you* yourself won't have any influence over her?"

"Influence? Like they have influence? What do you mean? I wouldn't change her like that. I'm a *widow*."

"I'm not accusing you of that," my great-grandmother said. "You said that, not me."

Now, I don't want to give the wrong impression of Aunt Teresa here. Even though she didn't like us to get any ideas from the pages of books like *Our Bodies, Ourselves* (if she only knew what lay nested between the pages of Anne's Young Lady's Li Brary), she was not a controlling person. The pope has always told me to feel guilty for Original Sin. The censors want me to feel filthy for looking at dirty pictures. When I got older, psychiatrists wanted me to feel strange about the way I acted, often out of that genius of desire. And even others, in the spirit of some kind of new age far worse than the old one, wanted me to feel only the joy of a child. Unlike these, Aunt Teresa, to her great credit, never told me how to feel. She just knew that there was no way to curb certain feelings. Feelings were the mystery that terrified her, like a god. She was as terrified as the pope and the psychiatrists and the censors and the people promising me a new age, but rather than force me into line with her, she preferred that I never open up Pandora's box.

"Why are you yelling at me?" asked Aunt Teresa. "I just want to make sure she doesn't get *hurt*. Is it so terrible to care?"

Nobody would back her up in this argument with my grandmother. We had all revolted, like Marsha's objects. We were all objects in Aunt Teresa's world and needed to be kept in line, an impossible task as impossible as controlling the abundance of fruit and corn and cider that flowed in, the monstrous cornucopia of Monsalvat, the genius and agony of desire and the hopelessness of consuming it. Marsha was right: everything was alive and kicking back.

When Marsha came back to the house in the late morning, full of praise about Philly and Millie, she brought back *Our Bodies* for Anne (who thanked her and was nice to her for the rest of the weekend and talked about perverted boys with her). She told my great-grandmother that Millie had secretly, for years, wished she could replant some of the flowers gone wild in her old bed, and my great-grandmother said by all means, tell her she can have as many as she wanted, as long as she didn't dig up Chester in his burlap-lined grave.

We left the next morning, laden with jelly and fruit and canned tomatoes and corn.

I was tired and let Marsha drive. I climbed in the back-seat and hunkered boomerang-shaped there with the bags of cider and donuts and sweet corn we picked up on the way home.

"They were very nice," Marsha said.

"Oh, don't lie," I said. "You don't like Aunt Teresa. You spent the whole weekend with those lesbians just to avoid Aunt Teresa."

"Millie and Philly are lesbians?" Marsha said. "Hmm. I just thought they were Polish or something."

I dozed off after a while, and I did not know that Marsha got into a minor accident with a tailgater until the broken jug of cider, cracked on impact, seeped under my collar and made my hair stick to the vinyl seat. I never heard Marsha blame the driver; she just assumed the car had a life of its own.

CHAPTER 8

In a World of Men

If the boys weren't killing themselves for their girlfriends, they were driving under the influence and crashing their souped-up cars into trees, eating too much greasy food and dying of choked-up arteries, suffocating themselves on cigarettes, or running into the woods to hunt, only to be shot by trigger-happy fellow huntsmen who saw only enough of those camouflage coats to think it was foliage itself, the decoy tragically convincing. This was the slow death of peacetime, the reason men secretly hope for a war so as not to fade ignobly. Men are as emotional, as passionate as women, but they bury it in strange places, or they boil it down to mere lust, craving, like too-sweet candy, and in order to avoid the dulling of the senses, they run themselves into trees—the last great passionate sensation.

Not long after my Labor Day visit with Marsha, I returned for the opening of deer-hunting season and met Kelly, Anne's boyfriend. I liked his name's ambiguous gender. I can't help thinking that having a name that could be a girl's name affected him, maybe sissified him a little. He reminded me so much of Tommy. He was a champion cross-country runner for Lumen Christi, Anne's high school, but he was kicked off the team for mysterious reasons. He told Anne only, and Anne told me after I swore never to tell.

He had shaved himself. Not his face, but his whole body. Although the act seemed weird—did he think it would make him more aerodynamically sound? (Around that time, Mark Spitz won gold medals at the Olympics swimming with a mustache, while Don Schollander shaved himself and was beaten.) But if that were so, the fact that they kicked him off the team seemed weirder.

I could just imagine it. The scene in the locker room after a real meet, Kelly stripping down and heading for the showers, the odd looks, the sheeny ceramic cup of his underarms, the bewilderment. And then the indignation. Did he think the lightness of his hair, so close to the color of his skin, would make it less noticeable? Was it that noticeable? I asked Anne.

"How would *I* know?" she protested. "Do you think I'm some kind of slut or what? *God.*"

Other than that, Kelly was a normal, friendly guy. When I first met him, he was always grinning, not a fake grin but a real one, a bashful one like somebody just caught him singing to himself. "Michael Bellman?" he said. "Bellman is a better last name than Kaiser. You were lucky. Kaiser sounds like a dictator," he said to me.

Anne butted in. "Bellman sounds like the hunchback of Notre Dame."

When the TV was on, Kelly was the kind of guy who liked to point out outrageously stupid lines of dialogue to me and make noises in the back of his throat like he was scandalized. He liked me, which always surprised me. And he loved to hunt. He asked me if I wanted to come up to Monsalvat two weeks later, to go deer hunting.

"Watch him," Anne warned me. "Kelly is a total pervert."

He grinned at me and stuck his long torso out, so it looked like a rickety baby's belly.

．　　．　　．

I will admit it. Once I folded up that picture from the drug-store and put it into my warm pocket, once I knew the thing existed, I had an immediate sense of connection with others, however invisible, who were like me, who craved centerfold shots like I craved them. Then I craved for community, I craved those others. And with that connection and self-knowledge, I began to lose something else that was very precious: my sense of the perfect unity of all objects.

Not that it went away just like that. There are several moments I can remember in which I made lightning-bright connections like the one I made in the drugstore. I remember the day I thought, "I am thinking that I am thinking," and it was like swimming just below the surface of a deep blue pool, looking at a submerged version of myself. And even before that, I remember writing the word "God" with a lower-case "g" and waiting for the bolt of lightning to zip through the window and split me in two, burn me to ashes, and leave my clothes fresh and clean. That is when I started getting tired of church. When I wasn't split in two.

This age, when I knew I was thinking that I was thinking, it was an age of exaggeration. If Uncle Tom and I had speared the carp when I was umpteen, I would have said that the carp was six feet tall. That the hole we dug for Chester was ten feet deep. That I broke Anne's arm in the fight. That Tommy spoke softly to me in the dark.

Measurements must be made.

I exaggerated in order to be noticed, to be believed. It is a kind of sincere lie. It is also a way of trying to feel things as strongly as I did when I was younger. Awareness of the self dulls the senses. It makes the world a world of parts.

For example, I hated my chin. I had a copy of the *Boy*

Scout Handbook which showed boys in their various stages of development. Hair growth, shoulder breadth, penis length were charted on three boys, one aged 9–12, the second 12–15, the third 16–19. If I backed up far enough away from the mirror, naked, feet buried in shag carpeting, and held the book out at arm's length, I could make myself exactly the same size as the third boy, and I would compare my hair and my shoulders with that drawing.

It was this passion to be normal that led me into so many activities that I would not do for myself. Kissing girls. Spearing carp. Hunting deer. It was part of my double life, to know all of those activities while seeking out my real desires in private.

Deer hunting in the Kaiser family was a complicated tradition. It involved the women sitting in my great-grandmother's living room on Sunday screaming bloody murder (*there*, there is some of that exaggeration) that no husband of theirs would be out in those woods with a hundred other drunken maniacs shooting at anything that will move.

Uncle Tom would turn to Aunt Charlene and laugh.

"You may think I'm joking, Mr. Man, but I'm dead serious," Aunt Charlene said, and took her cat-eye glasses off for effect. "So join a bowling league if you want to be a sportsman. Go watch some football."

Aunt Charlene's own husband was no longer interested in hunting, because he once went out and got frostbite on his toes. He never saw a deer. Whenever these arguments came up, he would leave the room or pretend to watch the television, even commercials, very intently. Aunt Charlotta's husband was mostly sick and arthritic by that time. That left Uncle Jimmy and Uncle Tom to battle it out. Aunt Mary was bad at browbeating Uncle Tom, and sided with him. And Uncle Jimmy would simply look at the ceiling to ask his dead wife permission. She always said yes.

The Kaiserbroads never said anything against Kelly going hunting, since he was not in the family. Aunt Charlene would say in a stern and jokey way to Kelly, "I think you're crazy. I think you've got a *screw loose*." And Kelly would disarm her with his grin.

And after that, not only did the men go out hunting, sometimes they talked my aunts into registering their own names for a hunting license so that each of the men could shoot two deer instead of the prescribed Michigan state limit of one per customer.

A deer had to be tagged by the registered hunter who shot it so that it could be cleaned and sometimes mounted.

"Think of it this way, Teresa," Uncle Jimmy said, "you won't have to buy meat all winter long if we get more than one deer apiece."

"What if everybody did what you're doing," Aunt Teresa said. "Then there wouldn't be any deer left."

Uncle Tom said, "Teresa, remember last winter when you nearly hit that deer on the way home from the grocery store? Remember how shaken up you were? Remember how it was dark, and you could have gotten yourself killed as well as the deer? Well, that deer ran out into the road because there's *not enough room* in the woods. There are so many deer out in those woods this winter that there won't be enough food to go around and half of them will starve to death anyway. Sometimes you've got to take the law into your own hands."

That convinced her.

I remember standing in line with Aunt Teresa at the bait store where people applied for hunting licenses. She was applying so that Uncle Tom could kill two deer. She was wearing jeans and sunglasses so that she looked sporty. That is the thing I remember most about her applying for a license. Except that the man at the counter said, "So you like to hunt?"

"Yes, it's very relaxing." She smiled.

The guy didn't ask her any more questions. He knew what she was up to. I think she believed she had fooled him, but I knew she would go to Confession right after the bait store to confess the grievous sin of lying.

I got myself a hunting license with equal ease. Whereas my uncles had to participate in the long-drawn-out war to earn the right to hunt, and whereas my cousins nearly my age were never allowed to get licenses until they were eighteen, I think there was a certain amount of relief when I expressed interest in hunting with a rifle.

"I'd like to go myself, maybe," I offered, after Aunt Teresa was talked into registering and they were moving on to me, begging me to give them my deer tags.

"You would?" Uncle Tom said, like he was saying, "Well how about that?"

"You would?" Aunt Teresa said, like she thought I was telling a lie.

"Don't give the kid a hard time," Uncle Jimmy said. "The kid wants to hunt. If he wants to hunt, let him hunt. There's always an extra gun lying around."

We got the license and then I showed Uncle Tom the clear plastic pocket to be pinned onto the back of my coat, which would hold the fluorescent orange number.

"You can use Tommy's stuff. He's already got all that. You can use his coat and camouflage, too, it ought to fit you by now." It was hard to believe that it had been more than three years since Tommy was last heard from. To everybody else, he had stopped growing, his clothes now fit me. It was like he was dead. It seemed so much like he was dead that Uncle Tom could say his name out loud, without stressing or whispering it.

"Aren't you going to buy *me* a plastic pocket?" Aunt Teresa flirted.

"Buy your own," Uncle Tom said.

She did. I went down the aisles full of tackle, hunting supplies, and live bait. I have always liked bait stores, even if I don't like to hunt and fish. Crickets chirping like cages full of night. Treacherous six-hooked artificial lures. Bins of minnows separated by size. Bobbers. Buckshot. Arrows. Sinkers. I like hardware stores for the same reason. All these parts, parts greater than the whole. Since I cannot attain the whole of things anymore, my adult life has been comforted by these parts. If these objects would not speak to me individually, there was at least the noise of so many of them, lined up, organized, in chorus on the shelves, the noise of parts, a noise not so much different from the crickets bripping blackly on those shelves.

Aunt Teresa leaned over a huge tar-bottomed tank full of frogs. There was some netting and sometimes a frog would try to leap out, but it banged its little head on the net. I stood next to Aunt Teresa and looked in with her. "Bait," I told her.

"I know," she said. "It sounds silly, but it doesn't bother me when you boys go out fishing with minnows for bait, but little frogs . . . just look at their eyes, and those little delicate hands."

I peered closer and suddenly all the frogs looked terribly desperate to me. They were gulping with fear instead of just gulping to breathe. It was those hands, like Monstro's eye, the familiar thing that I connected with, webbed, green, but still, they were fingers. I thought I might tear off the net and help them escape. But that seemed so pointless that I thought I might cry instead. I felt a lump in my throat. I was a frog, too.

But then I looked over at Aunt Teresa, and she was crying her eyes out. She was even sobbing, and she didn't care who saw her.

So I burst out laughing. I laughed and laughed, like I'd dived into a deep pool and swam and swam toward the surface and then took in all the air I could as I came up. She glared at me through her teary eyes and frowned. This was the beginning of a time when I would never cry again. Embarrassing tears, tears that looked as bad as my chin in that mirror, were not nearly as easy as boisterous laughter or shouts of anger. The adult of me was bigger than the child; it was *easier* to be the adult.

While we were still in the bait store Uncle Tom said to Aunt Teresa, "Give me your tag." She nearly lost her mind.

"Tommmmm," she hissed, "people will hear you. I can't believe you. I can't believe you. Do you think people are deaf?" He pulled the tag out of her hand and we all heard the guy behind the counter laugh.

■   ■   ■

Uncle Tom, Uncle Jimmy, Kelly, and I took a boat up the Higgins Riverway from Clear Lake to Uncle Jimmy's favorite hunting site.

I had no idea it was going to be that cold. It wasn't any colder than it had been on previous days, but I would touch the sides of our boat and feel the cold metal, and the wind whipped through all the layers of coats and sweatshirts and sweaters. I started craving small breaks of sunlight that poked through now and then. I spent a lot of time looking at the sky, waiting to get warm, hoping it wouldn't rain. And I had to go to the bathroom. To this day, I have a tremendously large bladder, having exercised it so much during those hunting and fishing trips.

Uncle Jimmy and Uncle Tom were drinking a lot of beer, and I was hoping Uncle Jimmy would drive safely. I knew all about boating and hunting accidents. He yelled at me, "How you doing, Dutchman?" and I would nod and smile so that he would leave me alone. Uncle Jimmy had given me a baseball cap with his company name sewn on it. It kept my hair stuck down and would have protected my eyes from sun, if there had been sun. Sometimes the wind almost blew it off.

Kelly mostly looked ahead, into the wind, and grinned. He was being shy, except that he had no trouble calling Uncle Jimmy the Fattest Man in the World when he wanted his attention.

"What're you so quiet about, Laughing Boy?" Uncle Jimmy pushed Kelly at the shoulder, which gave easily to the thrust.

"I'm not quiet, I'm praying," Kelly said.

"You'd *better* say your prayers," Uncle Jimmy said. "You're going to spend the next three days hunting with *Kaisers*."

"I'm praying to Saint Eustace. He's the patron saint of hunters. He was a heathen until he went out hunting one day and saw a vision of the crucifix between the antlers of a deer. Then he converted. Then he was tortured and roasted alive."

"That's pretty sick," said Uncle Jimmy.

Uncle Tom didn't talk much. He never talked that much. Uncle Jimmy landed the boat where a slough formed, a small waterway that fed into the lake. This was Uncle Jimmy's favorite place to hunt. Deer came here to drink. It was easy work to bag the game. Uncle Jimmy said he didn't like sweating when he hunted. His energy was for himself and his own needs, he said, not the deer's.

Before unloading any gear, Uncle Jimmy pulled out another beer.

"Wait a minute, Jim," Uncle Tom said. "We've got things to do."

Uncle Jimmy scowled.

I couldn't believe how wet everything was. If I sat down to rest too long, either on a log or on the ground, water seeped through my layers of clothes and I felt suddenly cold.

It would be hard to keep warm and clean for three days. Three days! No tent of my own, but I was sharing it with Kelly. The clouds were lower, and grayer. It was magnificently dismal and bleak, almost joyfully so.

"When will we get to hunt?" I asked.

"No big hurry," Uncle Jimmy said. "We've got to get set up, and drink."

"I'm set up. Can I go out?" Kelly said. He had already pitched the tent we were both going to stay in. I was more interested in setting out my sleeping bag and hanging out getting warm than tromping around in the swamps.

"If you want," Uncle Tom said. I marveled at how little my family was concerned with Kelly's health and welfare. Kelly must have figured on this, though, on the misunderstanding of his own parents—that he was going out hunting with two responsible adults, one a policeman who handled guns on a daily basis—and the misunderstanding of my uncles and aunts, who felt no right to force Kelly to do anything. Kelly slipped through the cracks, and before I could ask him if I could follow along, he was off into the woods, alone.

Uncle Tom and Uncle Jimmy sat on logs arguing about the beer. Both of them thought the other was in charge of getting it. Now, after two six-packs, their supply was almost gone.

"This is going to be a great hunt," Uncle Jimmy said.

"That's great," Uncle Tom said. "And it's going to rain soon."

I wanted to go off, to see them now, the herds of deer and wolves and bigger animals. I also wanted to catch up with Kelly. I had my gun slung over my shoulder, and Uncle Jimmy showed me how to load the clip and shoot it. I won't lie, I liked the way it kicked back in my grip when it went off. It had a power of its own, one of the last objects that still spoke to me as they used to. I didn't plan on shooting anything. I just wanted to catch animals in the real world off guard. I wanted to hide behind a rock and know everything.

Uncle Tom waved me away without looking at me. "Don't get lost. We might leave you behind if we decide to move upriver more, right, Jim?"

Uncle Jim nodded. I started over the rise between the shore and the birch and spruce forest. I felt the boots like lead weights. My ankles weren't very strong, but I liked the feeling of taking my boots off after walking around in them for a long time like this. My legs would feel light as feathers after my walk. My coat texture shrieked against itself in rhythm as I moved my arms back and forth, quick pendulums.

I ran through the dead woods, and leaped over shallow puddles and streams that were almost hidden and flush with the ground. They nearly tripped me before I saw them. Each spring the lake flooded this lowland, and it took all summer to dry out before the snow filled it again. The thought of that cycle depressed me. Violent changes in weather are not actually radical, they're inevitable. Spring floods and winter storms were mannered and predictable. I wanted real surprises.

I leaped on spongy mounds that were once tree stumps, trying to avoid falling knee-deep in swamp water. Pale green beads of duckweed grew over the ponds, and moss and ferns grew along the sides of soft rotting logs and even healthy trees. Nothing was sure, except the gun that was making a bruise against my side.

There were spiderwebs, secret in the trees, and although the mosquitoes were gone for the winter, there were small black insects that fell from bare branches into my coat and on my cap; the webs tickled my face and I imagined small, poisonous, colorless spiders running down my neck and nesting in my armpits and groin, biting and burrowing. I slapped at my face crazily when I felt the slightest tickling sensation. Crows were flying, sorry excuses for birds.

Where were the deer? Where was Kelly? I started to sweat from moving. I was a little lost. I stepped up to a mound where a strong V-shaped birch tree bent in two directions over the swamp. I wedged myself between the trunks and rested, hugging the tree and picking at the peeling papery white bark. I pulled away layer after layer, but didn't seem to go deeper into the wood. It seemed I could peel away forever.

I was uninspired, no matter how hard I tried to be. The only thing I could think of was all the water, the rotting wood and the flooded ground, the mold and the spiders. And crows. The crows were driving me crazy with the wish to be symbolic, but I wouldn't place them. I got off my perch and kept walking, getting used to the weight of my boots.

I didn't see the thing until it was too late, until I was right up on it and couldn't avoid it.

Half in and half out of the swamp water, a buck, dead for some time, maybe as long as a year, lay on its side. The bulk of its body had pushed away tall reeds and bushes, clearing a space around it like walls. It had struggled, because it had mowed down everything in front of itself as well. The rack of the buck curved up in two plates, and I stared at them for a long time. Its insides were nearly as liquid as the swamp.

"Saint Eustace," I said aloud. Saint Eustace the unbeliever, a heathen hunter who came across a great stag, standing in a golden clearing, and between its antlers, he had a vision of Christ on the cross, a conversion. I thought of praying to this dead deer. If I spoke to it, perhaps it would not speak to me, to my desire, but turn my desires to a kind of reason that would go to Saint Eustace, or at least to the objects that no longer spoke to me.

Catholics often rely on the intercession of saints and are often laughed at for not having a direct line to God, but God is so often the sum of His parts, I've found, and only once in a great while does He become whole. I suppose that's what somebody calls miracles. Here in the woods, with the dead stag before me, the whole was greater than the sum of its parts.

I don't know how many reasons there were for why it affected me like that. It was a dead animal, no big deal.

But I couldn't help but be glad and generous at that moment, and for that moment I felt no personal desire. There was so much filling my eyes and mouth and ears and nose, gifts of the sensual world, all gratuitous, all spendthrift. I thought, maybe I need God to exist not so that I would be split in two for spelling a word with a lower-case "g," or for making sense of this chaotic world, but to have somebody to thank for a moment like this, this inspiration, to thank for these *parts* when they assembled themselves momentarily into a whole, decaying deer—to thank for this gift.

The eyes of this deer had been eaten out, and it was decaying in the acid water and earth. It had stopped stinking long ago. Bones of the skull shone through, near the mouth. It was rotting into pieces, into details. I wondered if it didn't actually drown—but then I saw the arrow in its flank.

That was what spooked me, like the humanlike eye in Monstro the whale, or the webbed hands of frogs—that arrow, man-made, that order in the wild.

And then I heard the gunshot, just at that moment, and the yell that was not joyous or agonizing, only strange. It was surely from Uncle Tom. The deer before me became confused with some deer my uncle may have shot somewhere within earshot. I wanted to see the new deer.

In order to avoid leaping on the rotting mass, I had to change course and my mind blurred with decisions. The gun over my shoulder made me lose my balance. I leaped into open water, and stood, stunned, up to my thighs in swamp water, sinking in the muck. That was how the deer had died, I thought in a moment of panic, but I pulled one leg free by grasping a branch. My leg made an obscene sucking noise in the mud and I found myself black from the knees down. I felt the water burn through, cold on my groin. I yelled at the same time I realized I had to find my own way back to camp. I ran, the orange hunting license pinned to my back flapping like a useless broken wing.

As I ran, even more clumsily, feeling my fingers ache with cold, I thought about Saint Eustace. He suffered for his conversion. I decided that maybe it was not the Catholicity that was important to me, but the suffering. In times of real suffering, there was no time for thinking about anxiety, no time to think about the way time worked, of the whole flying into pieces as it seemed to have been lately. There was only animal pain. I ran through the woods, thinking, I am really suffering now, this must certainly be purifying, a kind of prayer, a place between passion and reason. I tapped it out on my mental typewriter: I am suffering.

■　　■　　■

I was running toward camp, and Uncle Jimmy was yelling to me. "You won't believe it, it's the biggest one I've ever seen. I saw him first but your uncle Tom took one shot and got him. I did see him first, though. Got to be sixteen points on him. He's back in the woods pulling him out—go give him a hand pulling him out."

When I came closer, covered with mud, Uncle Jimmy said, "Hey, Dutchman, what happened?"

I made little sentences for him between exhales of breath. "It's real cold. It's not going to dry. We've got to go back.

Back home. I could die out here. Of exposure. I admit it. This isn't for. This isn't for me. I'll be no fun. If I stay out here. With you guys." I doubled over, my hands on my knees, my lungs burning, my throat tasting raw and bloody. The mixture of sweat and swamp water made me shiver. My bowels felt loose.

"Well, don't worry about it, we have to leave now anyway, to get that deer back to civilization. Enough venison to feed us all winter. Go help your uncle. Tugging on that carcass'll keep you good and warm. He's down over the bank, by the swamp. Where's Kelly?"

"I don't know," I said.

Uncle Jimmy put his rifle into the air and shot it off, and yelled, "Kelly! Kelly!—Kelly!—Kelly!" He sounded deranged. I lugged my sodden legs down over the hills to find Uncle Tom. The sooner the deer was hauled back, the sooner I could get warm.

■   ■   ■

I saw the deer first. A huge rack with points in the shape of scooping hands. The eyes wide open. It could still be alive, I thought. I stopped a few yards away from it, and looked at its unheaving body. Then I stared at the face, which I thought would give itself away if it were actually playing dead.

Then I noticed something else lying near the deer—it was the fluorescent orange hunting license lying in leaves. I thought at first it had fallen off my own jacket. The leaves were not leaves; they were the camouflage pattern of a coat, and of pants, too.

Uncle Tom's face was on its side, in profile, and his hands looked as if they were blanketed and pillowed by leaves. They looked like they had been plucked bloodlessly from his body, like parts, and cast among the leaves. I thought of the other strange natural sights I'd seen, the praying mantis in my grandmother's flowers; a bumblebee which I swore was blue but had turned out to have been seen by the light shining through blue glass upon it; that rotting deer; and here, Uncle Tom's face and hands.

But the face was quivering, and his body became whole again when I noticed the shaking.

I went up to shake him, to say something wise guy like, "No lying down on the job," or something. I put my hand on his shoulder, freezing cold and mucky, and his shoulder bucked wildly in my hand.

"Oh, no," I yelped, and then I cooed, "What's wrong? What's wrong? What's wrong?" to him, trying to calm him as he shivered. "Uncle Jimmy, please, help?" I said in a normal tone of voice.

He wouldn't stop shivering. I thought of taking off my coat, but I was freezing to death myself. My nose had been running for so long that the stringency of it had made my upper lip sting in the raw cold. That was the pain I thought of the most, then. That was the sort of pain it looked like Uncle Tom was suffering, wincing in the wet leaves next to this huge dead deer. I would not give him my coat, though.

Given the choice offered to me years ago by Aunt Teresa on Anne's Confirmation day, no, I would not die on a cross if it meant I could take away the sins of the world. Aunt Teresa would like my new answer.

Uncle Jimmy ran up. He seemed to know what happened right away, which is why I think I suspected him, why I thought he was responsible, for several hours. Anybody who knows something right away is never innocent. He said, "He's had a heart attack. He strained himself trying to move that damn animal."

"A heart attack? What can we do?"

"Get him back home as quick as possible. Help me carry him to the boat. Then I'll take him up the lake."

"What about Kelly?" I asked. "Where's Kelly?" I was obeying, grabbing my part of Uncle Tom to haul him.

"Can't find him."

"Kelly! Kelly!" I screamed, then said to Uncle Jimmy, "We can't just leave him."

"So you stay here and wait for him while I take Tom back. I'll come back for both of you as soon as I can."

"I'll freeze to death! I'm all wet!"

"Climb in a sleeping bag. There's a change of clothes."

He motioned me to move faster with my part of the load.

"How can you be so calm?" I wanted to yell at him. "How come you can think of what to do like that? You must not care very much. You must not care, if you can be so calm!" We kept hauling him like a dead animal toward the boat, Uncle Jimmy carrying the most weight himself by the shoulders, while I held on to the muddy boots. Things kept falling out of Uncle Tom's pockets and I wanted to stop and pick them up, knowing they'd be hard to find later in these leaves. I said, "How can you be calm?"

Uncle Jimmy didn't answer me. We loaded Uncle Tom in the boat. Uncle Jimmy covered him with his own coat.

Uncle Tom stopped shaking for just a minute, and looked right at me, like pain went away that fast. He eked out, "It's a big deer, sixteen points, isn't it?" and by the time he finished his question, his face knotted up again, collapsed like a rotten apple, and he wasn't able to hear me agree with him.

Uncle Jimmy pushed the boat out onto the water. He'd revved up the motor and pumped the little rubber ball on the gas tank and was already moving out when he finally said, "I'll be back as soon as I can. See if you can round up Kelly." And he was gone, the boat sped down Higgins Riverway smoothly, and I thought how graceful the Fattest Man in the World seemed to me, for the first time, ever.

I thought of those bad Japanese movies where a helpless maiden in a white gauzy dress stood abandoned on the shore of an island populated by giant prehistoric reptiles. I felt like her.

■   ■   ■

Kelly did not come back by dusk, nor did Uncle Jimmy. I had stripped out of my wet clothes, warmed up in a down-filled sleeping bag, pulled some dry clothes into the bag with me to warm them up. Then I went out and yelled for Kelly some more. Then I went to look at the new dead deer. Then I went about looking for the things that fell out of Uncle Tom's pockets. The only thing I found was his lighter, which was shaped like a small pewter tombstone, encrusted with odd-shaped pieces of turquoise. I opened the lid and closed it; I liked the way it scraped shut so snugly, barely closing itself on a little hidden spring. It smelled like half-burned, half-fresh butane.

I gathered up dry wood and made a fire with the lighter, a big one, and put a ground cloth down next to it, with my sleeping bag, and fed the fire anything around that burned, and waited for somebody to come back, or for the rain to drench me.

Mostly I thought about old things, not about the situation at hand. I couldn't believe I was feeling a loss of childhood so soon in my life, as if the best things were over.

Objects were only objects and I wanted more sensual experience, my body wanted to call up those sensations remembered best by childhood. Then I was happy with the feel of wood or the scaly surface of a frozen carp or the taste of gum on the back of address labels. Now I desired more plainly—I desired Kelly, for one thing. It was a desperate lashing, a base and banal need of the body.

It grew dark, and still Kelly didn't come. I ate cold food out of cans for something to do.

In one way, I couldn't wait to be old, not at the beck and call of my body's needs. I hated the way I was becoming a slave to it. After all, I already knew what it would feel like to be with Kelly or any man, it would not be a surprise, really. I would know what it felt like, not only because of the hormones, but because my body shivered in that cold, felt pain. I thought how a heart attack would take my mind with it if I died. I think the notion of an "old soul" comes from what is actually the quality of early sentience—Aunt Charlene and Aunt Charlotta thought I was the sensitive introspective child, and I immediately moved into a nostalgic mode once I knew I was thinking that I was thinking. So I always seemed an old soul. It is simply something else.

I fell asleep this way, and decided to climb into Kelly's sleeping bag with him when he came back.

■   ■   ■

I woke up and it was very dark, and the fire was only three or four embers, red and variegated like red-hot corn on the cob, undulating in color with the wind. I woke up because somebody was singing softly under his breath.

It was Kelly. It was too dark to see what he was doing, and I wondered if he could see me. I was afraid he might step on me and fall into what was left of the fire, but I liked hearing him sing in a haunted, whispery sort of way. I could almost hear him grinning. "My funny valentine," he crooned.

Then he said, "Is that you, Mike?" and I knew he was grinning.

I was quiet for a minute, half pretending to be asleep, half trying to figure out what time it might be, and whether what I thought had happened had happened. "Yes," I finally said.

"What the heck's going on?"

"Did you get lost?" I asked.

"Nope. Just a diehard hunter. I wait till the last possible minute. Did you guys get anything?"

I was quiet for another moment. Then I stood up with my sleeping bag still around me, and hopped toward my tent. "Uncle Tom got a sixteen pointer."

"Sixteen points? No way. Have you seen it? Is it sixteen points or was he just telling you stories?"

"No, it's sixteen points. I'll show you in the morning. I'm going to sleep." I zipped up my tent. "Good night," I said, through the mildewy canvas.

"Good night," he said.

I wondered whether he would come into the tent. I waited and it seemed like we were both being more quiet than a person is normally, like we were both sneaking around. I got on my coat and boots and came out to him. "What's going on?" he said.

"Well," I said, "Uncle Jimmy just took Uncle Tom back to town. There was something wrong with him."

"Something wrong? Like what?"

"Like he had a heart attack or something."

"Or something?" Kelly said. "How can it be 'or something'? Did he get in the boat himself, did he make the decision to go back, or did the Fattest Man in the World carry him there?"

"Carried," was all I could say.

"Oh, man," Kelly said, and swung his leg over the log he sat on, went into Uncle Jimmy and Uncle Tom's tent, and slept there by himself. I cursed my uncle for having a heart attack and spoiling my chance.

In the morning, Uncle Jimmy woke us both up and told us Uncle Tom had died in the night when he got to the hospital in Monsalvat. We broke camp and left without taking the new dead deer with us. I know I should have been shredded by Uncle Tom's dying, and I was, but more than that, I was wondering whether Tommy might come home for his father's funeral. He would *have* to come home for that.

CHAPTER 9

A Funeral

Uncle Jimmy told me that while Uncle Tom lay in the hospital, not quite dead, Aunt Teresa had rushed up to the emergency room with Uncle Tom's slippers and an economy-size jar of aspirin. These tokens got to me, the very uselessness of those comforts, like a Band-Aid on a severed leg. It's the one time I ever cried during the funeral.

"I don't understand it," Aunt Teresa said. "He wasn't fat. Jim is fat. Jim's the Fattest Man in the World." (It pleased Anne to hear Aunt Teresa use her own moniker for Uncle Jimmy.) "And he wasn't overly uptight, he was a very calm man. Mary's more uptight than Tom. And he's not that old. Mother is his *mother*, for Pete's sake, and Mother is still alive."

I looked around the room to see if Uncle Jimmy, Aunt Mary, or my grandmother was offended. But feckless Aunt Teresa seemed the most offended. She didn't know what to do with herself. She had nothing, really, to take control of. She was as futile as her aspirin.

There was a sort of mystique around Kelly and me when they brought us back from the hunt, because they were already over the initial shock and we were still wearing camouflage. Even my parents had already arrived from down south, even though they left Hugh with the neighbors. Everybody kept quizzing me as to what Uncle Tom's last words were, which I've described before, and perhaps I made those words up to please them, and repeated the lie so many times it became the truth. "It's a big deer, sixteen points, isn't it?" "Isn't that just like him?" they said fondly, as if these were sweet last words, as if his last words were, "Tell Mary that I have always loved her," or "Tell Tommy that it was all a big mistake."

Well, it *was* just like him. I have for a long time accused all of my family of not showing enough feeling. But now I know that it is the contrary, that these quiet people are so full of great feeling that it is too much, that Uncle Tom died of a heart attack because he put a lid on so much in a seething pot, until the pot boiled over and his heart quit on him.

More family began to arrive in Monsalvat. My golden grandfather and grandmother came in, this time wearing a lot of pastel clothes. My grandfather wore a pink shirt and everybody gave him a hard time. It was mostly because of them that there was no room for me at the house. Kelly was the one who suggested I stay at his house.

There is a certain kind of festivity that comes around family deaths, because, other than weddings, it is the only compelling reason to bring the most far-flung relatives to one location. Huge meals were served, long lively discussions— mostly funny reminiscences of Uncle Tom—took place, and all of Aunt Teresa's rules about keeping shoes off in the house and keeping the younger children away from the upstairs were ignored. There was hardly any consideration of whether or not I should stay with Kelly for the weekend, only a consent. Even Anne slipped away from the house: she planned on staying with him, too.

■ ■ ■

Anne and I went with Kelly in Kelly's father's car the night after we came back from the hunting trip. Anne sat next to

Kelly in the front seat and he kept putting his hand on her knee. I sat in the backseat and leaned forward, between them.

Kelly was wild. His father owned the pharmacy where Anne had stolen the condoms and I had swiped the centerfold, and Kelly showed me that he had the keys to the place, jingling them in my face.

Kelly's parents were well-off. They had a house right on Round Lake designed by a private architect. His father worked at the drug store, and his mother made cocktails. They were funny to be around, and happy to let me stay over. They were Catholic but only had two kids, Kelly, and his older sister, who had graduated from high school and was living at home while she went to the junior college.

Kelly's mom waved her hand like she was saying, "Oh get outta here" every sentence she said to me. "You should see us"—she waved—"we go to church. We sit in the pews, next to these families. All of those families, they got enough people in them so that they could be a baseball team. We got enough for maybe bowling. They're all jealous."

Kelly's sister said, "Oh, be quiet, Mom, we'd be just as big as them if you hadn't had your tubes tied."

Kelly told us right in front of all of them that his sister was into the painful truth. Anne said that she could see why.

Kelly's mother asked us what we wanted to do. She opened a closet just off the kitchen, revealing a huge pile of board games. "We've got *Parcheesi*, we've got *Trouble*, we've got *Chutes and Ladders*, we've got *Clue*, what else? We've got *Twister*! Have you kids ever played *Twister*? I love that game. Let's play." She was trying to jiggle the *Twister* box from under the others, precariously stacked, without letting go of her martini glass.

Kelly's sister said, "Come on, Mom, you're being very embarrassing." Some of her mother's highball—that's what she called it—sloshed over the edge. Kelly's sister said, "Honestly, Mom, you drink too much. Maybe you're an alcoholic, have you ever thought of that? Maybe you should go to an AA meeting or something."

Kelly's mom stopped wrestling with the *Twister* game. "Alcoholic?" she yelled, running up the privately designed grand stairway. "Would an alcoholic do this?" and she hung upside down, in a dress, her knees wrapped like pipe cleaners around the banister.

Anne laughed the loudest, which made me stop laughing, and look at her and say, "You shouldn't laugh so much, your dad is dead."

But the house was a place of delirious intoxication. I liked the big banister, the nice things. We all sat around in the room that wasn't the dining room but where Kelly's family usually ate, and there was a gaudy cockatoo in a cage there. It sat next to the phone and squawked, "Flatiron Drugstore! Brawwk! Flatiron Drugstore!" when the phone rang. It also imitated the sloshed, cackly laugh of Kelly's mother.

Kelly's dad said, "Kelly, why don't you kids go stay in the carriage house out back? There's more room and you'll be out of your mother's hair." He meant we'd be out of his hair, but we didn't hold this against him.

We shuffled out pretty quickly. Kelly grabbed the cockatoo's cage and brought it with us. It laughed uproariously all the way down the lawn to the lake's edge.

The carriage house was actually a guest cottage right near the lake, where you could not see the house because of several groves of trees. There was a fireplace in one corner and two small bedrooms with single beds. It smelled like people used it often to change into and out of their bathing suits: vaguely mucky, seaweedy, and damp, even late in October.

The first thing Kelly did was pass two tablets to each of us. "What's this?" I said, trying not to sound too alarmed.

"Just codeine, won't do anything but make you relaxed," Kelly said.

"You know, codeine," Anne said, swallowing hers without the help of water or anything. "The stuff the doctor gives you when your teeth get pulled."

I swallowed mine, too, mostly because I didn't want Anne to make fun of me. I could have used some water.

Kelly turned on two rickety space heaters at opposite corners of the room, and the coils began to glow red, throwing off more lurid light. Soon, though, it was comfortably warm in the cabin.

In the farthest corner of the cottage, there was a pine-wood bar, unfortunately empty except for an old bottle of lime-flavored vodka. Kelly drank most of the vodka really fast, and then it was gone. Anne said, "We keep trying to buy booze at the tackle shop up the road, but the owner just laughs at us."

Kelly stopped smiling for a minute, and said very seriously, "I hate getting laughed at."

The inside of the bar cabinets were lined with Christmas lights, those big bulbous outdoor ones, and when Kelly turned them on, I was hypnotized. I thought I saw little animals scuttle in the corners, under the colors of the lights and shadow.

Kelly staggered back to where the cockatoo was. He opened up the cage door and it carefully sidled out and scaled its way to the top of the cage. It screeched, "Brawwk, Flat-iron Drugstore," as soon as Kelly hit a sofa, instantly curling himself into Anne's arms. Anne suddenly seemed older. She petted him, ruffling his hair, for a long time. He pointed to the place he had just been like it was a faraway place. "They don't work."

He meant the Christmas lights. "Sure they do," I said. "They work beautifully."

"Aw, no. No. It's like when we went into that liquor store and told them that we were eighteen. It didn't do us any good, because it only made us sound younger. Those lights won't do us any good. It only makes it seem darker."

"Then let's turn them off," Anne said. She was sticking out her finger and letting the bird nibble at it.

Kelly turned them off. We sat quietly in the dark, all of us on the sofa. I was so close that I could feel the air that surrounded Kelly, the air he heated with his body. "Can't see a damn thing," Kelly slurred. I think I was starting to feel the way he sounded. "Turn 'em back on."

He got up himself and turned them on, then came back in the festive, splotchy light. On the walls of the cabin, I saw framed pictures torn from a magazine, pictures of dogs of all breeds sitting around poker tables, playing cards, and smoking cigars. Trying to imitate Kelly's Cheshire-cat grin, I felt my gums go dry, exposed to the open air. I started naming off the kinds of dogs I remembered. "Bulldog. Collie. Great Dane. Schnauzer."

Anne and Kelly were making out right in front of me.

Kelly pulled out a joint, lit it, took a drag, passed it to me. I let him. I had never smoked pot before. Of course I coughed, and didn't feel anything. So I inhaled again and again, and when it started to take effect, it was very dramatic. Like my blood was replaced with some colder or warmer chemical. I could almost see the direction the smoke went through my body, spreading wider and wider, and moving toward two centers, to my stomach and to the base of my neck. At the same moment, the cockatoo took wing in a flurry of feathers the colors of hard candy, and circled the room wildly. When it went away from the Christmas lights, I thought it might as well be a bat, wheeling and wheeling in the dark.

We all three lay on the sofa forever. Then Kelly got up. "Want to see some cool stuff?" He went to a closet whose door matched the pinewood paneling in the wall, like a secret. Inside was a huge steamer trunk, which he dragged out, sloppy on codeine and pot. "Here," Kelly said. "My parents had a Halloween party here this weekend."

I rolled off the couch to inspect. Anne hung back whistling for the bird. The trunk was filled with costumes. Holidays, I thought, nothing but holidays with Kelly. We went through dozens of masks, simple ones and ones with feathers, faces of robots and clowns and princesses. I imagined the room full of grown adults wearing robot costumes and Dracula capes, drinking lime-flavored vodka in this cottage. There was a strange costume that neither of us could figure out what it was supposed to be, even after I put it on. I had to take off my pants to put on the purple tights, and the top part was covered with stuffed shiny fabric versions of cherries, grapes, and pears. The mask was in the shape of a pineapple. The hat was made of stiff giant plastic leaves. "Look at me," I screamed. "I'm sangria!"

"Shh," Kelly said, pointing to the couch. Anne had passed out. "You'll wake her up. She's been up for two days." Then Kelly put on his own mask. "Look at me, I'm a princess."

We were slow from the codeine but giddy from looking at each other in our outfits, and both of us started hopping around in little dances, like our feet were bruised or we'd been bedridden for three days. Kelly grabbed my arms and improvised a waltz.

I laughed through the mask, I could feel the sweat form on my upper lip and collect on the smooth white interior of my pineapple face. I had a small mouth hole, and I liked the way my lips and tongue sometimes rubbed against the edges of the hole. In the close space around my face, I could hear my own taste buds rasp along that opening. Up this close, the eyeholes of my mask only faced the eyeholes in Kelly's mask. I said, through my mask, woozily and wooingly, "Ah, my leetle princess, you are zo light on zee feet."

Kelly swatted me at the grape cluster that covered behind me like a bustle. "Fresh fruit!" he yelped. Then the princess tripped me onto the couch and fell on top of me. Our masks clacked together, and through the small mouth holes, our two lips met.

At first, Kelly kissed at me in the role of the princess. I thought it was funny. He said, "Ah, my leetle princess, your leeps, zay are zo sweet, sweetair zen sangria!"

Then I felt Kelly search with his lips to get through the mouth hole of the mask, the two layers of mask the only thing keeping him from kissing as deeply as he wished. He held me tight, under the shoulders.

Cushioned by giant stuffed grapes and cherries, I thought how comfortable this was, the weight above me warm, the Christmas lights glowing, the glimpse of the bird feathers through the corner of my mask, the pressing of the mask against my own. Even the lips next to mine seemed something besides lips, a different kind of flesh, flesh that performed acts that I could not recognize but easily participated in.

But Kelly's eyes, through the eyeholes, looked straight into mine with the familiarity of being in control. Kelly knew what he was doing, sort of.

I pulled his ear close to my mouth hole and whispered, "Why did you shave yourself?"

"I thought I had crabs." He pulled me up, and I stood, my feet covered in purple tights, on the tops of his two feet. He walked me like this into the bedroom and closed the door.

Kelly never took his mask off. There was a lot of light coming in from the driveway near the house, ghost light or strong moonlight. When he took off his clothes, which he must have done with a lot of grace because I never knew he was doing it, he jumped into my bed, there being two twin beds, and lay on top of me. I felt him smooth all over, and in that strong light I could see his skin a little darker, rose brown, where the band of his underwear usually rode, although he didn't have those indentations people usually get from wearing underwear all day. I thought of the appendix scar Tommy had, how it burned pink when he had been running or when he got mad at Aunt Teresa. There were no markings anywhere on Kelly's body, he was perfect. He reminded me of an android in a science-fiction movie.

"Aren't you glad I shaved?" he asked. "Now I can be anybody you want me to be."

"What do you mean?"

"I can be a princess, if you want. Or any girl you ever thought of. Who's your girlfriend? What does she say to you? How long is her hair? Is she as smooth as I am? I can be her, okay? Or anybody else."

I was tempted. I was tempted to ask him to be Tommy, to talk like him and to act like him, and I could imagine him, but he didn't have the scar, he didn't have the jacket, the snake, none of it. I ran my hand down his belly anyway. When I touched his belly button, half-inny, half-outy, he was covered in a sheath of goose bumps.

"What makes you feel good?" he asked.

"I don't know," I said. I knew, but I didn't like the question.

"Because I can do anything you want. That's what I'm here for. Like God. I'll be all things to all men. You like that? Isn't that what everybody wants? It's the thing I always liked about God. Isn't that what you like about God?"

Like a dog, I thought, eager to please everybody. All things to all men. But that wasn't what I liked about God. I liked him like I liked the cockatoo, bright, wild, kind of noble, unable to be anything but itself with its obvious colorings and plumage. In a dashiki or a sangria costume, I was unable to reinvent my gray self, and I have always been more comfortable with those who could only be themselves, however much bravado that cost. Tommy was a great cockatoo flown from his cage. Kelly was a dog in human outfit, smoking a cigar and playing cards for now, or changing into anything I wanted him to be.

We did things together that night (it was my first real time, but I was not innocent. I had read enough books like Anne's *Nurse and Her Stud*, I knew what I was supposed to do), but it seemed like role-playing, and the masks didn't help. Never could I take my mind off of the fact that this wasn't Tommy, and Anne was sleeping in the next room. That was the beginning of a strong resentment I had against Kelly. Maybe it wasn't fair—maybe I held it against him that my first time at kissing was not with Tommy, but I also resented his eagerness to please. It made me feel invisible. He kissed glass. I decided that I was a victim of his cruel sentimentality. When we were finished, I went over to the other twin bed and fell asleep without taking the sangria costume off.

In the morning, I came out into the pale room. The Christmas lights were still on, and I saw Anne trying to shove the cockatoo back into the cage. It was a hard fit and she swore while she did it. She said she had a terrible headache. But later that day, the day of her father's funeral, she took me in a corner and reminded me of what a crazy fun time we had in the guest cottage.

She was also like the bird, she had force of character she couldn't hide or change like a dog, and maybe that is another reason why I always respected Anne, in a strange way. She could not change either. Even so, I reminded her that she had a terrible hangover and passed out before any of the fun even started.

"What fun?" she asked, narrowing her eyes in that mean way.

"Kelly took advantage of you," I said slyly.

■   ■   ■

In one of his more articulate moments, Uncle Tom had requested to be cremated. He didn't want anybody spending a lot of money on him, and this was cheaper, he said. He had taken care of all of his own funeral arrangements, paid for it in advance so Aunt Mary could fall to pieces when the time came, as he guessed she would. That is the reason why they showed his body, at the funeral home, in a cardboard box.

What I guessed was that Uncle Tom, calculating the cost of embalming and preparation, did not want his body shown at any funeral home. But Aunt Mary and Aunt Teresa did. According to the funeral home, however, a body could not be shown in a coffin unless the coffin was purchased. There were no special "show caskets." None of the Kaiser family was interested in shelling out money for a coffin that would only be used for the showing. The only thing the funeral home had to offer was the packing box that a regular coffin had been shipped in.

What I remember about certain moments in Monsalvat, except for what I have told before, is often rudimentary. Vividly, I can remember parts of rooms and people, while the rest falls away like dead space, cotton wool, a netherworldy fog. To be honest, most of my grandmother's house is not firm in my memory, except for all the old deep-grained mahogany wood of wainscoting, pedestals, banisters, door frames, and wrought, turned fixtures. From the waist up, I cannot see the house; the ceiling disappears into the bleary night. Which may be why things look bigger in memory than they do when they are actually revisited.

So what I remember clearly of Uncle Tom's makeshift casket is the huge brass staples that held the flaps of cardboard together and adorned his head and feet. Looking in, I swore he smirked at me, like the box was his last, best joke. The staples could have been used on any other kind of big box, boxes for refrigerators or washing machines. Boxes I used as houses and spaceships as a kid after they were discarded, and staples I eventually scraped myself on, somewhere.

Aunt Teresa tried to pile up flowers in front of the box, to hide it.

Let me see. Aunt Teresa and Aunt Mary were not upset about the box, while the rest of the siblings were furious, livid, which is why I believe they made that decision of showing Uncle Tom in it. Everybody was livid, that is, except my great-grandmother and Aunt Charlene, who started laughing over Uncle Tom's body and couldn't stop herself. She laughed and tried to hold it in, but snorted through her nose. Aunt Charlotta and her husband stood on either side of Aunt Charlene and glared at her from both directions, and Aunt Charlotta even started hitting her pretty hard in the shoulder, hissing desperately, "For God's sake, don't you know how to behave when your own brother dies? For God's sake, Charlene, please stop. *Please.*"

"I can't help it, I can't control myself," Aunt Charlene lamented. "I'm trying not to think about it, I'm trying to think about how sad it is, but then I look at him there and it's just so ... funny. I can't control myself. It's like picking scabs." She started laughing again and ran past us out of the room, outdoors.

Aunt Teresa said, "Let her go."

Aunt Charlotta said, "I think this is just horrible. They could've at least put a piece of nice fabric underneath him to hide the box. Who's responsible for this? Mary? He looks ridiculous."

"It's not him anymore," Aunt Teresa said. "He's not actually there. Tom is somewhere else now."

"Well, he still reminds me of him, and that's all that matters to me," Aunt Charlotta said, and stomped off.

I went back to get another look. The longer I stared at him, the less he did look like Uncle Tom. While Uncle Tom was alive I wasn't allowed to stare at him for so long, it was impolite. Now I studied the parts of him, nose, lips, ears, hair.

He had a very neat widow's peak I'd never noticed before. They had combed his hair in a different way than he'd ever combed it himself, a better way, I'll admit, but that made him look different, too.

There are certain people in my life that I see best in my memory in the dark, in the immediate illumination of spearing lanterns, or in the lurid paisleys of Christmas lights, or the gentle weak pulse of a praying-hands night-light. Memory, like my memory of the wood in the bigger-than-life Monsalvat house or of the staples in the box, is often strengthened by poor, limited lighting.

My great-grandmother came up beside me, and leaned over the body for the first time.

She stood there, over the cardboard box, and I thought about what it would be like to outlive your own child. It hurt me to imagine it. I figured my great-grandmother would handle it better than I. Instead, she shook her head and bunched her face and said, "Oh no. Oh no. Oh no. Oh no."

I had thought she would have something smart to say, something wise and ironic; I had thought she would be able to pick up even this horrible little moment like a piece of her mismatched china or the cracked praying hands. But now I began to wonder if my great-grandmother *ever* did such a thing, if she was ever ironic and objective. Maybe she was just so subjective and committed that it seemed as if she were sage.

"Oh no, oh no," she said. It was the wisest thing I ever heard her say.

All around us people dressed in black lined up to look at Uncle Tom. They stood like they were buying tickets for something. Everybody tried to ignore the cardboard box, as if it didn't exist.

Philly and Millie came, and Philly even wore a dress, which made her look like a man more than any pair of overalls had. Millie kept calling Uncle Tom "Mr. Fixit." Kelly's mother and father came, and they brought the biggest bouquet of flowers in the room. Kelly's father offered to be a pallbearer, but since the cardboard box had no handles, there wouldn't be any body carried away. My golden grandfather and grandmother did a little cophilosophizing over him, as did several off-duty policemen standing nearby. Anne was respectfully quiet, and herded her younger brothers, sisters, and cousins around, until Kelly eventually came, grinned at me, paid his respects to Aunt Mary, then took Anne away. Uncle Jimmy wore a dark suit that made him look like a monumental maître d', greeting people at the door and showing them to the cardboard casket, probably warning them what to expect. Aunt Mary was always surrounded by six or seven Kaiserbroads, including my own mother. I heard at least three of them ask her whether she wanted something to drink. Aunt Mary looked very bony. She looked like she could use a back rub. Aunt Teresa grabbed people by the shoulders and pulled them partway to herself to give little air kisses. She didn't want all her makeup messed up.

I could never accuse these people of not having enough feeling. Their hearts had to be put into all kinds of cages, into makeup and black suits and cat-eye glasses, into laughter and concern over thirst, bravado police stories, even the nervous twitching Aunt Mary defended herself with. They had huge hearts that required huge cages. They couldn't wear their hearts on their sleeves, the vulnerability would destroy them instantly. So they locked them up, until they burst, beating and beaten.

My grandmother sat alone. Aunt Teresa was talking with out-of-town relatives, ones I was supposed to know very well, cousins who knew exactly who I was and when the last time I blew my nose was, who said, "Hello, Michael, How are you doing, Michael," as if they knew I didn't know what their names were, and were challenging me with my own.

I sat in a chair, flat against a wall draped in wine-colored velvet curtains, and lined myself up with my grandmother's chair. Her purse was black like her dress and it sat in her lap like a pillow. I said, "I don't know half of these people."

"Some are from the police department. Some from the parish. Some are his friends. It looks like a great party, don't it? Like it's his birthday."

I reached deep into my pockets, mostly because I wanted to put my hands somewhere. I felt the lighter in my pocket, and the tip of the reefer, which seemed obscene in this place, as obscene as the cardboard box.

"Why isn't Tommy here?" I asked, matching obscenity for obscenity. "It's his father, shouldn't they let him come, even if it's just for the funeral?" This close, I could see that my grandmother's dress wasn't just plain black, but was embroidered, like a secret, at the buttonholes with shamrock-shaped designs. My eyes have always been snared by patterns, and they cloverleafed infinitely around the button at her collar.

"Well, he would be welcome, if anybody could find him. Nobody can."

"No?" I asked. "Not even you? He never writes to you?"

"No," she said.

"So, Tommy doesn't even know he's dead. He won't know unless he calls."

"No."

"That's not fair," I protested.

"There's nothing you can do about it," she said. "There's nothing you can do about most anything. You always get surprised."

"I hate surprises."

"No you don't," she said. "I know you. You love surprises. For as much as you plan for things—and I've seen you plan—you'd rather be surprised. You'd rather have something unplanned happen."

I dug deeper into my pockets. The lighter I found while

hunting was still between my thumb and forefinger, and I'd traced the outline of the raised turquoise pieces for so long that the tip of my finger was actually sore. I quit tracing it with my finger at the same moment I quit following the pattern of my grandmother's embroidery with my eye. I pulled the lighter out and put it on top of my grandmother's purse. "This was his. You ought to have it. You'll take care of it better than I will."

Without Anne to keep them under control, a lot of the six-year-old boys and girls were getting restless and practiced sliding in their good patent-leather shoes on the funeral home's slippery parquet floor. "Jesus Christ," Aunt Charlene said. "We're going to have more than one funeral if you kids don't knock it off."

■　　■　　■

The funeral mass in the church was like any other mass, with an extra piece of prayer thrown in. Aunt Teresa said that Father O'Hara was a little disturbed by Uncle Tom's choice for cremation, as it wasn't something the church supported, but Uncle Tom had always given his share to the collection basket each week, was a big supporter of the athletic boosters at Most Precious Blood High School, and always volunteered to help work the tables at the bingo games, so nothing was really said out loud. The cremation was ignored like the cardboard box.

I still have the memorial prayer card they handed out, I slipped it into the Bible Aunt Teresa gave me for my Confirmation years ago, a special "red letter" version that zipped up like a diary and had all the words Jesus ever said in bold red letters among the more regular black ecclesiastical phrases. On the front of the prayer card, there was one of those round-faced depictions of Saint Thomas, the famous doubter, holding a T square. He was the patron saint of architects. I thought of the shed Uncle Tom built behind my grandmother's house, ribbed and framed and unfinished forever in my memory, another hand-built cage.

Uncle Tom's final funeral arrangement was a request that his ashes be scattered over Round Lake, his favorite fishing and spearing lake, and, unwittingly, the lake near which he died. On All Saints' Day, Aunt Mary looked uncertainly out the window at the early-November dreary cold. At this time of year, under a sheet-metal sky, trees looked their ugliest, twisted metal wrecks that groaned in dead air.

"What do you suppose we were supposed to do if he died in January," Aunt Mary harrumphed nervously. She patted her hair where her nurse's cap was usually pinned. "Dig a hole in the ice and dump his ashes into it?"

"That," Uncle Jimmy said, "would have been a hell of a lot easier."

He was right. The wind whipped off Round Lake in merciless sheets. Uncle Jimmy told Aunt Mary she was in no condition to sprinkle ashes in an open boat in November. Instead, he recruited me and Anne, and we pulled out the rowboat that had been put up for the winter.

Uncle Jimmy and I took turns rowing the boat. Anne was going to do the scattering. It took us a long time, because the gale-force winds kept blowing us back to shore. I had no gloves, and my knuckles turned a bilious pale green yellow. There were no other boats on the lake except for a lone police boat, which headed right toward us, maybe desperate for company.

Anne said, "Ain't this against the law?" as the police boat came closer.

"What, boating?" Uncle Jimmy said. "Do you need a license to go boating?" The wind made my eyes water. Anne was dragging her hand on top of the water. I told her she was slowing the boat down.

"The water is warmer than the air," she said. In her lap,

she carried the ashes. They were not in a beautiful chalice like I'd imagined they would be, but in a flimsy pink cardboard box—another cardboard box!—the kind they used to cover cakes at a bakery.

The police boat pulled alongside us. I recognized the policeman as one of the guys who had come to Uncle Tom's funeral. He recognized us, too, and saluted Uncle Jimmy and tipped his hat at Anne. She blew him a kiss.

When he'd gone away again, Uncle Jimmy made me stop rowing. He pointed at Anne. "Okay, kiddo, bombs away."

Anne said, "The none-a-yuh have any respect for the dead." She looked at me with her narrow rat eyes.

I should say that I do not mean to be entirely derogatory about Anne's rat eyes. There is something appealing about small eyes on older women, they get wetter and less narrow, and I know that when she grows old, she will look nicer and nicer, which should be a comfort to her. And the same goes for Uncle Jimmy, who was immensely fat, but never complained once about being cold there on the lake. His heart, sunk deep in that much fat, probably felt cozy all through the trip, while I shivered and rowed furiously to keep warm.

"It's just ashes," Uncle Jimmy said. "That's not the dead."

"It's not ashes, it's my father."

He really couldn't say much to that. He suggested, though, that she lead the three of us in prayer. She said she was in no condition for that. Then she opened the box. Immediately, a big wind gusted off the water and lots of ashes got under my down vest and in my lap, and in their laps, too. We were all surprised that we could recognize bone fragments, but not even Anne said "gross" or anything.

Anne said she could see why Kelly's sister was interested in the ugly truth, but when push came to shove, Anne would not draw attention to things that were truly awful. I know she was just as upset as I was by the bone fragments and ashes in our clothes, but she was learning the limits of her own politeness, and in a strange way, that was a comfort to me; in a strange way, I knew she had a fine apprehension of real beauty and real horror, and how we sometimes have to live through both, without discussing it. The Kaisers never discussed beautiful people, or they did only as a passing detail—"you remember that real handsome boy, that Kelly boy?"—or Chester's horrifying illness. For all of Anne's loud-mouth honesty, she was becoming as puritanical as Aunt Teresa, separating her own language from the body and its natural, sometimes disgusting functions.

She nearly fell in, trying to reach low over Round Lake. She ended up dumping the ashes instead of scattering them. No ceremony. We watched a muddy blob of Uncle Tom sink into the dark water. She dropped the carton and Uncle Jimmy had to maneuver the boat so she could grab it out again. We were afraid we'd be fined for littering.

I thought for a moment of a time years ago when I'd lost the frozen carp here, somewhere in the weeds, and had the dream of the fish man, tearing at his own gills and hair.

We let the wind blow us back to shore.

Uncle Tom had been cremated on Halloween. All over the neighborhoods in Monsalvat and back in my own hometown, people had cardboard skeletons plastered to their front porches, grinning merrily at trick-or-treaters. People wonder why other people get big egos, and yet the whole world seems to be paying attention to a person's private world, the world that I thought was invisible.

CHAPTER 10

The Jack of Hearts

I have gotten better at it as I've grown older, getting over somebody, or some unrequited thing. To tell the truth, at first I didn't even know that my prime lusts were of an aberrant kind—I did not know enough to perceive myself in any sort of category. I was too focused upon the object of my affections. The categories come later, with loss, and the speech you learn in order to lament the loss.

Tommy had been out of the picture for years, though he was still everywhere: old photographs, the inscriptions in books, personal belongings left behind. He was in any image, for instance, that was religious in nature. I was especially spooked at the images in Slavic religious icons, with their dark-ringed, sleep-deprived, saintly eyes, and tugable beard tufts. Even their hands were held up with two, three, or four fingers, and I thought of Tommy giving me the peace sign. I thought that if I were a decent enough artist, I would make a painting in the style of one of these icons, in alabaster and gold, holding as his symbols a book of citizenship (a sign of his martyrdom) and a boa constrictor (one of the martyred).

It was especially painful to play solitaire and turn up a jack of hearts (ugh—of *hearts!*) in the Dondorff Centennial deck, holding in one hand a scroll and using the other hand to hold his own heart. That, I couldn't pass up. I swiped him from the deck. For a time, I was taking the jack of hearts out of every card deck and had, in my old cigar box, almost a deck of jacks. Thirty-eight and growing: it became a hobby. It became impossible to find a deck with fifty-two cards in the house—any house—my own or the one in Monsalvat. Is this the sort of displacement of affection that leads to fetishism? The Bicycle jacks were my least favorite, however plentiful—they were too simple and schematic. On the other hand, I had one jack of hearts from a nudie deck that Uncle Jimmy owned, and it was just as rudimentary a drawing as the one in the Bicycle decks, but I got a special secret thrill from the fact that it had a naked lady on the back, a lady I had no interest in. She also stood guard over the secret deck, in case anybody came across the jacks, to explain my desire for the cards. In the cigar box, I always placed her on top.

One day in the spring after Uncle Tom's winter funeral, Aunt Charlene, who cooked at the Saint Mary grade school cafeteria, and started and finished her day by driving a minibus full of far-flung students to school and home, was finishing up her bus route. She had about five kids left and they were forced to drive slowly down a one-lane road behind a truck with its tailgate down and barrels full of some sort of chemical loaded in the back. Aunt Charlene didn't get the license-plate number, but she did remember the truck was in disrepair ("If you got rid of the rust, there'd be nothing holding the damn thing together") and it had a sign on the back that read DANGER: HAZARDOUS CHEMICALS.

The warning signs against catastrophe in the industrial world always seemed to involve hands. I have seen farm machinery, printing presses, and auto-assembly plants with huge machines, filled with rollers and blades and hydraulic vises, and they all have directions on the side of the machine for removing "foreign objects" from within the gear work, if such objects should get caught. Usually, it is a hand, rolled tortuously back and forth among the gears, broken back and forth, as if these machines were built to replace the medieval inquisition. The sign, I knew, for corrosive-chemical hazards—it must have been corrosives the truck was carrying, since it would explain the rusted-out truck—was a hand open palm upward, as if asking for alms, with a droplet bearing down on that palm, and a small dip in the hand, at the point of the chemical-drop trajectory, to show that the hand had been eaten at, worn away.

It was too dangerous for Aunt Charlene to pass the trundling truck with a bus and children, so she followed the long road behind the truck, semipatiently. The truck hit a bump, and one of the barrels popped its lid and splashed viscous green chemicals all over the windshield of the bus. Aunt Charlene swore in front of the kids and then apologized to them, then she got out of the bus with her squeegee and scrubbed down the chemical gunk so she could see.

She immediately lost her voice.

"I thought it was God's way of punishing me for swearing in front of the kids," Aunt Charlene said, after telling the story for the millionth time.

She had to get a very expensive antibiotic from her doctor, and soon after seeing him, she began to run a high fever. She thought it was the antibiotic making her sick. She only got her voice back after a week. Aunt Charlotte said she ought to sue.

"Sue? Sue who? The doctor? I don't even know what was in the truck."

"That's right, you could be dead by Easter," her sister said.

"Then what's the point of suing?"

"To leave money for your family, stupid," said Aunt Charlotta. She lit up a cigarette. They had a competition to see who could smoke the most. Aunt Charlene was quickly falling behind, in her condition.

For some reason, the poisoning of Monsalvat, both chemically and mentally, came hand in hand with Tommy's flight from it. Aunt Mary was not around to be Aunt Charlene's home nurse during the loss of her voice, and because it was spring break, I spent a lot of time with her. As her voice improved she taught me quite a few off-color jokes.

I actually enjoyed hanging around with her. She was the least squeamish of my uncles and aunts, probably because she spent several years living on a cattle farm with her husband, until they sold it, three or four years after I was born. One of my earliest memories was being knocked down on their farm by a beagle they had, named Jake the Snake.

Bodily functions were no problem for her. "Christ, Michael, I could tell you some horror stories about medical problems. With cows! This throat thing is nothing. You want to know the grossest thing I ever saw? A cow with an infected horn. No kidding. Turned black. The vet drives out to see what the problem is, cuts off the horn with your basic hacksaw, sticks a tube down into it, a straw, you know—and he *blows*. Like he's blowing bubbles into a milkshake. God! All this infection and pus, what a smell, comes running out of this poor cow's nose. Oh God, Michael, I thought I was going to throw up right there."

"Wow," I said.

I had to laugh, it was so awful. She was surprised, as people are, to find that the regular everyday things she had experienced in her life might be interesting to somebody else. I was a captive audience, and that only fueled her stories.

And whenever Aunt Charlene talked, she was always wanting to yell, first because she was a Kaiserbroad, second because she probably had gone deaf around so many tractors and combines in those farming years. Now they throw earmuffs in with tractor purchases. So it hurt Aunt Charlene to be talking to me, but I think it hurt her even more when she was *not* able to talk.

One day, I came in with her favorite afternoon drink, lemonade with Ancient Age. I was experimenting with alcohol then, the sweeter stuff that didn't really taste like alcohol but gave off the same chemical effect—blender drinks, sloe gin, and now these. I'd make half again the amount Aunt Charlene requested, and slug it down quickly in the kitchen before bringing hers into her bedroom. Now I know she must have smelled it on my breath in those times, unless the toxic chemicals messed up her other senses, too.

I went in, where she lay on top of her bedspread in a pair of long shorts, and I handed her her portion. She took a drink from the glass, smacked her lips, and said to me, "When I start drinking these, Buster Brown, you know that summer is coming."

"When you start drinking these," I said, "I know you're feeling better."

"You're darn tootin'."

I started emptying ashtrays into an empty bowl. She was smoking more, which meant she was feeling better, too. Catching up with Aunt Charlotta.

She took one of her antibiotics with the lemonade drink and said, "I know this is what's gonna kill me. I figure the price on these little blue babies is about seven bucks a pill. What I got into on the road must've been potent stuff."

"Aunt Charlene," I said, "have you ever read any of those reports about people getting cancer at an early age from being around too many chemicals? Like pesticides in crops getting into the watershed, stuff like that? Dry-cleaning fluid in the backyard?"

"What are they teaching you kids in those public schools?" She narrowed her eyes half-jokingly. She'd lit up another cigarette, too.

"Nothing. They never talk about that at school."

"Then you've been reading your Aunt Teresa's *National Enquirer*s, haven't you?"

I told her I hadn't, and besides, if it were in the *Enquirer*, I probably wouldn't be so worried about whether it was a problem. I said, "It's just that what with PBB in all our cows"—a bad thing to say to Aunt Charlene: some of their own cows had gotten their feed mixed up with fire-retardant chemicals just before they sold the farm, and Aunt Charlene and her husband lost thousands of dollars in the sale because of it—"and I see Uncle Jimmy spraying down Grandma's yard with weed killers and kids just roll around in it before it's even dry, and then they put all this green gunk in barrels and you lose your voice...."

"What's your point, hon?" she said, flicking the ash away.

"Well, doesn't it make you want to, I don't know, find out?"

"You've got a nice bedside manner."

"Doesn't it make you want to move away? Everything seems so poisonous around here."

"Where would I move to, dear?"

"I don't know. The ocean. Where would you go if you wanted to get away from poison?"

"Hawaii," she said right away. "Only, it's getting to be so damn commercial, they say."

"No, not for vacation," I said, "But a place you could live. A place where they're not so worried about killing weeds."

Aunt Charlene puffed up a pillow to rise up on. I was focusing on the little blue varicose veins that lichened here and there about her knees, in order not to look at her face. She said, "How come you like weeds so much? What have weeds done for you? I say good riddance to them. You are a pill, Michael. An expensive blue pill. You'll be out protesting for weed rights behind your mother's back before too long. I'll tell you what: You ought to try living on a farm for a couple of years. Then you wouldn't be so fond of your weeds. One little crop failure due to ragweed or quack grass, and you'd change your tune real fast."

I didn't answer her. I probably posed my question in a

wrong way. I should've asked, if you were a weed, and they were spraying everywhere to get rid of you, where would you try to live? In the cracks of a city sidewalk? In a fallow field in Montana? Where was Tommy?

"Honey, do your aunt Charlene a favor," she said, taking a drag on her cigarette and exhaling like a movie star, "Get your aunt Charlene another lemonade. And find me a good deck of playing cards—this one's only got fifty-one."

∎　∎　∎

After a while, I thought that everybody was trying to hide information from me. I was sure that everybody in the family knew Tommy's whereabouts, and nobody was going to tell me. To this day, I'm not sure whether or not that is true. It would have been easy to keep me in the dark, somebody who only visited during holidays and vacations. Of course I was paranoid. One thing different, though, between then and now, is that then I believed it was a unified conspiracy among them all, and now I know, for sure, that if they did know of Tommy's whereabouts, they never talked about it among themselves. That piece of information was either too unbearable for regular family discussion, as so much was, or it was kept like a sacred object, a trump card, a right bower (the jack of hearts!) to be discarded in a deft play, but secreted away until that time, whatever it was.

This I didn't think at that time, though. But I did know that in order to dispel the paranoia, I had to attempt to make somebody, anybody, tell me what they knew.

Of course, Anne would be easiest. She would, ironically, tell me anything, as long as she knew it could be possibly painful information. But therefore Anne would know nothing, because everybody, including her brother, knew she had a big mouth. That was something the two of us had in common: our big mouths. What, after all, have these hundreds of pages been otherwise? My big mouth has gotten me into trouble in a lot of ways. There is a margin, in many situations, between what is public and what is private, different for every person.

During Aunt Charlene's illness, for instance, I went to visit Philly and Millie, because I had found a huge new interest in their lives, both public and private, and in certain ways, theirs were open books. When the biggest secret in your life shoulders its heft out into the open, the margins of your own privacy are pushed into another arena.

"Hey, Mike, how's the family?" Philly asked. She asked only after eagerly telling me, in excruciating detail, the events of a trailer trip the two of them had taken into the Southwest for two winter months. "Was it clean?" I asked. "No, it was so dusty!" Millie said.

The baseball game was playing on the radio again, spring preseason exhibition rounds. Al Kaline was messing up royally, and Millie kept saying, "Oh, fudge! Come on, Al, get it together!" I imagined they had tape recordings of baseball games to play in those down hours, in the winter, on their trips in the camper trailer.

"Oh, they're okay," I said. "Aunt Charlene is not so hot."

"I've noticed she's been pretty scarce. What's she got?"

"Poison," I said. Out the window, I could see a beautiful weeping willow. Willows loved this whole area of Monsalvat that was close to Clear Lake, with the spongy-wet acid loamy earth and mild breezes. I liked to climb in willows, except they were places infested by a kind of small black bug, the size and shape of ladybugs, only plainer, more liable to bite, or escape a slap.

"Poison!" Philly said.

I told her the story of the bus and the barrelful of chemicals. Philly shook her head. "The world is going to hell in a hand basket, my friend."

Millie popped in, "All around us—*nature*—and they're hacking away at it. Nobody likes a good surprise anymore.

They'd control the weather if they could. You know, Michael, we should learn to enjoy the weather more, because we can afford to. People who are outside a lot tend to hate weather. Farmers hate it. They don't want any surprises. Airplane pilots, too. Fishermen. Meter maids. Sailors. But we sit in the house all the time, we ought to appreciate all that phenomena." Millie waved her hand at the weeping willow, as if she were clearing the window so I could see it better. I wondered if I would enjoy the willow more if somebody exterminated all of its black bugs for me.

I thought of the way Aunt Charlene cursed rainfall, or a late-April snow, and how she always turned to the weather report on television, or in the paper, first.

I said, "Have you ever thought of running a farm? I have. Or going to live in a big tenement in a city. When I think of my future, I think I'll be completely on my own, one way or another, in some wild environment." For Millie, I added, "With lots of surprises."

"What's the matter, Mike," Philly said, "are you sick of Monsalvat?"

I'd begun to think seriously about what I'd do in a year or so, out of high school. When I brought up college, a thing rarely done in my family—in fact, I would be the first of all of my family to get a bachelor's degree—Aunt Teresa said, "Why don't you do the sensible thing, and go to the community college? You can stay with your parents and tuition is dirt cheap!" "Sometimes," I said to Philly and Millie, "I think Monsalvat is sick of me."

Millie said, "We're not sick of you, Michael. Let me get you some root beer." Their refrigerator was well stocked with pop and beer.

I blurted it out right then, my own private life. It was now or never. There were a combination of reasons why the time was right in that cabin, with the root beer and the attention—first of all, they said right up front that they weren't sick of me; then, there was that lack of avenues available to express my desires; then, here was the thinnest of opportunities to express desires to these two (hopefully) like-minded women; and finally, here was a chance for the quelling of my growing paranoia. I said, "I thought I'd go out and find Tommy somewhere."

"Find Tommy? Why?" Millie asked.

"Where would you look?"

"In the woods. On a farm. In a city. Did he ever tell you where he wanted to go?" I said "ever" like I was pleading.

"The marines," said Philly, right away.

"Well, he definitely changed his mind about that," I said. "Do you know the real reason why he left? Why he didn't join the marines? Did anybody ever tell you about my letter?"

"Your letter?" Philly asked.

I told them everything, things that nobody knew until now, I even told them about saving his cigar stubs. I unloaded my world like I was unloading Philly and Millie's filled refrigerator—beers and root beers all around. I didn't tell them about the stolen playing cards, however; I knew even then that there must, at all times, be a residual secret in my heart. Otherwise, I'd be forced to do something else that would be considered aberrant, in order to restock on an emptied secret world. If I told them about the cards, then I would have to lie, or steal, or do some damage, again.

I told them everything else, though, up to and including my recent discovery of the drugstore magazine rack.

I don't know what I expected them to do. I'd never planned it that far. I'd never *planned* it, except in a very abstract way, this telling. I supposed that anything they might do would disappoint me. They would discuss my state of mind, perhaps, or ask who else in the family knew, or was I sure? Maybe a lecture on their hard lonely life, and a discussion of whether it was worth it.

Instead, Millie said, "When I was your age, there was a person who I loved. And that person lied to me. That person left me, too. It darn near broke my heart."

"Such a sloppy bunch, you Kaisers," Philly said. She got a whiskey bottle off the top of the refrigerator and poured me a shot glass full. I started to cry. Sort of a sob, it was, the sort I hadn't had since third grade when I missed my bus home from school. I'd never had straight whiskey before and it burned horribly, so my attention was taken up with being strong enough to down what seemed like an endless shot of whiskey. Getting it down, getting a glass of it, in general, and being treated like an adult, these distracted me from my big-mouthed pronouncements. For once, physical pain rescued me from mental torment.

This is how my adult tastes—fetishes—have come to me: hard straight liquor, asparagus, olives, black coffee: these items have presented themselves as the best aspect of a terrible situation. Later, in college, sleep-deprived before an important lecture, I went to the student union and bought a newfangled coffee flavor, "mocha," which I thought would make it taste like hot chocolate. So confident was I that I didn't even doctor it with cream and sugar. Trapped in lecture, I discovered its true nature: strong black coffee, bitter as rusty metal and tar, extra large. Faced with this or certain nap time, I drank the coffee. By the end of class, I was a changed man. So, too, with this simple shot of whiskey poured by Philly, I was becoming a changed man. And it took my mind off my big mouth. Already, I was regretting it, hoping perhaps they'd forgotten what I just said.

"Mike," said Philly, "from what I know about Tommy, I'd say he probably isn't going to look you up anytime in the near future."

"Yes," agreed Millie, "Tommy's quite a womanizer, as I remember."

"He never had a girlfriend," I said hopefully.

"No, he never could make up his mind," said Philly. "He strung 'em along for months and months. He was a real lady-killer—among other things," she added, for me.

"He was a weed," I said.

"A weed?" said Philly.

"He could never please his folks, so they dug him up like a dandelion," I said. "They all hate him, and it's my fault."

"They don't hate Tommy," Millie said. "I've heard any one of your aunts wondering out loud where he could be, wishing they could get in touch with him. I've heard them."

"Really?" I was sniffing up the last of the crying, finishing off the whiskey. Relief washed over me, very unreasonably, the best kind of relief. Add to it the fact that I looked up just then and caught the mopping, undersea motion of the big wilty willow tree.

"You're sure you don't want to go after this Marsha girl?" Philly asked. "She's a looker. I like her better than Tommy any day!" She winked. Millie smacked her in the arm ineffectually. Al Kaline whapped a very successful line drive, and the announcer was excited about it, as relieved, maybe, as I was. "It's a line drive to right field!" he shouted.

■　■　■

A day after, I came back from the Monsalvat Plaza, where I'd spent the afternoon at the tulip festival, and bought some piece of junk. I went to check on Aunt Charlene, to see if she wanted one of her special lemonades, but she seemed very mad. At me.

"What have you been doing today?" I asked.

"Visiting," she said. She was wearing the same shorts she wore the day before, and sat on the top of her bed in the same position. She seemed an aging mandarin, deciding punishments. Her voice was brassier today, almost back to normal. She was pulling idly at the little cotton pills in the bedspread texture, and making the headboard squeak by moving the bed back and forth. She was impatient to get out and on with her life, her smoking.

"Visiting? With who?" I asked.

"Philly and Millie dropped by. Left a pie."

"That was nice of them." I blanched, probably looking monstrously guilty. "I saw them yesterday and they were worried about you."

"Wasn't that nice of them?" Aunt Charlene said.

"Do you want a lemonade?" I asked.

"No," she said. "Michael?"

"Yeah?"

"Do you know what it means to have a personal life? Have you ever heard the old saying 'Loose lips sink ships'?"

"Yes," I said.

"Yes, what? First of all, Buster Brown, nobody here hates Tommy. If I knew where he was, I'd go right out now and get him."

"I don't think he would come," I said. I know that if my mother heard that, she would have called me a smartmouth at that point. But Aunt Charlene couldn't say that because she wasn't my mother, and the Kaiserbroads respected the boundaries of parenthood.

"No, he probably wouldn't, the little asshole," she said. "Yes, I'll have one of those lemonades," she said, after a minute.

I was happy to leave the room for a minute. I made the drink extra strong. That was a secret command she'd given me, and I picked it up loud and clear. When I came back to her, she was calmer.

"Look, Michael. Millie said she was worried that you thought it was your fault that Tommy left. Don't you worry about it. And please, this is a family matter, it's private. Have you ever heard the old saying 'Blood is thicker than water'? Those two ladies are real nice, but honey, they don't know you from Adam! Don't go discussing private things with people. It's none of their business."

I agreed. I turned red. I left the room, and didn't come back to her during that stay—not alone, anyway.

Finding the line, by tragic and embarrassing accident, between a public and private life, as I discovered with Aunt Charlene, was to find out what a person cared the most about. Aunt Charlene muttered loudly about being overworked, bad bowling scores, Uncle Tom's hunting accident (too dramatic, if private, to pass up as a good story), even about Tommy unzipping his pants on stage as a child, but she was as silent as a grave when it came to what she construed as dire information: the way she lost her voice, the way we lost Tommy, the weeds of the family.

That secret margin is as individual and idiosyncratic an aspect of Aunt Charlene's life as there ever shall be. To find that place with somebody close is always painful and is a transgression on an intimacy. When it is stumbled over, like a gopher hole, one thing is lost—the hiding place; at the same time an equally important thing is found—the hidden object. Trust is lost, and make no mistake, lost forever. But the key to another person's heart is found, and the responsibility for holding on to it is engaged until the end.

Still, for those of us who wish a private secret could be made public, for any reason, but mostly because it is too big an elephant to hide, too naturally needful of open space, we hope we are often spoken of, and when that private beast walks into the open, never to return, very few other secrets matter much.

I cannot help but believe that during all that time he was gone, Tommy hoped we talked about him daily, forlornly, and publicly, that the Kaiserbroads spun a boisterous tale of the wicked one, a tale they repeated nightly over beer. He would have been disappointed, I think, to find the conspiracy of silence surrounding him, and that the mention of his name in the outside world was an embarrassment, a sunk ship.

Nevertheless, a few months later, I struck upon the desperate notion of putting a personal in the newspapers of a dozen major cities, simple, all capital letters, reading, "TOM KAISER, SON OF TOM KAISER OF MONSALVAT, MICHIGAN, PLEASE CONTACT MICHAEL BELLMAN AT HIS HOME ADDRESS." I wanted it to go into a Detroit paper, and papers in Boston, New York, Miami, San Francisco, Seattle, Toronto. Through desire's genius, I went so far as to hunt down the addresses and rates at the public library for all these and more. But I never sent them, I chickened out, afraid that some other Kaiser would see the personal somewhere.

I asked Aunt Mary why Uncle Tom's friends at the police department couldn't make a search for him. She was reluctant to answer me, but then said, "You know, I've already done that. But these things take years, and so far, they haven't had any luck." All of my efforts were like torches cast into a black and bottomless well. I was playing solitaire with a not-quite-full deck of jacks.

CHAPTER 11

Hopeless Cases

In my grandmother's living room, over the television, there was a print of a painting from some fifteenth-century master named Stephan Lochner. I found the same painting later at a library, in an art book. It is called *The Last Judgment*. In it there are hideous demons, some with second faces on their bellies, battling angels that had perfect complexions, battling for the bodies—more clearly than for the souls—of mankind. The obviously ugly versus the obviously beautiful.

The angels looked like Kelly: porcelain, smooth, shaved, somebody else's perfect idea of what is beautiful.

Above everything floats Mary, Jesus, and probably John the Baptist, in that order, and the damned humankind look up at Christ as if he betrayed them. But in case anybody wondered, the evidence of their sins is quite obvious: bags of money, crowns, dice, obesity, drunkenness, decorations for the bodies, not the souls, proof positive of sins of the flesh. You can't make a necklace out of dirty thoughts.

What horrors the lately saved endured as they were snatched from the jaws and claws of those six-faced slimy monsters! I'd steal looks at that painting for years, piously giving my attention to Jesus and Mary, but after that, after my dues were prayed to the Holy of Holies, I'd treat myself to the pictures of the monsters, imagined before nuclear waste, imagined before mustard gas.

The angels reigned over that painterly sky, but the demons abominated the earth and castles.

I could hear music when I looked at *The Last Judgment*, heavenly choruses and low chants trying to outsing each other. The angels pierce the air with nattering castrati melodies. The demons rumble great feral plainsongs, voluptuous, hairy, toadlike, lecherous songs. Men's voices, oh, definitely bass men.

The angels, sylphlike, embrace the newly arrived holy humans like old sorority sisters with wide eyes. Below, the demons stare fish-eyed, those eyes unrelentingly lidless.

In seventeen years of visits to Monsalvat, I'd done my first thieving, drinking, gambling, swearing, and stealing the Virgin Mary's crown in a house that cared so much about my spiritual well-being. And secretly, I thought the militant demons were much more interesting. Bad, but more interesting. This has resulted in a secret love of horrible zombie movies, in which the living are eviscerated and devoured by the rotting dead. How beautiful, some corrupt part of me says, how beautiful, to see the beautiful mutilated by the ugly. If you can obliterate a beautiful thing, I figured, then it's yours, you've got the upper hand over it.

Are the beautiful really beautiful?

Anne obviously thought Kelly was attractive, or at least harmless, because the two of them were an item for quite a long time. After Uncle Tom's funeral, Aunt Mary went on a monthlong tour of Reno and Las Vegas with her Sweet Adeline group, a gaggle of frosted-haired skinny women who sang together, into each other's ears. She left Anne, almost eighteen, in charge of her younger brothers and sisters. If there were any emergencies, call Aunt Teresa, the note on the refrigerator said, and following that, a list of casinos (Bally's, Caesar's, Tropicana) on the Sweet Adeline itinerary, with hotel names and phone numbers. This was how Aunt Mary grieved for Uncle Tom, how she kept from having a nervous breakdown.

Kelly practically moved in with Anne. It wasn't so much that he came over every day, Anne told me, it was that he just never went home. It was only a matter of time before the eager-to-please Kelly pleased himself into Anne's pregnancy.

■ ■ ■

"I know you've come to me for support, but I'm having a real tough time with this, I really am. You are almost an adult. Your mother has given you responsibility for your entire family, and how do you deal with that responsibility? You *don't*. That's your *whole problem*. What kind of an example do you think you're setting? What have you done in front of your brothers and sisters that I don't know about? Never mind, I don't want to know."

"Nothing that they don't already know about," Anne said defiantly back to Aunt Teresa. "If you think I feel bad about what you're saying, you're crazy, because at this point, I just don't care anymore."

"You'd better start caring, little lady! You'd better!"

That is what Anne said the conversation was like when she knew for sure she had become pregnant. "That's your whole problem, that's your whole problem," Anne mimicked, her upper lip up like a largemouth bass's. "God, *so stupid*."

By the time I saw Anne, she was beginning to show a little. It was in the spring, Easter weekend of my junior year of high school, and although word had gotten to us that Anne was "in trouble," she had been carrying the baby for four months before I had a chance to talk to her about it. By then, everything was a mess, nobody would lay off her. I had to take her for a ride in the shuddering pale blue car to get to talk with her alone.

I remember she was wearing jeans and a thick ski sweater with dozens of multicolored nubbins on it. She was trying to draw attention away from her pooched-out stomach with that busy design, but it didn't work.

Anne loved talking to me about it as we drove straight out of town. All through our conversation, I kept looking down at the evidence, rising like bread dough in her lap. To the Kaiser family, nothing was really wrong, nobody was really mad at her until she started showing. *Then* it was terrible. Aunt Charlene hadn't talked to her in two weeks. All Aunt Teresa would do was whine and yell. When Aunt Mary returned from the tour, she cried a lot and wouldn't come over for the Sunday after-church boredom.

Uncle Jimmy was good at acting like nothing ever happened, even when Anne's gut was sticking out of her blouse. It reminded me of the cult of silence around Tommy and the imposed ban on the bodily functions described explicitly in *Our Bodies, Ourselves*. And they had successfully kept the information from my grandmother. "You have to tell her," I said. "Eventually, she's going to figure it out. She's not stupid, you know."

"No, she's not stupid, but she is getting pretty blind."

"She'd be on your side."

"Just leave her out of it, okay?"

I drove some more. "So. What are you going to do? Are you going to marry Kelly?"

"I don't know. Maybe. He's rich, you know." We stopped at a light.

"His dad is rich." The light changed.

"Same thing."

"But do you love him?" I waited until another stoplight before asking that question.

"I don't know. Do you?"

I looked at her. I stepped on the gas. I knew he told her about the night before the funeral. He had probably told her as soon as I'd gone home after the funeral. That was one more reason for my not liking him. I had a ton of reasons for not liking him, and none of them had anything to do with feeling protective toward Anne. "No, I don't," I said.

"Just because I did it with him doesn't mean I love him."

"So if you don't marry him, what happens with the baby?"

"It becomes a bastard." She emphasized the word, made it sibilant. I winced. "Everybody's so full of ideas about what I should do. Get married. Don't get married. Finish school and get married. Get a job so I'll get insurance. Don't get a job and don't get married and use Mom's insurance. Give it up for adoption. Marry after the baby's born. Blah-blah-blah."

"You know," I whispered, "you don't *have* to have the baby."

She was upset by that, but not because it was a horrid idea. She was just getting more and more upset in general, talking faster and faster. I drove to match her mood. The car began to shake like it might fly apart. "I know, I know. I've thought about that. Did you know some people can get rid of it by taking a bath in scalding water? Ouch. I can't do that. But where would I get the money? Nobody in this family or in Kelly's is going to pay for my baby killing."

I hesitated, but then I said, "What about Tommy?"

"Would you shut the hell up about Tommy!" she yelled, looking like she might force the steering wheel out of my hands. "All you ever say is Tommy Tommy Tommy! Shut up. Shut up. Shut up." Then she started crying, really loudly, really recklessly, like she didn't know where she was going with the crying.

I pulled the car over to a gravel turnout. I let her grab me and cry and she got my shoulder so wet I could feel my shirt becoming sopping. I patted her on the back and it was all very awkward.

A car went by and honked. I figured we must have looked like lovers holding each other, pulled over along the road because we were swept up in so much ardor for one another.

She was right, though. All I could think of was Tommy. He had set the tone for passion, and to this day he affects the patterns love makes on me. I wrote Tommy letters. I have written hundreds of love letters by now, ones that go unsent and pile up in boxes. When I got in trouble at school, I got in trouble for passing notes. ("Do you like me? Check box: yes/no/maybe.") When I left home for good, I wrote long letters to Anne and my grandmother and had nothing to say, really, but said everything. I never wanted a letter back, I just wanted to talk, repeat stories I'd heard, sing like a bird that's not trying to fill up an empty space, but is so full of a full world that it overflows. Onto the page.

I was obsessed with Tommy, and that does not mean I was always saying Tommy Tommy Tommy. The fact was, there were long stretches when I did not think of him, but then another disappointment would come, a disappointment like Kelly, and my mind would return to Tommy in full force, that old scab gouged. I spent years forgetting and remembering, forgetting and remembering, heartthrob that cycled over years rather than minutes. And I found that if I sat down to write a letter, I was spending the whole time remembering and not forgetting. On the page I could concentrate, I could pray, and that was less painful than the constant forgetting.

Memory is not nearly as painful as forgetfulness.

Anne stopped crying eventually and then resented me for seeing her cry. She said she had already tried to find Tommy, had even gotten an address from Uncle John, my grandfather who made the military a career in California. But the address was two years old and it was the same one which had done no good in bringing Tommy back to the funeral.

We started driving again and there was more silence until

I said something I was afraid she would mock. I said, "Have you tried praying to Saint Jude?"

"Oh, great," she said. "Patron saint of hopeless cases. Thanks for the vote of confidence, Mikey."

"Well, have you?"

She was starting to bug me by pushing the cigarette lighter in and pulling it out. She threatened to brand my arm with it. I slapped her away. She said, "I'm not superstitious and I'm not stupid."

"I am," I said. "Sometimes, I will walk into Grandma's living room, and I'll see some picture of your father, and I'll think, If I don't touch that picture in the next ten seconds, my heart will stop, just like his did."

"You're very weird, Mike."

She didn't know it, but I had driven her to the outskirts of Monsalvat, to an actual Saint Jude's Catholic Church. That had been the secret of the whole drive. I hadn't planned to talk her into it, because I knew she would say it was a stupid idea. This was my version of brute force. We were already halfway there by the time I brought up the idea.

But she must have sort of known that this was my scheme, she must have intuited it like I always know when I'm being taken somewhere. She liked, for the moment, I think, to be taken, to not be the perpetrator of evil. I was driving the car. I was holding the evidence, for a change.

I swear it was more than a coincidence that Saint Jude's was on the outside of town. Families like my own made a place for dirty laundry. There is a natural desire for gambling, lustfulness, gluttony, sloth, but that desire has been made ugly in order for it to be kept under control, and kept at arm's length, in the desert at Las Vegas, an outpost for sensuality. Saint Jude's was another outpost, a place to leave guilt and find forgiveness for all that vice.

Saint Jude's was like a regular church and had masses like a regular church, except that there was a special room on the side of the building, with a separate entrance, which housed a shrine for Saint Jude. In the middle of this round, window-less room was a life-size golden statue of Saint Jude, patron saint of hopeless cases. Like the center of a man-made flower, he was surrounded first by a tiered bank of votive candles in see-through red shot-glass-sized holders, flaming up like the musical strains of choruses. As a border, an octagon of pews flanked the statue. The room blazed in a lurid red and gold, medieval luxury. Against the walls were piles of paper almost to the ceiling, which were all the appeals that had been made by people who sought help in their troubled times. I won-dered how many of those appeals were made by Kaisers, Un-cle Jimmy for his dead wife, Aunt Teresa for Chester, Aunt Mary for Tommy. Here, at the edge of town, was a heap of anonymous secrets, a spiritual Las Vegas. I knew I'd never find the particulars in this hagiological bureaucracy, but it maddened me to know that such appeals might exist, secrets revealable, at arm's length, like a library without a card cat-alog.

The room's roundness and the endless stacks of paper made us confused, and Anne and I, every once in a while, lost our bearings, and got dizzy. We were the only ones in the shrine that afternoon.

"This is the place where deals are made," I said.

"Deals?"

"Sure. You make a deal with Saint Jude, and if he helps you out, you publish a little thank-you note to him in the pa-per for services rendered."

"I haven't got enough money to be paying for an adver-tisement to thank a dead guy," she said. "And this isn't even my church. I don't even know who this guy is." She pointed up to the statue. He was holding a boat in his hand.

"Have you ever thought of praying to your father?" I asked.

"No, I never prayed to him. I prayed for him, sort of."

"Sort of?"

"Yeah. I made deals with God. I sat up that night he was dying at the hospital and I thought, What would I give to keep him from croaking? My left arm? My eyeballs? Would I die in place of him?"

Once, I thought, I told Aunt Teresa that I would certainly die on a cross if it meant that it would take away the sins of the world. Would I give my left arm for Uncle Tom?

Anne had opened up her purse to take out some change. The inside of the purse smelled like spearmint gum, which seemed sacrilegious in this room of powdery incense and paraffin. "I thought about it," Anne said. "And I had terrible thoughts. I knew that I wouldn't die for him. I might not even give my left hand. Maybe a finger, I don't know. I'm terrible, aren't I?"

I was thinking of my own sacred and profane prayers. I would pray at night to see a naked man the next day. I prayed to hear from Tommy.

"No. It's funny, though. There was this guy I read about who had cancer and he prayed to God, and said that if God cured his cancer, he would have himself crucified every Easter. So they gave him a bone-marrow transplant and he got better, and so now he nails himself to a cross every year for Easter weekend. He's probably hammering himself in place as we speak."

"That's really stupid," Anne said. "So you think I should promise to crucify myself so that the baby doesn't cause any more problems?"

"No, I'm just saying. This guy made a deal. I make deals all the time. Modern science makes it so you can make even more deals. Science makes me superstitious—I could say to God, if this guy doesn't die of cancer, I'll give up my bone marrow. You can give blood. You can donate your eyeballs to science. It's like a deal you make." But I was thinking, I will pray to Saint Jude myself. I will make a deal: if I could see Tommy one more time, I would agree never to see him again.

"I'm not superstitious, Michael. There aren't any secret charms." And as she said that she pitched her change into a tin tube, stovepipe black, knelt down at a bank of votive candles, lit one, and began to pray.

She prayed as if she were pitted against the candle, as if she were in competition with it. The candle, like any sacred object in this church—the statue, the rosary, the paintings, the cross, the cruet, Bibles, bells, vestments, missals, pattons, they were all a clutter that stirred up superstition, competition, challenge. Evidence. If I did not touch the picture of Uncle Tom, my heart would stop, too.

Anne got up and left the shrine, and I followed. We walked into blindingly bright daylight. Neither of us daubed ourselves with a cross of holy water, so our prayers to Saint Jude were probably jinxed.

■　　■　　■

"So will you marry her?" I asked Kelly. We were helping Philly and Millie rake the dead leaves and pine needles out of their lawn on Easter afternoon. The ladies were paying us five dollars an hour. Uncle Tom probably did the job for free. We'd been at it for two hours, and we were both sweating as we heaped the leaves into a wheelbarrow. I've always enjoyed sweating in cool air. The rest of the family had gone out to Round Lake that day—the whole town of Monsalvat had, in fact, because a huge run of speckled bass had mysteriously appeared there. As fast as they put their hooks into the water, they pulled out huge fat fish. So other than the zwitching sound our rakes made on the sickly grass, we worked in a dead and silent world.

I could see at Kelly's wrists how the grime collected in

those lines where a person might use a razor blade to slash them open.

"Maybe," he said. It took me all afternoon to ask him, and this was how he answered me. Eager to please, like a dog, and I felt like slugging him.

"Well, are you or aren't you? I mean, it's going to be your kid, too."

He looked at me like a dog, with a kind of pleading face, like *I* had made an ultimatum, that I was some sort of last word, and spelled his oblivion. I was the object pitted against him.

But I didn't feel sorry for him, the way most people always felt sorry for Kelly, so sweet, so kind. I wanted to be mean to him, to beat up his empty face so that it was ugly, or at least something rather than nothing, so that I could begin to love him, as I loved all broken things. I inherited that desire for chipped china and faded photographs and watermarked doilies from my grandmother, from the Kaisers. I have no use for the wide-eyed beauty of angels. If I made him ugly, he was mine.

I leaped on him, and grabbed him by his sweaty T-shirt. "I know what guys like you are like," I said. "You look like you're poor little Kelly and you've been mistreated, and you think you're making everybody happy by being like God, all things to all men and all that crap. But all you are is selfish. You figure that if you don't do anything, that if you don't make any of the decisions, then you'll be Mr. Innocent. Meanwhile, Anne's got a belly the size of a truck she's dragging around, she's got the evidence, and she *can't* be innocent. *God,*" I said, "you're even afraid having any hair on your body will make you a suspect."

He grabbed his own shirt sleeves out of my hands and set himself up again while saying, "Geez, Bellman. She told me you were a weird guy. What are you *on?*"

I wanted to cry, but I pressed. "Are you going to marry her? Or are you going to help pay to get rid of it?"

I probably shouldn't have avoided the word, but it was as foul sounding a word to me, too. I should have said "abortion," and if I were seven years younger, more innocent than I was, I would have.

"It's none of your business what I do," he said, and stomped out of my reach. I looked him up and down. For some reason, I thought of Kelly's parents when they found out. I imagined Kelly's father walking out of the room in disgust so he wouldn't have to hear the rest of the problem, and his mother cackling, along with the cockatoo, over the martini. The thought made me push Kelly down again into the leaves. I fell on him and had the advantage all along, not because I was a skilled fighter, but because I really wanted to hurt him.

Philly came around from the other side of the cabin, wearing her overalls and fuzzy gloves the color of new tennis balls. I got up off Kelly. Philly pulled her wallet out and handed Kelly some money. "You boys did a great job, why don't we call it a day?" Kelly thanked her, never looked at me, grinned for her—this time I saw how the sides of his mouth drew back wolfishly—and walked down the road. Pieces of rotting leaves stuck to his back, but he didn't dare brush them off.

"Come in the house," Philly said to me. She pulled the rake out of my hand like I was going to use it against her.

Inside, Millie was sitting over a small table that fit in the kitchen only when the leaves were down. What did they do when they were serving dinner to company? I wondered. Millie was adjusting the tuner, listening to a Detroit Tigers exhibition game. I did not like baseball, but the sound of a game reported on the radio was soothing to me.

Millie said, "Michael, you're all sweaty! I'll make lemonade. Tigers are ahead, three–oh. They're going to have to work for everything they get now that they lost the Bird." Mark "the Bird" Fydrich was another crush I'd had, part of a long line of mythic heroes like the Hardy Boys and the Man from Atlantis, with his smooth muscular body and terrifyingly webbed hands. "You play baseball?" Millie asked.

"No, I'm uncoordinated. I run in the summer and I swim in the winter."

Millie brought back a tall turquoise aluminum glass, its lip curled out like a flower petal, full of lemonade. The metal seemed even colder than the lemonade, and together they tasted as tart as iron, as cold as blood. Millie ran her hands down my sweaty arm in a half caress. "Gad's, you're soaking wet. I can tell you've been working hard."

The truth was, it was too cool a spring to actually work up this kind of sweat. I was sweating from wrestling with Kelly.

"When I swim, I sweat, but nobody can tell," I said. "Nobody knows how hard I've been working when I'm swimming."

Philly sat across from me. She must have thought I was possessed, insane. I said, "When I go underwater, I can scream my head off, but nobody can hear me. I punch at the water like I'm killing somebody, and nobody can tell." Violence was all around us, Millie once said.

Philly leaned back. "What's going on, Mike?"

I told her Anne was pregnant. It was old news, they'd talked to her quite a lot about it. I told them I thought Kelly ought to help her out.

"Do you think she wants to marry him?" Philly asked.

"Is this a trick question?" I asked. "Have you already asked her that question?"

"No, I swear to God," Millie said. "Philly's just asking."

"Well, she hasn't really said she loves him." I said. "She never did seem very crazy about him. But that's just how she is."

"Well, that is just how she is, but that means there are other ways of telling what's on Anne's mind. She never tells you what she's really thinking. But I can tell you what she thinks." She tapped the side of her head like she was playing her trump card. "Woman's intuition."

■ ■ ■

"I think I've got it all figured out," Anne said to them all. It was Easter and it was dusk. All of the Kaiserbroads had gathered around her at the kitchen table and Anne sat at the head. Clockwise, it was Aunt Mary, Aunt Charlene, Aunt Teresa, Aunt Charlotta, and, wonder of wonders, me. Anne called me in for moral support. "They'll tear me to shreds," she said, "unless they have to behave for somebody."

I kept my hands busy rolling boiled and colored Easter eggs under my hand, across the pitted wooden table, shelling them, dousing them with salt, and eating them in two bites. After three of these, Anne moved the bowl full of the eggs to the other end of the table.

Aunt Teresa was fidgety. She kept getting up and going to the sink to run water. Aunt Charlene and Aunt Charlotta were plowing through a pack of cigarettes together, passing the pack back and forth, accordioning half-finished butts into a clear blue ashtray that had different moments from Jesus' life illustrating the edges, in gold, the crucifix in the very center, radiant light looking more like a cartoon character's sweat drops flying outward. Aunt Mary had bought it for Aunt Teresa when she was in Las Vegas, as a souvenir.

"I saw it in the shop and I thought of you immediately," Aunt Mary said to her sister-in-law. "Isn't it beautiful?"

"It's hideous," Aunt Teresa said. Because she was nervous, because she could not concentrate on being polite, I think she was honest for the first time in her life. I have learned over time that it is dangerous to buy into other people's collective idea about what is beautiful. The way I have always looked at beautiful people has been superficial—it's easy to see what is attractive at the skin-deep level: skin. But as years go by, my love of my homely aunts and uncles, the puzzles with pieces missing, the cup with the cracked handle, these are not broken, they are broken in. I have no use for beauty. I am much more excited by what my aunts disagreed about in considering what was beautiful: the hideous ashtray, the new paint job on the neighbor's house, the extravagant vase.

Because Aunt Teresa said the ashtray was hideous, the twin aunts made a project of defacing it with their cigarettes. Over the course of the ensuing conversation, the crucifix was permanently obliterated with gray ashes. Aunt Mary looked as pale as the day when she had petted the already dead Chester.

Aunt Charlotta said to Anne, striking another match, "And how have you figured it all out?"

"I'm not getting married," Anne said. "And I'm keeping the baby. I'll move into this house in the spare room and help Aunt Teresa keep it clean. That way I'll finish school and maybe go to MCC."

"Oh-ho-ho," said Aunt Teresa. "Have you discussed this with your grandmother?"

"No," Anne said.

"Discussed what?" my grandmother said. She had been in her living room with the television turned up, so she had no idea this meeting was taking place. Up until then, nobody wanted her to know anything. Not Anne, not the rest of them. I said, "You'd better tell her the big surprise," I said to Anne, trying to sound optimistic, trying to make it sound like she bought a new expensive coat that looked great.

"Big surprise?"

"Grandma," Anne said, "You're going to have another great-grandchild."

She shuffled over and sat down next to me. It took her a

while to shamble and settle in and let her round head peer close to Anne's belly, but she did all this and said, "You?" without gasping at all.

"What do you think of that?" Anne nodded.

Everybody looked at both of them. My grandmother raised her eyebrows and it reminded me of my own mother for a moment. "Well," she said, "I guess what goes around comes around."

Quiet. Then Anne said, "What?"

"Well, how do you suppose your brother Tom got here? How do you think your father got here? A bunch of accidents, that's what half of this family is!"

Aunt Teresa groaned and blanched. Aunt Charlene said, "She's really gone crazy." But Aunt Mary revived, and leaned forward. "Tom was no accident." She said it like it was revenge. "We knew exactly what we were doing—and so did you—and so does Anne!" My grandmother nodded.

Aunt Teresa got up again, this time to walk out. But Aunt Mary said, "And so did Teresa," which stopped the exit.

"Oh, my God," said Aunt Charlene. "Mass hysteria."

Aunt Charlotta said, "Pass me those cigarettes."

"No," Aunt Teresa said. "No. There *is* a difference. The difference is, we all got married. We took responsibility and we got married for the sake of the children."

"Oh, bull," said Aunt Mary. "You got married because you wanted to, and because nobody else wanted you to. I'd like to know where your kid is if you were doing it for his sake?"

"Him," I couldn't help saying out loud.

My grandmother said quietly, "She put him up for adoption." She got rid of the evidence. I thought, There must be some unsigned appeal in the shrine to Saint Jude, in Aunt Teresa's handwriting, begging for a way to marry that sharp-clawed Protestant man, dead anyway since I was born.

Anne said, "Well. This is great." And she got out of the house and halfway to Philly and Millie's cabin before I heard her crying. Everybody stayed in their seats and didn't speak. I think everybody grabbed a cigarette out of the pack, because it was empty. I crumpled the wrapper, for something to do. I turned to Aunt Teresa and trembled, because it was the first and maybe only time I ever spoke back to her. "Then why have you been so hard on Anne?"

Aunt Mary answered my question. "Because that's not the way I raised her."

Oh, yes it was. We were all raised in that sanctified house to desire and laugh and win hearts and make something beautiful for ourselves, and there was nothing terrible about that. Pummeling beauty into Kelly was a dream I had, getting past the skin-deep attraction to the viscera, like I was a flesh-eating zombie sifting beneath the skin of the living. Who else but the religious would mar the surface where sins of the flesh show as easily as the porcelain skin of angels, what else but religion would make a crucifix an image of beauty, one more powerful even than Christ's transfiguration, his bodily ecstasy? Where else are we supposed to go to find a tangible soul if it's not under the skin, among the organs, asleep in us all like a baby?

Perhaps, in that painting of the Last Judgment, I did see myself as one of those demons, who were dutifully showing how real ugliness, like supposed beauty, was only skin-deep. Underneath us are organs, wombs, and all their natural functions, sworn to silence (I could not say "abortion." I could not hear the word "bastard" because it sounded awful.) because they shouldn't be seen, relegated to a no-man's-land between what they call good and what they call evil.

I am my innards, down to the hairs on my body. I was given all this, all this body, and I was raised to tread a line somewhere between the obvious sins of the Last Judgment and the anonymous appeals to the patron saint of hopeless cases.

I got up and walked, myself, next door, letting the storm

door slam shut behind me. I left the house with my aunts still in council, their conversation murmuring at my back like sylph song, as they leaned toward each other and embraced each other's shoulders, like old sorority sisters.

CHAPTER 12

The Heretical Teachings

"Nay but, O man, who art thou that repliest
against God? Shall the thing formed say to him
that formed it, why hast thou made me thus?"
ROMANS 9:20

If I had been asked then, I would have said: *here*, here is
where I purposefully walked away from the Catholic house
and family in which I grew up. I really thought I did, too. As
if I were ever in it in the first place. Bolstered by a conversation I had that evening with Anne on the chilly porch,
when she offered the devastating opinion that there was no
God, there was just all this (sweeping her arm phenomeno-
logically over all that, in the Monsalvat night). When I looked
into the night, I saw a promising abyss of surprises, like a
dark lake full of fish and dogs and deer and snakes. I became
confident after that by depending upon my own two feet, and
I walked out of that Kaiserbroad Council.

I left my sorority-sister aunts in that kitchen strung out
across wooden chairs like dolls that had gone crazy and then
wound down, heads on tables and weeping over the backs of

chairs and over each other, legs splayed out or buckled under, hands on head or knuckles dragging the tiled linoleum floor.

I thought I left, but I know I never really did. Anne and I strove away from the puritan rules of house and church, tried to be ugly as possible with our own sensuality, and flaunted it. I spent years thereafter exploring dark corners, she spent years in loveless quarters. But I, the ugly sensualist, was not walking away from the house, was not defying it, but moving through different rooms in it. The pimps, the men in raincoats, the heavy breather on the other end of the line, the pornographer, those are also members of the Monsalvat household, in an uglier guise. The demons of *The Last Judgment* belong there, in that house.

For a while, my whole family went a little crazy. Aunt Charlene got in a fight with Uncle George and slept on the couch for a month. Aunt Charlotta got a bad home perm in her hair and had to have it cut out. At my great-grandmother's house, somebody left a box of crayons in the dryer with Aunt Teresa's whites: her bras, slips, and socks. Aunt Mary (never a Kaiserbroad by blood but a half-breed like me who clung tenaciously to that whirling centrifugal ball of aunts), began to confide in me for a time.

She must have sensed that I was the right person to be an outcast with. On my visits, she would linger late and seek me out and offer me coffee or tea or whatever she was drinking. She always wanted to tell me stories, but never stories about Uncle Tom or Anne or Tommy. They were always stories about her Sweet Adeline trips or something particularly grisly she claimed to have seen as a nurse at the hospital. I actually liked her yarns about disgusting medical emergencies, the way I liked anybody's boastful stories—Uncle Jimmy regaled me in the same way by lamenting the big buck we left behind when Uncle Tom died; I beat my breast telling him about the carp that got away. He never believed me. "That sounds made up, Mike. I think you're full of shit."

But he was the one that always brought up the carp, he always encouraged me to make the carp bigger in size, the loss more tragic. In the same way, I encouraged Aunt Mary to tell me her stories.

The evening after the council, when Anne closed herself in the pale blue room, Aunt Mary sat with me and drank crème de menthe and vanilla ice cream, a concoction she called a "grasshopper," and told me about her trip to Las Vegas. She was proud of the innovations she had picked up on her trips through the Las Vegas luxury hotels, like taking the flower that garnished her room-service breakfast and putting it in her hair, a trick she continued now at home with sprigs of brittle baby's breath, or the lilacs that smelled like Chapstick. There in the kitchen, she wore a small wildflower and sat like she was balancing her head on her neck, and I noticed that her eyeshadow matched her flower and her dress, a fuchsia hue. My grandmother sat with us, too, dozing.

"It was all so *nice*, Michael. They taught me to play black-jack and I won twenty dollars. We saw a big show with waterfalls and airplanes landing on stage with showgirls without anything on top—you'd love that, wouldn't you? You men are all alike—and they served us a surf and turf—a whole lobster tail!—for five dollars. The casinos were full of lights and slot machines for as far as you could see. There were no windows, so you couldn't tell whether it was day or night.

"It was all so nice, and convenient. They'd make change for you like that." She snapped her fingers. "You could even cash your paycheck right there. And there was room service in our rooms and each room had little bars of soap and a bathing cap and a little sewing kit and a Bible and little cabinets full of snacks and pop and liquor and that's where I learned to make a grasshopper, when I was at the blackjack table and winning like crazy and the waitress brought me a free drink to congratulate me on winning and I said my God that's so good what's in it? And she gave me the recipe and I suppose I was paying so much attention to her directions that I stopped paying attention to the blackjack table because I started losing again.

"But you know, it was all so nice, they even had peacocks walking on a lawn so perfect your uncle Tom would have cried. The peacocks were blue and shiny like the lining of my coat"—she flipped out her coat draped over a chair between us—"and there were white peafowl, too, they looked so perfect and nice. Like heaven, I bet. But you know, I really like a bar of soap that's been broken in. I like it when you've washed with it a few times and all those pointy edges are rounded off and it rolls all over you"—and she stopped for a moment, looked at her empty grasshopper glass, and got up to blend herself a new one, powdery green—"and every day I'd come back to my room and there would be this new bar of soap all wrapped up, and they threw away the old one. Now first of all, that's just plain wasteful, but I tell you, I prefer a bar of soap I can call my own. It makes me feel more at home. No matter how nice things were, they made sure I knew I wasn't at home, that this was somebody else's house. Here, Michael, have a sip of this, you're going to love it." And she handed me the drink. It tasted as chalky as a digestive, warm as fever.

"And then do you know what happened? Those beautiful peacocks started to molt. All the feathers started pulling away and they got so ugly. Great big bald patches here and here and here"—she illustrated on her own body—"and some of them went into *heat*. They started chasing the peafowl around, trying to get at their butts. Isn't that just like the world? You try to make things look nice, and the peacocks start to molt and look all scaggy and chase the other birds' butts!"

My grandmother said, out of the blue, "That's what nature *is*—a big scaggy peacock chasing after your butt."

■   ■   ■

So I chased after the ugly. Ugliness has not as much to do with quality as it does with quantity. I mistook the abundance of the world—mismatched porcelain, collected praying hands, newspaper clippings—with the consumption of the world. I consumed, I inhaled. I rummaged in dozens of human bodies for the things they might carry, including their souls, and made objects of them, commodities that might be acquired with a payment of some sort.

Once I knew there were others like me, I went to the places they could be found, the rest stops, the library washrooms, the public parks, sleazy bars, the ugly places. Not that the people in them were ugly. Even the most jaded men and women I met, dulled or gray or dusty—or worse, those who preened themselves into somebody's else's idea of beauty— there was always something particular and amazing about each one of them that I discovered while rummaging, however briefly, in their lives, as if they were boxes full of belongings.

My hormones made me monstrous. I sprouted pimples, then lost them in a matter of a week. They made me in turns ugly and attractive and had me in their possession, as did the other juices that flowed through me like medicine. But the thing was, I *wanted* to feel ugly, I wanted to be one of the demons in the picture in my grandmother's living room.

It became summer, the one before my last year of high school, and I stayed with my grandmother and Aunt Teresa because I got a job at a golf course in Monsalvat. I would ride a big lawn mower all day and I wouldn't be able to sleep at night. I took to running at night. I would slip through my grandmother's porch door, opening it by inches so that it didn't squeak. Once out there, I would run through the

Monsalvat subdivisions, taking sidewalks and trails, spooking family pets and watching the fireflies swarm over the marshes. As the night grew still I would shuck off what little clothes I was wearing, the T-shirt, the shorts, and then I would be running with nothing on. The summer night air worming over my body felt obscene and perfectly pleasant, the way orgasms felt, the illusion of going very fast and going in slow motion at the same time, nearly—but not quite— jumping out of my skin.

I loved the night. It softened and blunted all the sharp things daylight showed, and showed the secret colors of things. There is an optical illusion I've seen in many books in which the American flag is printed with green and black stripes, with a yellow field for black stars. You look at it for a minute, and then look at a sheet of white paper, and suddenly, you see on the blank page the image of the flag in its red, white, and blue tradition. The cones and rods inside the eye have been worn out, and that's what causes it to see what was always there, hidden away. So it is with the night.

There was a park in the center of Monsalvat that was usually my destination for night runs. It was also the place where people like me prowled, usually for something anonymous, even silent. Others wanted to talk after a grope in the dark, to assure themselves that they were doing something human, perhaps. I liked the talkers. Whether they were telling me the truth or lying was beside the point. They were always telling me wonderful stories, like my golden grandfather or the Kaiserbroads on a drunken evening over beers and cards.

I complained about Kelly being this shaved-down alabaster hollow-cast dog, eager to please. I confess that I was eager to please, too, but I used my firm footing in my own desire as leverage for another's. I would quickly discern what my partners were looking for, hands, mouth, voice, movement, and exaggerate it, magnify the experience with my own. I pleased myself not by being the ventriloquist's dummy, but by being the ventriloquist himself.

■   ■   ■

Aunt Charlotta's husband, who worked on the assembly line at an auto plant, got laid off and started drinking all day long, instead of only at night.

"He's an addictive personality," Aunt Charlotta said. She wasn't embarrassed at all when her husband, Uncle Roger, flipped his Jeep on a back road because he'd had one too many. "We're lucky not to have addiction running in our blood—we'd be ruining ourselves with drugs and alcohol and who knows what."

Uncle Roger, who had checked into Alcoholics Anonymous and successfully pulled himself out of the mossy-walled well of drunkenness and my memory, said, "Naw, you're not addictive types, you all are obsessive. We talk about you in group all the time, you obsessive types. At least we can treat what's wrong with me. There's no hope for what ails your family."

"You think we're all weak?" asked Aunt Charlotta, slipping on her glasses. "You think we have trouble controlling ourselves?"

"Naw, honey." Uncle Roger sat up and drank a hit of black coffee, ever-present in his state of recovery. He was wearing a work shirt, despite his employment situation, and it was well pressed and immaculate in its own olive-drab way. His hair was combed straight back, shiny with Brylcreem. We'd never seen him so clean-cut. He looked like an alien. "I'm just proud of being strong enough to say I'm weak. To say there's something wrong with me. Honey, you just don't have a disease you can blame it on."

"Blame what on?" said Anne. "I don't know what's so great about trashing a perfectly good Jeep."

Uncle Roger said, "I don't see what's so great about having a mouth like yours, that you can't control"—and then he looked down at her belly—"or anything else like yours that's uncontrollable."

It was one of those moments that everybody could make a big deal about, or just let slide. Anne didn't cry or rush off or slap him up, though. And Aunt Charlotta simply said, "You ought to watch your own mouth, Mr. Man," to her husband, and then the subject was dropped.

I, for one, was furious with what Uncle Roger said. I hated to side with Anne, but I couldn't understand how his problem was a noble one—addiction—while Anne's (or mine), desire, was a degrading weakness.

Yes, of course, it was a puritanical instinct to deny the body its pleasure, but can desire ever really be controlled? I might have gone for years, for a lifetime, denying myself the thing I wanted most. I would have made a terrific priest. The ways of avoiding desire are actually laughably simple: remove the object of affection, or remove the self from the object. Or simply live with it under the same roof and gain a reputation for having a permanent sour mood.

But desire is not to do with choice, it's a mistake to think so. I could not simply choose *not* to be me, who is my desires. When I tried to avoid my desires, I only felt weak, and I thought the only way to remove the want and the weakness was to pull away from my aunts and uncles, and hope that my grandmother, who understood weakness best, would remain close by.

∎   ∎   ∎

It was sad to see Anne so listless. I wished she would torture a cat for me, but she sat on my great-grandmother's porch with lemonade and fanned herself on those summer days. I would come home from the golf-course mowing and ask her if she wanted to go to a movie, but she didn't want to do anything, not read, not walk, not argue, not watch television. She didn't want to talk.

Kelly stopped coming around, and I was afraid to ask Anne what she was going to do as her due date approached. Aunt Teresa tried to be nice once and said, "If it sticks out like that,"—pointing at Anne's belly—"it's going to be a boy." I suggested that we get a big sheet of butcher's paper and put it up and draw her profile on it once a week, to see how much it grew. Anne glared at me, which was mildy satisfying.

"What are you going to do with yourself?" I asked her, exasperated.

She was staring at the newspaper on that porch. Behind her, the measurements of my aunts and uncles yardsticked a frame around the rocking chair she sat in. She looked up. "I'm going to be Aunt Teresa," she said. "When Grandma dies, she will be Grandma, and I will be Aunt Teresa. Then when Aunt Teresa dies, I'll be Grandma."

"You'll make a terrible Aunt Teresa," I said. "I don't suggest you go for that one."

"Shut up, Michael. I'll do what I want." And she went back to gazing at the newsprint, which I could tell she was not reading.

"You act like somebody gave you a lobotomy," I said, but it didn't provoke a reaction, none at all.

Then one afternoon, I came home with pieces of grass under my collar and a sunburn on both arms, and Anne was gone. "Where did she go?" I asked Aunt Teresa.

"To a place where she'll have privacy until she has the baby. It's a good place and they'll take care of her and the baby." I thought about her a lot during that time, thought of her as dead as Uncle Tom, or Chester, or the boa constrictor. Once, I dreamed we water-skied together on Clear Lake, and she wiped out in the water.

She came back to Monsalvat in October, not pregnant anymore, when I'd returned to the southern part of Michigan. I heard it from my mother, who heard it from Aunt Mary: Anne was just fine and going to beauty school, seemed very energetic and her old self. She was even seeing Kelly again, and everybody always liked him, he was a friendly boy. He had a good job now and seemed to have grown up a little bit. Maybe they'd get serious, Aunt Mary was hoping. Maybe he'll ask her to marry him.

Anne gave the baby up for adoption. "Was it a boy or a girl?" I asked. My mother told me it was none of my business.

■　　■　　■

The only family member I had not moved away from was my great-grandmother. She seemed to have no fear of evil, nor any monkeylike aversion to seeing, speaking, or hearing it. Her matter-of-fact statement of children conceived out of wedlock in our family made that apparent to me.

One afternoon that summer, with the house still and the outside heat flooding into the house—was it good for the wood of this near-antique furniture? I wondered—I sat in the living room and talked to my grandmother about nature, the scaggy peacock, and desire, the bastard child.

"You don't hold it against them, do you?" I asked her.

"Hold what?"

"That they had children without being married first."

"Coulda been worse," she said, unwrapping one of her dietetic candies. She made a face when eating them, and I don't think she really enjoyed them. "They did all that out of love rather than hate. They coulda been thieves. Or killers."

"Sometimes people steal and kill for love," I said.

"Yes, that's understandable," she said.

"Love sort of makes you stupid, doesn't it?" I said. "Fools for love."

"Fools my eye," my grandmother said. "I never bought that old line. If you ask me, it's the other way around. My mind never worked so fast as it did when I fell in love with your great-grandfather. I'd say they ought to call you 'genius of love' because that's what you are."

"Genius?" I asked. I was on the piano bench only half listening, running my pinky up the keys, many of them chipped, a couple completely missing.

"I mean," my grandmother said, "once, I was eighteen and a French boy whose father was in Monsalvat to sell Christmas decorations moved to town. The boy had those lips like that actress, what's-her-name, has. And he didn't speak a word of English. I loved those lips. And. And his backside, you know? And I couldn't talk to him. So you know what I did? I zoomed right down to the library and asked the librarian about books on French. It must've taken me a day, two days tops, and I was speaking French all over the place. *Bonjour, monsieur, comment allez-vous?* Voilà, instant genius."

"Not *two days*," I said incredulously.

"I had to work fast, he was only staying for the summer."

"Some people will learn French," I conceded. "But why wouldn't he learn English?"

"Because someone always has to do the chasing. Someone always has to be the one to realize that life doesn't revolve around you. You and I, Michael, we're chasers. It's a lifelong thing. You'll hate it, but you'll always be one. It's a funny position to be in. It's like being out of control and in control at the same time. But sometimes you're the most powerful one when you're *not* in control. You get to dish out the goodies. You offer the wares. They eat it—they take, you give, but who finally gets? I didn't get the French boy, but now I know French."

"I think I know about pursuing. I've done my own pursuing."

"I know you have."

"Not just Tommy."

"I know you have. It's best not to say."

"I go out running at night—"

"I know you do. I saw you leave once. It's best not to let anybody hear you."

"But I want to tell you what I've been pursuing. You'll listen to me, you won't shut down."

"Michael. Sometimes I sit here and watch television and they show gory car crashes on the news or two people having at it in bed on my story, or they'll have people talking about their sex changes on the talk shows, and I wonder, why do people want to hear this? Why do they show these things? Isn't there any privacy? Don't you want to have some privacy? Don't you want something of your own, yours alone?"

I looked down at the threadbare carpeting. Around her feet, under her chair, the pattern had worn through. "I feel like there are some things that I only have alone, and just once, I'd like to not be alone with it."

"Michael. What you want to tell me about is your conquests. You want to tell me about serious things like you've been to the circus and you've seen some goofy spectacle. Don't sell yourself short. You're not a circus freak."

"I feel like a circus freak. One of a kind, you know, and alone."

"If you're ever in trouble, somebody will be ready for you, you won't be alone then. But some things, even when you're with somebody, you'll always be alone with. Let your pursuits be the things you will be alone with."

She reached for the remote control for her television and turned it on. "Everybody tells their secrets on these shows. Don't they know that without a few secrets, there's no good story worth telling?" I looked at her and went out the front door, and sat on the porch for an hour, feeling utterly betrayed.

She was that last best hope, and after that moment, there

was nobody to help hold together the two separate worlds I lived in. When I walked away from my grandmother, I turned my back to look at the chasm between me and the rest of them, and it seemed vast and dangerous. Of course, the Michael that I was was still around, and could be as charming as the Kaisers. And the Michael that I was was definitely a scion of that family tree, however gnarled and obtuse. Even now I will admit that my better qualities are direct results of being raised among them.

But there was a part of me, a large part, which they would not look at, or could not see, however big and obvious it was. I remember sitting in a dentist's waiting room once, with six other people, three men, two women, one a mother with her daughter. I watched one of the men look at the single woman; she smiled back, he wrote a note on a slip of paper, put it into one of the magazines on the waiting-room table, and I watched the woman pick it up, pull the note, read it, smile, and nod to the man. I saw another of the men open his cigarette case to smoke, and expose to the third man—and curious me—the contents of his flat gold case. Among the cigarettes was a joint; the third man raised an eyebrow, the other looked to the door; they exited and returned minutes later, a deal probably made. All that time, the woman fussed with her child and never saw any of this; I was a spy in the secret world and I never knew how others could not see it, too, and in fact went to great lengths to blind themselves to it.

Yes, that other Michael was often sordid and unlikable, but mostly to attract attention to him, me. When I went away, I thought I could leave that family, choose or refuse it like a career or a coat. Family is fate, Lord knows; I could've put a nuclear bomb under the bunch of them and there would still remain that blasted husk of Kaiser, in poisoned air.

Family must stand for duty and honor and fidelity, to counter desire's wild selfishness. But isn't there in desire itself duty and fidelity? When I see a person engrossed in their passions—a welder concentrating on a joint, a musician laboring a tricky chord progression—I tend to love them for being so true to their passions, their obsessions. To watch Uncle Tom build the shed, to help Aunt Teresa dust her praying-hands collection, these made me fall deeply in love with them.

If a person knows their true desire, then they show a kind of necessity to follow after it. There is no real choice to make between the fidelity to desire and the fidelity to duty, however right that duty is; one must follow the obsession. And succumbing to desire is not an exhibition of weakness, it's the final caving in of long isometric force against inner walls. To proclaim, for instance, that I was gay meant not only to break down the steel walls others put up, but the second, stronger wall I put up within myself.

People who know their own wild desires seem to be the people who know of all the secret worlds in dentist offices and elsewhere. To expose the secret world is to show how wild desires *are* lovable, beautiful, desirable.

And even now I don't know if there is ever a way to show people how to see the secret world, those who have not seen it. Tell all the truth, but tell it slant, said the reclusive poet, but I recall my high-school shop teacher, a hirsute man with muttonchop sideburns named Mr. Sexton, his regulation tie forever tucked between the top and second buttons of his dress shirt to keep him safe from the lathe and planer, who took it upon himself to provide a certain kind of enlightenment to the twenty-odd yahoos in our class. Each day, before sending us to the machines to construct tissue boxes and wall hangings, he would stand in front and read a chapter from *Jonathan Livingston Seagull*, which must have moved him deeply in the privacy of his own life. Most of the class snickered or shot rubber bands, until finally, Mr. Sexton snapped his dog-eared paperback shut and shouted, "All right, you clods, there's no hope for you—go do your work," and we all broke up, donned safety goggles, and went to the machines. Even I, who perhaps *should* have been hoped for, who tried to be spiritually enlightened, who tried to see him while others rendered him invisible, even I admit that for all my effort to listen, Mr. Sexton and his book bored me silly. Perhaps all of this, too, will bore a person silly, illuminate nothing with a too-bright light.

But I was blinded myself in my single-minded mission to break with my family. I was on a conquest, discovering the dark new world, and I left my grandmother and the others high and dry.

I never was able to get close to my grandmother again. That is more than punishment enough for the likes of me.

■ ■ ■

Let me tell you about one of my conquests. One night, on a night run in Monsalvat Park, I met a man named Hollander. Even in the dark, I was attracted to his hands. They were huge and blocky like the sawed-off butts of a two-by-four, pale in the palm, with three deep creasemarks where it started folding into a fist. He was huge, corn-fed, boisterously healthy, blocked out in great geometric shapes: along with those big-as-brick hands, he had an inverted triangular torso that narrowed to a point at the waist, cylindrical head and neck, eyes like beads, and straight, thin straw-colored hair. He liked to talk, too.

I said, "How come you're so big?"

He told me that when he was young he was small and skinny, and he used to feel infested. He said his older brother told him things he learned in science class. He told him about earwigs, usually living in that corn, now burrowing into his brain when they got in bed at night; about trichinae worms that crawled in the cracks of his bare feet, got in his bloodstream, lodged in muscle, and tore away at the tissue until he got puny and weak; and about segmented tapeworms that ate most of the food in Hollander's stomach. His brother told him that if he felt close enough, he could feel the worm tickling his trachea as it inched up for food. That was why Hollander was skinny, he told him: because of the tapeworm; why he was stupid: because of the earwig; why he was weak: because of advanced trichinosis. Hollander decided to bulk up.

I felt a worm inching up my own trachea as he told me this. "But you can't bulk up your hands. Your hands are just naturally big."

He made a fist with his right hand and held it up in the night. He leaned over and kissed my neck and said, "They say your heart is as big as your fist," and then he held it up to his own chest. "Let me see your hand." He grabbed mine and exposed the palm. "It smells like soap. Look at your life-line. Look how long it is. Look at it."

We walked along in the dark, the humidity wrapped around us like a wet washcloth. He was slow, lumbering, and that made me feel even more energetic and fidgety. "Do you come to this park often?" he asked. Before I could answer, he said, "Not me. I can count the number of people I've done it with on one hand." This was a boast, I now realize, a way to keep the crazy universe finite, under control. "Do you want to come over to my apartment?" he asked me.

"Okay," I said. "But I can't stay all night." Although the idea appealed to me.

He lived on the other side of the park, near the fair-grounds where the Carp Carnival and Petunia Festival was held. All along the way we walked, there were purple petu-nias, so dark that they looked like ragged swatches of velvet. Hollander said they smelled bad, but I couldn't smell them.

His apartment was narrow, like a hamster run. A long hallway fed off into the kitchen, the living room, and the bed-room. In his room, the first thing I noticed were two pairs of dirty socks, and an unconnected telephone at the foot of the bed. Streetlight bled in at a weird angle through a leaded window, and that depressed me.

"Excuse the digs," he said to me. "It's small but it's clean. No cockroaches. I made sure they sprayed in here for cockroaches."

I hadn't even thought of cockroaches, but now I looked everywhere for them.

We sat very awkwardly on his bed. He put on this music, this old Broadway musical. The songs were inappropriate and by turns rambunctious and tender. "You don't have clap or anything, do you?" he asked me out of the blue.

By then I had traveled through that passage that seems prevalent among every boy after his first two or three sexual experiences; I had panicked at the slightest itch and the least amount of burning while urinating—I had already convinced myself that I had gonorrhea and syphilis and crabs and even strange exotic diseases nobody had ever heard of, listed in my health textbook years before. I had gone to an anonymous clinic after walking around the block about twenty times, only to be laughed at by a nurse who had seen a hundred guilty boys in her time slip into her shop. Now I was confident that I had nothing, but I said to Hollander, "No, but why should you trust me?"

"Well, you look perfectly healthy."

"I've got acne."

"That's perfectly healthy," he said. He put his hand on my knee. I felt my heart race. He leaned over and kissed me briefly, then moved his mouth down my chin and throat. It was nice not to be making these moves. He removed my shirt, then pants, then his own. He smelled like lemon and sweat and salt and saliva. He tasted like pure copper and pure blood. Then he pulled away. "There's something I like to do," he said. "You won't think I'm weird if I ask you to do something I like to do, would you?"

"What is it?" I was excited and terrified at once.

He got up and unlatched the door so that it was still closed but a little bit ajar. Then he started stacking up objects in the room against the door. A couple of chairs, a tennis racket, a stack of books, a small coffee table, all towered precariously. He picked up the unhooked phone and stopped to put the receiver to his ear like a seashell, like he was going to hear something. Then he stacked that on the very top. Then he tied a string to the doorknob and handed me the end. "I want you to hold on to this string, and when I start coming, I want you to yank on the string real hard."

Then he turned the light off and the only light came from the leaded window and the streetlight. Hollander blocked my light with his head. He was over the top of me, and had both of us in his two big hands. As he worked over the both of us it was like I wasn't in the room. He began to breathe heavily and swear, swear in rhythm, swear loudly, and I knew he was almost ready.

I grabbed the string hard and yelled out, "Hey, what's going on in there!" which he hadn't expected, and the sound of my own voice with the tumbling of the furniture and books surprised even me, and we both felt it at the same time. It was as if the tumbling sensation inside me was in him and in all the world, as far as I could see and hear. I thought of my grandmother in that moment, which sounds terrible, but I remembered how she said that there were some of us who had to be the chasers, some of us had to step outside of this Copernican universe in which all the objects of the world revolve around us.

I stopped being a child when I realized that the universe was not Copernican, and that it was actually a relief—a freedom—to revolve around other bodies, and to travel, spin, and chase.

"That was great," Hollander told me. "How did you know to do that?"

"Lots of practice," I said. I know he wanted me to seem as innocent as he wanted to seem. But I had taken what I wanted and given as much, and I didn't want to seem anything.

"Lots of practice?" he said. "I thought you said you didn't go to that park very often."

These days, from where I am telling all of this, there is a terrible virus that would probably make a man like Hollander curl up into a ball. I've met men like him, who carry in their pockets thin purple slips from a doctor's blood test that reads "No evidence of HIV serological contamination," and expect their lovers to believe that truth as easily as Hollander believed that the smell of soap on my hand was proof enough that I didn't go to the Monsalvat park often.

I try to be charitable, because he wishes we were all permanently innocent, the way my aunt Teresa wishes. But there is something so vicious and calculating to me about shutting the eyes to evil—as if none of us ever knew of it, as if evil visited us from the underworld and that this is not a place where angels and demons don't *come from*. To believe that such creatures dwell in the celestial heavens or the bowels of the earth, and do not live and breathe and are human in form, that is a mistake. To deny ugliness's existence is a profound ugliness, for at least the ugliness I pursued had its own genius, and its own strange beauty.

"You know," I said to Hollander, "you can go ahead and pretend that you can count the number of people you slept with on one hand, you can pretend that you're pure and naive and have a heart as big as your hand, but there are a lot of different kinds of diseases you can get. You can be dead in the head as much as you can be dead in the ground." Perhaps I didn't say that. But the words in my memory belong in that room, and they must have seemed apparent to him as well. I picked up my clothes, dressed, and walked out, pushing books and tennis rackets away. When the phone hit the ground behind me, it jangled, like somebody was calling.

I left and walked all the way home, not realizing how far away from my grandmother's house I'd gone. On the sidewalk, along the side of the fairgrounds, I found a dead baby bird, featherless and skinny. It looked obscene and sickening. When I came back in, it was almost daylight.

In the bedroom, with the help of weak dawn light—the praying-hands night-light had burned out and gone unreplaced for years now—I held out my hand and wondered which of the two creases was my heart line, and where it intersected. I wondered how long I could keep my perfect skin from blooming with disease. Home might help me live forever, but how could it, I wondered, when it was already so far away? How would I be able to see an accident coming when it hit me, when it was so dark in my own room? I was not a genius, I did not feel any kind of love enough to make me smart, and I would die of stupidity, I thought. I made a fisted hand and put it to my heart and thought, That big.

■　　■　　■

I am older now, don't live near Monsalvat, am done with college and moving here and there. Home since then has been my body. It is attracted to certain things, it has prejudices. If you want to know where it is that I'm telling this story, I would have to say that I am telling it from my body. My body often wishes that it was younger, when sensation came more naturally and was not contrived and schemed away. My body wishes it were satisfied with less. My body secretly wishes that it would grow old so that it would not be so enslaved by sensation, but it also secretly knows that it will always, in a way, stay young, crave feeling, no matter how old it gets. My memory grows wiser and older, but my body stays foolish and young. And yet I'm telling this story from my foolish young body, which will always claim innocence while my memory takes responsibility for crimes committed.

CHAPTER 13

Confession Again

Somewhere along the way to college, I decided to hate everybody in my family. It was the kind of hatred that I lavished on Anne's boyfriend Kelly, and when I first discovered what sheer comfort there was in hating the people I grew up around, the hate relieved me. Can it be that such hatred is a kind of love? Why would I pay so much attention to my family if it weren't?

I delighted in the litany of reasons why I hated them. I thought of demented Aunt Teresa, who told me years before that dinosaur fossils were not a real thing, that they were the work of the devil because God did not believe in evolution. Yet she believed that black holes in the universe, where stars were devoured, were actually doorways to heaven. She told me not to give to UNICEF at Halloween because they gave the money to needy children in communist countries. I remembered all these outrageous reasons with glee, like the Romans peering into the arena as the lions ate the Christians, covering their faces but peering through their fingers at the hideous carnage.

And once I set out to hate them all, I was able to stand clearly outside their circle. I became a kind of freak to them. I was not just the strange cousin who wrote the letter and talked to furniture. I was the articulate one. The one whose whole world was a confessional—Aunt Teresa, Aunt Mary, Uncle Jimmy, they were all afraid I might speak of their secret desires, or worse, of my own, and once you speak of secret desires and acts, you are most definitely guilty of them.

I loved to hate them, to walk around like a human bomb, the kind of bomb my golden grandfather told me about in his war, buried just below the earth's surface that explodes as soon as the foot steps off. The Kaisers were like the soldiers I imagined standing in open fields long into the night, for as long as they could stand it, one foot down on me, not daring to pull away. When would I speak? When would I go off?

Years go by; people go away. I went to a college that was far enough away, at the end of a tether, that when I heard about cousins and aunts and uncles marrying or dying or graduating or getting into trouble, I often mixed them up. I forgot, for a while, that Aunt Charlotta's husband died one summer while swimming on Clear Lake, that Aunt Teresa sat on the beach reading a trashy novel and saw his body wash ashore herself. I loved that lake. It was a calm place in my dreams. Other marriages and deaths were easier to remember.

I came home from my junior year in school to see Anne get married. Despite the disposition of her first child, she was very excited about having a somewhat pure start, and between her family and the well-off parents of the groom, they were having a huge wedding. That, and perhaps a funeral or two, was the only thing that could lure me back by then. It seemed that every time I came home, home was not where my parents and brother lived, but was Monsalvat, home was Saint Mary's Star of the Sea Catholic Church, with old Father O'Hara as pastor, who once heard my false confessions about committing adultery.

The day before the wedding rehearsal, I decided to scare Father O'Hara by walking into his confessional booth and sitting with him, talking to him face-to-face. I was going to get a charge out of saying, "Forgive me, Father, for I have sinned, my last confession was *five years ago!*" Perhaps I was hoping he would say something perceptive, something I'd missed in those days of disillusionment, but at the time I thought he might be too frightened by my boldness.

I walked down the aisle to the booth. The entire inside of Saint Mary's Church was lined with scaffolding. They were painstakingly cleaning the paintings of the saints and apostles on the high walls, and though Father O'Hara promised the Kaisers that all the work would be done well before the wedding, he hadn't counted on a labor strike that brought the work to a standstill for many months. On the circular wall behind the altar were brown-toned disciples of Christ, carrying sheep or crosses or books, all with beards down to their knees. What was most strikingly noticeable since the half-finished cleaning were the gleaming halos around the heads of them. They were shining all that time under the dirt, but now it seemed like they gave off their own light.

I walked into the confessional—it was a very hot day, which made the inside of the church smell of damp and the ferrous odor of the rusting scaffolding; there was no line of sinners waiting to admit their sins—and found Father O'Hara polishing a rifle. Tommy once told me years before that Father O'Hara used the gun to shoot pigeons that tried to nest on the head of the Virgin Mary in the alley between the church and the sacristy. He put the gun down and sat back in his chair, grabbing the two back legs of it in each hand, like he was taking off in a rocket ship and the g-force pushed him into that position.

"Hi, I'm Michael Bellman," I said.

"Hello?" he said.

"I'm Anne Kaiser's cousin."

"Oh," he said, like that explained everything. He even let go of the chair legs and pulled out his handkerchief. I noticed how perfectly his hair was combed; I would have said it could be a toupee, but it was definitely his own hair.

"I like what they're doing to the walls," I said.

"Well, you're the only one. Your aunt is going to kill me for having all that scaffolding up during Anne's wedding. And all I've gotten is complaints for the way the paintings look now."

"Complaints?"

"Nobody likes the halos around the saints. They think I've had the cleaners paint them on or something, they think I'm trying to *change* the walls or something, like I'm trying to make them less holy or something. But the halos were there all along. They're all mad at the clean gold halos, even though that's the way they're *supposed* to be." I remember a parable by Kafka about a leopard that leaped through a stained-glass window of a church and jumped onto the altar to drink from the chalice, did it a second time, and a third, until soon, the leopard's appearance was incorporated into the ritual.

"I've come here to confess," I said.

"Oh. You're one of those kids who like to do things the new way." In that time, the gleeful unbridled rules released by Vatican II not only took the babies out of limbo to Aunt Teresa's satisfaction, they also took all the exotic Latin out of the mass, brought in the touchy-feely strumming guitar masses, multicolored felt banners with HE IS RISEN and THE LIGHT OF THE WORLD, and face-to-face confessions. Not only could I sit with Father O'Hara and tell him my sins *mano a mano*, I could also go to Communion and hold out my hands and have him put the host into my own hands. I would touch the papery-bread body of Christ, and I could put it into my own mouth.

"I don't know if I want to do it the new way," I explained, "so much as ask you why the things I've done are sins. And I want to know why my telling you what I've done will make it go away."

"Let me tell you this." Father O'Hara started talking in a

teachy way, which made it hard for me to listen to him seriously. "I had this friend—well, maybe he wasn't such a friend—and he did something crummy to me. We didn't talk for about a week, and then he came up to me one day and started acting like nothing was ever wrong. When I walked away from him again, he accused me of holding a grudge. But I wasn't holding a grudge, I just wanted him to admit he made a mistake. I just wanted him to say 'I'm sorry,' because I really think he thought he was Mr. Perfect. I think that if you never admit you've made a mistake now and then, you really start thinking that you don't make mistakes."

"Is that it?" I asked him. I was looking around his tight cubicle. They had installed shag carpeting to absorb sound, and it smelled new.

"I think it's important to tell the truth, as much as you can," he offered. "Plus," he said, leaning forward to get his gun again, "plus, I really like a good story."

"True stories."

"Emotionally true stories. I like them jazzed up a little bit."

"What's the difference between lying and jazzing up?" I asked him.

"Context," he said.

"So," I said, running my finger along the pattern of the filigreed wainscoting, "You figure that this little booth is a good enough context for my telling you my horrible sins?"

"Horrible sins," he said philosophically, like he was underlining the words and making them a heading for a whole list of ideas. "I get old women on the other side of this wall"—he tapped on the starburst-patterned grating, and I thought, Here I am, a dozen years older and in the place where I saw the light come from while confessing to adultery and a number of other false sins—"women who confess to sins that aren't really sins. They confess that they forgot to take out the garbage. I get kids in here who tell me they've committed adultery and start making up sins to fill up the time. Those are the horrible sins to me, because they're insincere. Thieves and fighters and cheaters, they don't seem like horrible sinners to me."

"How can you always tell when somebody is insincere?"

He leaned forward. He started cleaning his gun again. "You're the kid who was with Tom Kaiser when he died pulling out that big buck, aren't you?" I nodded. "Do you believe in Original Sin?" he asked.

"No," I said.

"I do," he said. "Not the apple thing in Eden, but Original Sin. Original Not Innocent. Because you see, Michael Bellman, people think that if they don't say anything, if they never confess somehow, then whatever they've done never really happened."

"Tell me about it," I said. I was warming up to him.

But he was having none of it. "Oh, I'll bet you're just as guilty. There's also the type of guy who thinks that he can brag to me about his sins and that just because they sound like sins of passion, he's the victim. Do you feel like a victim of my church, Michael Bellman?"

I didn't know what to say. "I think you don't like a lot of the things I do. I think you think that the things that come naturally to me are unnatural."

"No." He thought about it for a minute, then he said no again. "Nothing's unnatural if you do it sincerely. And if you tell me stories about what you've done as a way to come in here and shock me, if you tell me about what you've done to brag, well, that's unnatural. Bragging is lying. Jazzing up is being passionate. That's the difference, I guess."

I thought about what my grandmother had told me about keeping my conquests to myself. I got up. "I've got to go," I said. "I'll see you later."

When I stepped out, I heard Father O'Hara slip the latch on the inside of his confessional door. An old woman crept into the passenger side of the booth. I was sweating. It must have been the heat. I looked all around me at the scaffolding, and felt like climbing high up into it. It looked like the scaffolding was the only thing holding the place up, like flying buttresses didn't work. It looked like the scaffolding was a kind of cage to hold the people in, to squeeze around them the way the crown of thorns squeezed tight to the Sacred Heart. It was so hot outside that the holy water in its marble bowl had dried up at the door.

■　　■　　■

"I can't believe you would actually choose red, white, and blue for your wedding colors," I said. "I can't believe you'd act like you were an immigrant or something."

"Shut up, Michael. Like you've got taste. I think it's only appropriate that those are my colors, since I'm getting married on the Fourth of July."

"I can't believe you're getting married on the Fourth of July."

"Shut up, Michael."

I never would have admitted it to her, but the dress was kind of nice, a simple white dress without much fringe, lacy sleeves, and a bold blue ribbon around her waist. She was showing me a picture of her bridal bouquet, which had carnations and roses and hyacinths. They weren't as bad as they could have been. It was the blue tuxedos for the groomsmen with matching blue shoes, and the scarlet dresses for the bridesmaids that were making me laugh at her. I was going to have to wear a blue tuxedo with matching shoes.

The trouble with being the smart aleck that I'd become was that I couldn't take anything seriously, and I missed taking everything seriously. I was a little jealous of Anne, jealous that she didn't have any idea that red was wrong on bridesmaids.

We were sitting in the chalk-blue bedroom with the burned-out praying-hands night-light. Palm Sunday fronds had piled up and sagged like scoliosis over the Last Supper painting. The room had never been painted since the summer Uncle Tom painted it for my visit.

Outside, it was early summer. The birches were full, the bluebells and four-o'clocks and sumac bloomed. From the bedroom window I could see cottonwood flying through the air and settling here and there. It settled on Clear Lake like summer snowfall. "Dirty trees," Aunt Teresa had said when I had come into the house the day before and told her how I had missed the puffed pods of cotton as much as anything, "all they do is make a mess for me to clean up."

Aunt Teresa came in the room. She rushed over to Anne and gave her a hug around her blue-sashed waist. "I think I'm going to cry," she said to Anne. To me she said, "I always cry at weddings."

"You're going to get water marks on my sash," Anne warned.

I wanted to be alone with Anne for a little while, so I got rid of Aunt Teresa by saying, "Gee, Anne, it's a good thing you didn't get married when you were pregnant. Then you would've had to wear spandex instead of red, white, and blue." Aunt Teresa shook her head, brushed her own dress in a downward stroking, and bustled out of the blue bedroom.

"So," I said, "who's going to give you away? Who's going to be your father?"

Anne turned around, and the dress made the same kind of *zwick-zwick* sound her Confirmation dress had made when she ran up the stairs to show me Aunt Teresa's bedroom. "You're not going to believe it," she said. "You're not going to believe who's giving me away. Guess."

"The Fattest Man in the World."

"No way. He's taking the pictures. Guess again."

"Philly and Millie."

"Ha-ha, very funny."

"Well, who?"

"Tommy!"

"Tommy?" By then, of course, I was over it, the whole thing, but it still made me stop to wonder. "Where did you find Tommy?"

"Turns out he was getting all our mail all along. He was in the marines just like Uncle John. Uncle John knew, but he promised not to tell. But when he found out I was getting married, he said he'd come for it."

"Tommy?" Tommy in a blue tuxedo and matching shoes. And a military haircut. And probably no neck. "Are you going to make him wear one of those tuxedos?"

"Aw, no, he'll probably wear his uniform and sword."

"What a good citizen," I said. "Tommy's a warmonger after all."

"Shut up, Michael. He was always a good citizen," Anne said. "You just thought he was a bad one, just like everybody else thought. He could have done good things until he dropped over dead and everybody would've still thought he was a crummy guy."

She went over to the bed and jumped on it, making the fabric whisk all around her. "I can't wait to see all the presents we get!" she said to me.

On the desk next to her gloves and veil was a *Bride* magazine. I pulled it open and idly flipped through pictures, curious about the journal's preoccupations, which were as foreign to me as those in *Playboy*. There were endless pictures of women in dresses with varying amounts of filigree. There were very few men in the pictures. Often, the woman models were walking down the aisle with a man, but the man was cut out of the picture at the arm: it only need be obvious that this young lady was being escorted, was bridal.

"Did you actually *buy* this?" I asked Anne.

"No, Aunt Teresa got that for me. And the whole pile

besides—" She pointed to a stack of magazines, stashed like pornography, on the closet floor. Anne grabbed a pencil off the desk and snatched the *Bride* magazine away from me. Using the eraser end, she proceeded methodically to erase the eyeballs out of the model bride, until she looked like a mindless zombie, a Stepford wife.

I giggled. "You know what she's saying? She's saying, 'Honey, after we're married, I'll make you a real nice Bundt cake.'" I took the pencil from Anne and drew bolts on the bride's neck.

Anne laughed and grabbed the pencil away, and began to black out one of her teeth. As she did I said, "You know, Anne, I knew where Tommy was, too."

"You did not."

"I did!" I protested, and grabbed the pencil from her for emphasis. "Years ago. I was in California visiting Grandpa, and I heard them talking on the phone." I started on a new bride on a different page, giving her a gaucho's mustache, then volunteering the pencil to Anne.

"How could you know they were talking to Tommy?" Anne asked.

"By the way they were talking. Grandpa was saying he couldn't talk long, and that he should call back after I left. He asked him if he was planning on spending his leave with them." Anne had drawn a long, stitched scar up the long neck of the blond bride with mustachios. I added the devil horns. We turned the page and began erasing the nostrils on yet another bride, to change it into a pig snout.

Anne said, sort of out of nowhere, or from the deep concentration of bride defacement, "You know, Michael, I know your whole story. I mean, I always thought queers were so *queer*, that they liked boys, and all. It made me so mad, sort of, that I wouldn't have any power over a queer, not in high heels, not even in lipstick. But now I don't think it's so queer."

I started up a new Bride of Frankenstein. This one got a little Hitler mustache. "Thanks," I said.

"Oh, no, Michael. I still think you're queer. I think you are so weird to be obsessed with just one guy, who you haven't got a snowball's chance in hell with, and who probably thinks you're the biggest dickhead in the universe. Besides, *God*, don't be gross—he's family." She changed the escorting male arm into a horrible tentacle that vined around her arm, suction cups and all.

"Is he married?" I asked.

Anne watched me finish the devil goatee on the bride. "Why do you keep changing the girls into guys all the time? Draw something else. Here, make her cross-eyed." And Anne drew googly eyes in the erased sockets of the zomboid model. She always did like freaks.

■　　■　　■

Father O'Hara was lecturing Kelly. "I'm not going to marry you tomorrow," he said, "if I don't see the marriage license. You should have brought it tonight and there wouldn't be all this tenseness. It's a rule I made a long time ago. No license, no wedding."

"Oh, that Kelly"—Kelly's mom, not tipsy this time but always seeming so—"he's such a cliffhanger. Aren't you, Kelly?"

Anne turned to Kelly, grabbed his hand, and said in her best matronly falsetto, "Oh Kelly, you're such a *cliffhanger*!" It rang in the scaffolded church and it bit the way it bit Uncle Jimmy when she called him the Fattest Man in the World. For the rest of the night, she kept calling Kelly a cliffhanger.

We were all there for the rehearsal of the wedding. It was going to be a full mass, which usually ran about an hour. Everybody's least favorite wedding was a Catholic wedding. But Kelly and Anne were both Catholic.

They both had had to go through the "Marriage Encounter," yet another new development brought about by Vatican II, in response to the alarming number of divorces going on. "It's just this stupid thing," Anne said, "where Father O'Hara asks you all these things about how much you get along with your mate. It's kind of like the 'Newlywed Game.' What's his favorite color, what's his favorite food, what's his favorite thing to shave his armpits with."

"Ha-ha, very funny," Kelly said. He was trying to get me to side with him, but I really always did hate Kelly.

I said to him, "So, Kelly, what *is* her favorite color?"

"Um," he said.

"Oh, that Kelly," Anne said, "he's such a cliffhanger!"

I stood with the other groomsmen in a row, and thought, All these guys are friends of Kelly's. Why did he choose me to be in there when he knew I didn't like him? Was it because he wanted one man from Anne's side of the family? He could have chosen one of her little brothers for that. Maybe all of these groomsmen were guys he also kissed at one time or another. I looked at them to see if they looked like they might have kissed other guys before. I really couldn't tell.

Then the organist started playing the Here Comes the Bride All Fat and Wide music, and I saw him.

Sometimes I will fantasize about what a person will be like before I see them. I will have very detailed ideas about how the person will sound, what the person will be wearing. And then, when I actually meet the person, I am often somehow disappointed, because the fantasy will not have been fulfilled. But the way I fantasized Tommy to look as a marine was exactly how he looked. Fully uniformed, including the sword, he stood tall and had a thick neck. His skin looked smooth and almost oily, and the creases in his neck looked like he had been eating nothing but grain for ten years. If I was disappointed by unfulfilled fantasies, I was devastated when my expectations were met. My great-grandmother was right: I did like to be surprised.

He looked at me, took a moment before he realized who I was, then he looked away. He brought Anne up to the altar, and hustled back down the aisle and brought back another woman with a lot of mousse in her hair, and sat down next to her in a pew to watch the rest of the rehearsal. He held the woman's hand.

Aunt Charlene and Aunt Charlotta were talking next to the candles. "It's so good to see Tommy again," Aunt Charlotta said.

"God, he's *huge*," Aunt Charlene said.

"I can't believe John hasn't told us where he's been." Aunt Charlotta sounded scandalized. "I feel like saying something."

Aunt Charlene held her hand up to her sister's mouth. "Forget about it, for God's sake. This is Anne's big day. Let's just enjoy it. We'll talk to John after the wedding."

"You're right," Aunt Charlotta said, and I could tell she would drop the whole thing, "He's just huge." I knew then that Tommy's return was no big deal.

■　■　■

The rehearsal dinner was at Tom's Tiki Room. This was a special restaurant with an exotic Polynesian theme—the restaurant where people took prom dates. They served drinks in goblets as big as fishbowls with names like Witch's Tit and the Sidewinder Fang. We all sat in big rattan butterfly chairs and ate seafood with silverware whose handles were shaped like South Sea totem poles. Behind the bride and groom and their parents at the long main table, there was an illuminated mural of a beach scene in which calm natives hulaed, roasted pigs, and repaired nets. Over the course of our meal, a hazy sun, like a halo, rose and set on the beach scene, then rose again.

Kelly sat next to Anne, cracked crab legs, and dipped the meat into a fondue pot full of butter. At some point he knocked over the pot and the flaming can of Sterno, and Anne's dress was ruined by the butter. She thought it was hysterical; so did he. "Oh Kelly, you're such a cliffhanger!" she yelled. Kelly's mother laughed like we weren't laughing at her, so then it seemed like we really weren't.

Next to me, Tommy sat with his wife, Kim. Kim actually sat next to me—they had switched the seating cards so Tommy didn't have to sit near me. Kim kept talking to me and then tried to draw Tommy into our conversation, but he kept getting out of it by toasting the future bride and groom and clanging on his glass to make them kiss.

"Tom's Tiki Room," Kim said. "So does that mean you own this place, Tommy?"

"Sure, I've got a lot of hobbies."

"One time," I told Kim, "Tommy used to raise snakes. Did he ever tell you about his snakes?"

"Oh God, Tom," she said, skimming both hands down her breasts and into her lap and up again like she was a human roller-coaster track, in mock revulsion, "I knew I'd hear all about your seedy past if I came home with you."

"He used to smoke cigars," I said. "Does he still smoke cigars?"

"No!" she said in disbelief. "Have you got any other secrets you want to tell me about, honey, before I get to them first?" she said to her husband, patting him on the back of the neck.

"Michael," he said to me for the first time, "just shut up."

Kim was surprised at the way he sounded. "Honey," she said, "I'm only joking. Michael's joking, too. We're just playing around." She refilled his glass and he stood up to offer another toast.

"When I first heard my little sister was getting married," he said, "I thought, Uh-oh, how can I get to this guy and tell him he's making a big mistake? He doesn't know what he's in for." Everybody chuckled. "But now I found out that they've been going out for five years. Five years? If he doesn't know what he's in for now, then he must be retarded!"

"Cheers!" Uncle Jimmy yelled.

I thought, What a clever family I have.

■   ■   ■

We were all getting dressed in the church basement when Kelly came to me. "Why didn't you come to the big bachelor party last night?" he asked.

"I didn't want to see you all embarrassed," I said, trying to figure out how the cuff links worked. He reached over and tried to help me, but I told him that I had it and pulled away from him.

"Want to see what we did last night?" he asked, then licked his lips like it was something I especially missed out on. "Want to see?"

"Okay, Kelly, let's see."

He rolled up his sleeve. On his pale hairless biceps, he had had a tattoo made, one of a Sacred Heart, with a crucifix over the top, only, instead of a crown of thorns around the middle, there was a big sash like Miss America might drape over herself, and written on the sash were the words "I love Anne." It was still scabby and bloody. "It hurts like hell," Kelly said to me. "It's a good thing I'm drunk, or I'd be crying right now."

"If you don't take care of that, it's going to get infected," I said.

"Don't worry about me," Kelly said. He scratched at his tattoo and it started bleeding a little where a scab was ripped away. "Is that all you have to say about it?"

I shrugged. "Is this some sort of proof of commitment for you? Some sort of heart-on-your-sleeve gesture?"

He rolled his tuxedo shirt sleeve down with brisk twists. If he were walking, he would have been stomping. "Bellman, I don't get you. Why do you hate me so much? What is it that I did to you? I didn't get you pregnant."

I didn't flinch. "It's very complicated, Kelly. It's about as complicated as the reason why you wanted me to be one of your groomsmen."

"That's not complicated. I wanted you to be a groomsman because I wanted you to like me. I like you, after all."

"Oh, no you don't," I pushed at him. "That's just the point. You don't like me a bit. You just like me to like you. And I won't. No matter how you try to please me. People won't always like you just because of the nice things you do."

Tommy came down into the basement for a few minutes, but he was already dressed, and when he saw me, he went upstairs again.

The church was boiling hot. I was roasting in the tacky tuxedo. The shoes were not only ugly, they didn't fit me.

Father O'Hara gave a strange, boring homily, full of big general words without examples. He shouted it, paused between phrases, and swung his sentences like pendulums. "Love each other in all the ways. Love each other in all the places." It was hard to pay attention. I could see that he was proud of his sermon, and didn't know that he was boring.

After that, Aunt Charlene led out a choirful of cousins and second cousins, aged five to ten, and she directed them furiously from the organ loft as they choked out "Amazing Grace" in a frightened monotone. We nearly drowned them out by shifting in the pews. They sang "Rock of Ages," and a few people clapped for the rickety, quiet choir.

I could hardly see anybody in the church, they were blocked by all the scaffolding.

■   ■   ■

The band for the reception was a group of high-school boys from Monsalvat. They called themselves "Show Your Work." They complained about having to carry their amps and speakers so far up to the clubhouse because there was no way for the car to get up to it. Anne and Kelly had rented the Knights of Columbus hall on Clear Lake, which had a lot of signs up for bingo and a computer printout banner that read JESUS LOVES THE UNBORN.

People piled up their presents on one table, ogled the four-tiered wedding cake on another, and took ham and turkey slices from a third, and sat down in big clumps at the long tables. There were several kegs of beer. Uncle Jimmy and Philly presided over their taps, taking turns pumping and pouring.

When the band started playing, they only played honky-tonk tunes, fast and loud. Their speakers were blown, had been for a long time. Nobody could hear the lyrics. The singer was too close to his microphone. He sang like machine-gun fire. I kept wondering why nobody cared what they were saying.

All the time, I kept trying to track Tommy down, but he always started dancing with his wife or went outside just as I fought through the crowd to get him.

I watched my gangly teenage brother Hugh go up to a scared-looking girl his age sitting next to her mother. He asked her to dance, and she trembled and looked up to her mother.

I was caught by a hand in a netted web of gauze studded here and there with small wads of thread, white like clover. Anne shouted over the band's din, "Michael, come see what I got for getting married." She led me across the room to the pile of gifts. Of course, there were the appliances. But it was the personalized gifts which somehow depressed me, made me sick to my stomach, a little. Uncle Jimmy had commissioned some local artist in the touristy part of Monsalvat's lederhosen-laden malls to draw silhouettes of a bride and a groom holding hands, their bodies in the shapes of their last names. Aunt Charlotta was in her ceramics phase, and gave them three ceramic coats of arms, which had been painted to look like old wood and tarnished steel.

Anne pulled out an envelope that was addressed "Kelly and Anne" in Aunt Teresa's unmistakable wispy handwriting—wispier due to the skips of an old ballpoint pen. Anne showed me the card, dully appropriate. There wasn't any money inside, but a handwritten note tucked in on a loose sheet of plain white stationery. "Kelly and Anne, Congratulations on this wonderful day in your life. I love you both very much. I know you have discussed other arrangements for homemaking, but I want to make you an offer. This is my wedding gift to you. Please come live in your grandmother's home. I have made out my will to give you full ownership of the house and all its furniture when I am dead. Until that time, there are two full bedrooms which are yours to live in. This will help while Anne finishes beautician's school, and you can begin to save money. Please accept this gift unconditionally. I think of both of you as my children."

I looked up at Anne. "So you *are* going to be Aunt Teresa when Aunt Teresa dies."

"No way!" She raised her eyebrows up into her veil. It was hot, but Anne refused to take off the veil. "First thing we do is repaint the front porch. Then we redecorate."

I thought of the demarcations on the doorway where my

aunts and uncles were measured during their lives. I wanted to defend the porch, and forgot for a moment that I hated my family.

Uncle Jimmy rolled over to us and grabbed Anne by the veil. "Time for the dollar dance, little missus. And I'm first!" He pulled out a ten-dollar bill and tucked it gently down the cleavage of her dress. Then he whisked her off to some unnamable tune butchered by Show Your Work. People cut in now and then, but Uncle Jimmy kept cutting back in and putting nothing less than a five-dollar bill into her dress. He must have given her a couple hundred bucks by the end of the dance. He came over to me afterward sweating like a pig, saying, "Haven't danced that much since Mary was kicking around." He watched me watch all the Kaiserbroad women. They were swaying together in a long semicircle, back and forth, like a demented Moldavian circle dance, around the best man and Kelly, who started to strip for them. When they took off their shirts at the same time, Anne shrieked when she saw the scabbed-over tattoo on his arm. She pulled him over to the side and the best man continued to strip down to his boxers.

Uncle Jimmy watched me stare at the best man and then he invited me outside where he had scotch and gin in big thermos bottles in the back of his truck. "Look at all this," he boasted. "I bought it with my pension." There were four full thermoses in plaid and black, and they were covered with the brand-name stickers from bananas. Over the years he had become the Fattest Man in the World with the help of a regular diet of two chicken-salad sandwiches, cake, pie, a thermos full of soup and another of coffee with cream and sugar, and a banana. He used his work thermoses for all the alcohol he'd bought with his pension. I sniffed each thermos. The gin smelled like coffee.

It seemed like it was getting too hot in the Knights of Columbus hall, because there were more people out in the lot than inside. A baseball game had started up. Groomsmen were playing in their blue tuxedos and cummerbunds.

I watched Tommy take his marine jacket and hat off. He was organizing a real game. Somebody suggested using the tuxedo jackets as bases. I pulled down the tailgate on Uncle Jimmy's pickup and got drunk, almost magically, drinking straight out of a thermos. Uncle Jimmy left to be shortstop. Father O'Hara volunteered to be umpire. By the time they were divided into two teams, there were thirteen people in the outfield. Every time somebody hit a ball, he was tagged out instantly with so many people fielding the ball.

Father O'Hara used his booming voice to shout "Ssssttrrrike!" and I could see him spit a little in the profile. Once, the priest called "He's *safe*."

Father O'Hara was dressed as usual in a pair of shorts and a black shirt with collar. They asked him to bat once, but he refused, and told them he was wearing his good clothes. They let him officiate, but they often ignored his ruling. He got upset when they didn't pay attention.

"Didn't you hear me? I said he was out!" He crossed his arms and stepped between the pitcher and batter.

"Out?" the batter shouted incredulously. "That ball was way too low." He threw the bat down. "Hey, guys, kill the ump! Kill the ump!" The team picked up the chant and gathered around Father O'Hara. Then the other team came in and joined, "Kill the ump! Kill the ump!"

"Wait, guys! It was a fair call—can't you take a fair call?" He had his hands in the air, and they shouted around him, closed in.

About twenty-five people picked up Father O'Hara by the legs and arms, supporting him along his back like pallbearers, shouting, "Kill the ump! Kill the ump!" They carried him down to the edge of Clear Lake. I heard Uncle Jimmy say, "Hey, let's baptize the padre!"

"Hey, you guys!" I saw him struggle as they carried him closer to the shore. "I can't swim—hey! I can't swim!"

There was a "one–two–three—heave!" and they thrust Father O'Hara out into the lake water, his arms and legs splayed as he arced and plunked. He went under and came up sputtering, slapping at water.

What we didn't expect, though, was the way his hair, so well set on his head, came undone. It was a long tail of brown hair that he grew in the back, and he always wore it to coil over his bald, shiny head, combed and set each day. Now his hair came down hippyishly. Everybody laughed, but they laughed in a different way, like they'd been caught picking their nose.

It probably sounds terrible, the way I talk about Father O'Hara, hiding his bald spot and shooting pigeons off the Virgin Mary's head and swiping the flasks of whiskey sneaked into church youth-group dances, but I don't think he was hatable. I liked him, I think. I liked him because of those things. People don't always hate people just because of the naughty things they do.

Plus, maybe he was right about Original Sin.

Tommy had stayed behind. He was coming over to Uncle Jimmy's truck because he knew that he had a mobile wet bar in the back. He looked like he weighed the worth of getting something to drink and being near me. He came over and pulled up a plaid thermos.

"Don't worry," I said, "I won't bite you."

He stopped what he was doing and cocked his head and narrowed his eyes at me. "Mike," he said, "when did you first realize that you were weird?"

What sort of answer did he want? I thought of talking to furniture, of lying to make myself seem believable, I thought of stealing centerfolds and writing letters, of praying to see naked men and dreaming of fish men. "I don't know. When did you first realize I was weird?"

"Not soon enough," he said. He took a long drink of straight scotch right from the lip of the thermos and looked away from me.

"God," I said, "you must really hate me."

He turned back and grinned that wolfish grin for the first time. "It sounds like you're hoping I hate you. Well, if that will make you happy, little man, then I don't hate you. I don't even *care* about you. I haven't thought about you, I forgot who the hell you even *were*. I think you're a real queer shithead."

I looked at him with as hateful a face as he was giving me. "I would really like to kiss you right now," I said. "A kiss full of all that hatred." He looked surprised and confused. I said, "I hate you as much as I hate this whole family."

"And you want to kiss all of them, too, I suppose?" he asked.

Yes, I thought. Poisoned kisses, kisses that awaken sleepers. "Yes. Maybe I'll go in there and kiss everybody square on the lips."

Tommy shook his head and put on his coat again, even though he was really sweaty. "Well, go ahead, Mikey. But you'd better be careful, because if you go around kissing everybody, they're liable to get the wrong idea. They're liable not to think you hate them at all." He walked away, but I caught up with him before he got too far and jumped at him, planting a wet one almost on his lips. "God, you're weird," was all he said. Then he punched me in the mouth. Then he walked away.

I could tell that he could have punched me harder, but all he did for the time being was make my teeth slice into my lower lip. Sometimes little cuts like that can hurt more than a broken bone.

In the hall, people were settling in for a long party. Somebody had gone out to get three more kegs. Anne and Kelly were sitting in chairs next to the disemboweled wedding cake. The little plastic bride and groom were on their side, half-sunk in a wad of pink frosting. Kelly had his sleeve rolled up and Anne had a first-aid kit opened in her lap. She was running a piece of wet gauze over his tattoo.

"This is going to sting some," she said, dousing the gauze with a bottle of syrupy yellow Merthiolate. "No. It's going to sting a lot."

I watched at a distance as Kelly sucked in air through his teeth. I watched with the two of them as the medicine stained his skin a pinkish red. Anne was like a tattoo artist herself, pricking into his arm a new red tattoo of her own design, without shape but as big as the already existing tattoo, but hers was clean and healing.

■　■　■

I got back to the old house again early, on my own. The punch in the mouth was really bothering me. Drinking liquor only made it sting.

The reception went very late. I thought then, Wow, I don't think I have ever been in this house when it was absolutely empty. But since my great-grandmother had died three years before, had actually done the thing Aunt Teresa warned her against doing, falling down the stairs and breaking her hip again, the house was not so much a forum for the Kaisers anymore. Aunt Teresa was being Grandma now that Grandma was gone, but her brothers were dying off and her sisters taking up ceramics and macramé. There was no heir to that household throne now, Anne gave it up by marrying Kelly. After Aunt Teresa, who would take the title? I wondered.

Sometimes I will fantasize about a place the way I will fantasize about a person as I remember them. Everybody knows that sensation of coming back to a place from childhood, remembering it as being huge and grand but seeing it now as small, simple, disappointing. Every once in a while, though, a person or a place will live up to my memory, or surpass my memory. The house in Monsalvat will always be a place like that.

When my grandmother died, I came home for the funeral. I had never talked to her again since the day she told me not to talk to her about my conquests, and I wished I had apologized. I had outlived hating all of them, and these days, five years out of my smart-alecky college days, I figure that if blood is not thicker than water, memories certainly are.

In science class, we learned about the Doppler effect: a train passes by with its whistle blowing. The sound of the whistle passes low as the train goes away. Sound and light and other waves sometimes zoom past me at a lower, graver level, and my grandmother's house will always grow larger, graver, and more hallowed as I go on, and does so with each of my visits to it.

People grow more profound, too. They resonate in deeper tones as they pass by. I have not seen Tommy since that reception day, but I hear enough about him to know exactly what he is like. He probably lifts weights and rides a motorcycle, but Kim keeps him in line. She probably is in charge of the checkbook and motorcycle payments. Every once in a while she will bug him about the snake he used to own, but he won't tell her about it. He'll think of me when she asks about the snake. I'm satisfied with that.

Aunt Teresa lives with Anne and Kelly in that house and keeps it up very well. She won't die soon; the gift *was* conditional. Aunt Charlene and Aunt Charlotta moved in together and play games with the clocks. Philly and Millie sold their cabin and live in a condominium, so Philly doesn't have to mow the lawn anymore. Anne is a beautician, specializing in haircuts for children. Kelly got a job as a bartender in one of the tourist bars near the lederhosen district, called the B-One Bar, or, in the vernacular, the "Bone" Bar. I went there after my recent visit to Aunts Charlene and Charlotta, with my now-adult brother Hugh, a Casanova of another kind, and Aunt Charlotta's son, Ed. They were very popular among the girls, regulars at the Bone Bar. They would come up to our vinyl booth and sample our nachos and ask either Hugh or Ed why they hadn't called lately, when would they call again? Kelly restricted his own pelvic thrusts to closing the cash drawer on his register after ringing up the drinks, which his hands were full of. Kelly and Anne have another kid, who was not given up for adoption. Weirdly enough, Anne is the kind of mother who I don't worry about, because I think she knows what needs to be corrected in a child's behavior and what must not. I secretly wish she had been my mother.

Aunt Mary had a big spread done on her in the *Monsalvat Citizen Patriot*, one about older women being active. She went to work as a ticket taker in a movie theater at the mall and was put on the board of directors for the Sweet Adelines, who sang and gave out scholarship money to promising young high-school musicians. I, of course, stopped hating them, because my hate involved spiteful kisses, and I began to enjoy keeping myself a secret, being one of the mysteries of the Kaiser family. Being a visible secret, I think, would remind them of certain stories that they would never retell until they became beautiful lies. In a family that loved to keep its memories locked in stories, I was the walking storybook full of unutterable tales, tales that had to be remembered, whether they liked them or not.

And as for my grandmother, I am sorry she had died while I was hating my family. I am sorry that I didn't get to tell her how I understood what she meant about not wanting to hear of all my shocking exploits, how I now understand that without a *place* for love, love looks like a freak show, love looks like a crime. Without a *place* for love, it's in purgatory. But when love has a place, a home, nothing I can do is criminal when done for that place.

People always think that once they've done something

wrong and admitted it, confessed it, the innocence they were born with goes away, like the halos around the pictures of the saints. The dust on the halos doesn't make the gold in the halos go away, the gold is always there, underneath. It always will be. Dirt and stains, sin and crime, are merely decoration, like the dice, crowns, and money bags surrounding the hellbound souls in *The Last Judgment*. One may be guilty forever, like Father O'Hara said, but one is also innocent forever.

That is what I wanted to tell my grandmother. But she is in heaven. She's in heaven or hell—they may as well be the same place, because to me, if you really want to know what I think, the forces of good and evil are pretty much the same and are dependent on each other. And God is among them, the good and the evil. And if there is a *place* for people who do good and do evil then they must share that place. All the rest of us are usually nice in the middle, we've put ourselves in a terrible purgatory, full of frozen carp and liquefied deer and smothered snakes and poisoned dogs, thinking that they're suffering under the view of God, but He's not there. God does not exist to pat us on the back when we're nice. We waste our time, in purgatory, being nice.

That is what I would have told my grandmother.

ABOUT THE AUTHOR

Brian Bouldrey's fiction, essays, and poetry have been published in the *San Francisco Chronicle*, *Crosscurrents*, *Nimrod*, and other literary reviews. The first chapter of *Genius of Desire* was a runner-up for the Katherine Anne Porter Prize for Fiction. The fifth and sixth chapters appear in Dennis Cooper's anthology *Discontents*. Bouldrey is also the co-editor of a literary magazine called *Whispering Campaign*.